THE
MOTHER

THE
MOTHER

A NOVEL

B.L. BLANCHARD

Published by 47North, Seattle

www.apub.com

Amazon, the Amazon logo, and 47North are trademarks of Amazon.com, Inc., or its affiliates.

ISBN-13: 9781542036535 (paperback)
ISBN-13: 9781542036528 (digital)

Cover design by Faceout Studio, Molly von Borstel

Cover image: © Shelley Richmond / ArcAngel; © Ildiko Neer / ArcAngel;
© Rolf Richardson / Alamy Stock Photo; © Social Media Hub / Shutterstock;
© Abstractor / Shutterstock; © LeksusTuss / Shutterstock;
© Chaikom / Shutterstock; © getgg / Shutterstock

Printed in the United States of America

For my mom, Shelly; and my sister, Abbey.
If we tried this, we'd be caught in five minutes,
but we'd laugh the entire time.

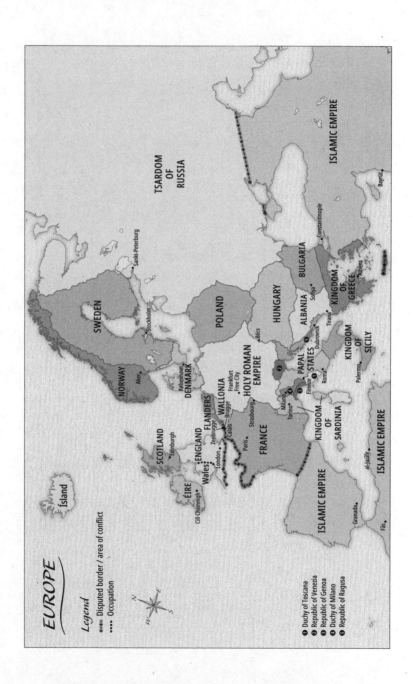

EUROPE

Legend

★★★ Disputed border / area of conflict
•••• Occupation

① Duchy of Toscana
② Republic of Venezia
③ Republic of Genoa
④ Duchy of Milano
⑤ Republic of Ragusa

Ísland

ÉIRE
Cill Chainnigh•

SCOTLAND
Edinburgh•

ENGLAND
Wales
London•

Calais•
Zeebrugge•
Brugge•
FLANDERS
WALLONIA
Strasbourg•
Paris•
FRANCE

NORWAY
Aker•

SWEDEN
Stockholm•

København•
DENMARK
Frankfurt
Free City•
HOLY ROMAN
EMPIRE

Sankt-Peterburg•

TSARDOM
OF
RUSSIA

POLAND

Bécs•

HUNGARY

BULGARIA
Sofiya•

Constantinople•

ISLAMIC EMPIRE

ALBANIA
Tirana•

KINGDOM
OF
GREECE
Athens•

Bayrūt•

KINGDOM
OF
SARDINIA

Milano•①
Torino•

④
Firenze•
①
PAPAL
STATES
Roma•

②

③
Dubrovnik•

KINGDOM
OF
SICILY
Palermo•

al-Jazā'ir•

ISLAMIC EMPIRE

Granada•

Fās•

ISLAMIC EMPIRE

That's my last Duchess painted on the wall,
Looking as if she were alive. I call
That piece a wonder, now . . . She had
A heart—how shall I say?—too soon made glad,
Too easily impressed; she liked whate'er
She looked on, and her looks went everywhere.
Sir, 't was all one! My favour at her breast,
The dropping of the daylight in the West,
The bough of cherries some officious fool
Broke in the orchard for her, the white mule
She rode with round the terrace—all and each
Would draw from her alike the approving speech,
Or blush, at least. She thanked men,—good! but
thanked
Somehow—I know not how—as if she ranked
My gift of a nine-hundred-years-old name
With anybody's gift. Who'd stoop to blame
This sort of trifling? Even had you skill
In speech—(which I have not)—to make your will
Quite clear to such an one, and say, 'Just this
Or that in you disgusts me; here you miss,
Or there exceed the mark'—and if she let
Herself be lessoned so, nor plainly set
Her wits to yours, forsooth, and made excuse,
—E'en then would be some stooping; and I choose
Never to stoop. Oh, sir, she smiled, no doubt,
Whene'er I passed her; but who passed without
Much the same smile? This grew; I gave commands;
Then all smiles stopped together . . .

—Robert Browning, *My Last Duchess*

Chapter One

Gregorian Calendar: Monday, 3 August 2020 (Feast Day of Saint Faustus)
Anishinaabe Moon: Manoomin Giizis (Ricing Moon)
Islamic Calendar: 13 Dhu al-Hijjah 1441
Chinese Calendar: Cycle 78, year 37, month 6, day 14 (Year of the Rat)
Hebrew Calendar: 13 Av 5780
Mayan Calendar: 13.0.7.13.2
Ethiopian Calendar: 27 Hamle 2012

Marie, Duchess of Suffolk, left Grayside in the middle of a clear and moonless night, having stolen the most valuable thing that her husband's family owned. As she did it, she thought of her mother and smiled.

If she was lucky, James would never know what she had taken. She did not chance looking back as she walked away. She knew that if she did, she would never have the courage to keep walking. And she had no choice but to keep walking.

It would hopefully be days before James even noticed she was missing. She and her husband did not normally share a bed—at least, not unless he was there to try to have sex with her. Otherwise, she was left unbothered, in a plush and comfortable room done up exactly as she liked it, in the opposite wing of Grayside—the name apparently chosen by one of James's forebears because of the mist that swallowed up the manor house and blocked the view of the sea. The name was apt in every way. Marie's life was bleak and gray; always had been. She wasn't the only one who held that opinion: before she'd married James, she'd heard others refer to the house as "Graveside." Marie had learned never to do so after she'd chanced saying it once in the presence of her mother-in-law, the Dowager Duchess of Suffolk, who still ruled the house and everyone in it.

She hadn't had long to make her plan to escape, but she'd used the short period of time well. Marie had tested how easy it would be to get out of the house without any of the twenty-six live-in servants noticing, which was roughly half the number actually needed to run a house the size of Grayside. The house was old, the money running low, and so there was no modern alarm system as would be common in comparable homes. It was cheaper to employ people from the village—ideally, those who had fallen behind on their rents and could serve as nighttime security in the Duke's home as payment. They were untrained, often drunk and then asleep. Perfect.

Paid servants were another story. They often had to support not only their own immediate families but also members of their extended families on their meager salaries. Any slipup in their performance would result in an unceremonious dismissal without pay. They had every incentive to ensure that Marie, like everything else James owned, was not misplaced. Marie felt bad that what she was doing was likely to cost many of them their jobs—probably all the maids who attended her. But not badly enough to stop. It was them or her, and she'd chosen herself.

After two successful sojourns from the house in the dead of night, with no one mentioning or noticing it, she had laid her plan. She'd acted withdrawn during the day, being less than pleasant to her husband and his mother, and made sure that the servants saw her looking unwell. If she were unwell, James wouldn't want to see her. It would also provide cover for what was to happen later, if she were to seem faint and confused. She was a woman; they expected it of her anyway.

She'd wandered in unpredictable directions on both nights so that her maids could say later that she had seemed unstable but would not be so concerned that one of them would be placed in her bedroom with her overnight. That had happened in the past, and she didn't wish to be punished like that again.

And tonight, once Marie had made it out of the window on the ground floor that was easily unlocked and not patrolled by anyone, she scurried over to the edge of the sharp cliffs that led down to the sea. Waves thundered hundreds of feet below her. England had many beautiful seasides, and none of them were in Suffolk. The rocks here were jagged, the cliffs were high, the waves were unforgiving. Each year, the sea reclaimed more and more of the shoreline. The nearby town of Dunwich, once one of the largest towns in England, had nearly disappeared after centuries of erosion. The cemetery was the most recent victim, and it was not uncommon to see bones jutting out of the cliffside. And as the cliffs crumbled into the sea year after year, so too did the size of Grayside's estate diminish. It was almost poetic, and had Marie read that as a metaphor in a book, she would have found it too on the nose.

Marie took the bundle of sleep clothes from under her coat—the ones that her maid had dressed her in earlier that evening. She removed the slippers from her feet, left one on the ground, then tossed the other over the edge. She lifted the robe high into the air and let it go—it billowed out like a white flag of surrender, and she let the wind carry it where it might. She took the nightgown and let it flutter down to the sea below. She turned before she could see it hit the bottom and, stepping gingerly on stones to avoid leaving footprints, walked barefoot as fast as she dared toward the road that led to the nearest village, Covehithe. From there, she could catch the train to London, where she might pass safely and anonymously until she could get across the channel. She looked up, longing to see some stars, but they were hidden by the mist.

As far as faked deaths went, this was probably not the most convincing. But it was in everyone's interest for her to be dead, so she trusted they wouldn't look for her too hard.

Once she was over the rise of the hill that hid Grayside from the village, she allowed herself a shaky breath of relief and put on a pair of old shoes she'd found in a toolshed. She hadn't been seen or caught. Marie wrapped the coat around herself more tightly, pulled a scarf from an inside pocket, tied it over her hair, and marched into the wispy embrace of the fog. She checked the watch on her wrist—four hours until the first train of the day, which would leave before sunrise.

Marie felt inside the pockets of the coat: the little money and jewelry she'd been able to steal; the paper that she'd folded and refolded so many times in recent days that it was now as soft as flannel; a small book from the library; and the most valuable object in the whole estate. She'd never wanted for a single possession in her life, and now she was down to just the essentials, ones without which she could not survive.

Marie shivered; she was used to being cold at Grayside, but this was new. But she embraced the discomfort, the damp, the fear in walking along an unlit road at night without directions. She'd left her phone back in her room—not that she'd ever been allowed to use it without supervision. In London, maybe she could buy a new one—one that would actually provide the freedom the politicians and priests all said was too dangerous for women to wield.

When she saw the first smokestack rising from the village, she felt hope for the first time in her life. Maybe, just maybe, she could do this.

Chapter Two

Like all good broodmares, Marie Kenfield had been raised to attract the most optimal male and bear his children. She was the third of three daughters of Thomas Kenfield, the Eighth Earl Kenfield—making Marie her father's greatest disappointment. When she was born, he was so apoplectic with rage that he beat her mother, Charlotte, as she lay in bed recovering from Marie's birth. He banished Charlotte from the bedroom while he very publicly carried on with other women—tenants, servants, daughters of friends—who bore him three illegitimate sons, just to prove over and over to his wife that it was her fault that she had not produced an heir to the Earldom, not his. He was Earl Kenfield, and she was just his useless wife. After years of such humiliation, when Marie was only seven years old, her mother had walked off the cliffs. Her body had been found by the children's nanny, Jane. Earl Kenfield had refused a funeral or burial on the Ellthrop grounds. Instead, he'd quickly replaced his first wife with Louise Goodman, daughter of his shooting friend Lord Goodman, Baronet. After a quick wedding in the chapel and a few more nights in the bed, Louise had given him what he'd always wanted, what the estate had always needed—a son, Marie's little brother, Arthur.

Until Arthur was born, there had been a very real concern that her father's line would end with him and that the Earldom would be inherited by his horrible younger brother, Edmund. Edmund was unsuitable for the Earldom in every way, being a "confirmed bachelor," as they called it in polite circles, and Earl Kenfield was not going to let a man like that inherit his title. Arthur had been raised as the favorite, with his sisters, Alice, Emma, and Marie, distantly behind him.

Despite being only an Earl, Marie's father was a close member of the King and Queen's inner circle, frequently socializing with them on holidays. To attract a husband, the girls had to remain untouched and unblemished English roses. And they'd grown up in the regimented and stratified society of the English nobility, one of the few left on earth that classified and ranked its members according to class.

Their mother, Charlotte, had been the most beautiful and desired woman in all of England. She'd chosen Thomas Kenfield, who, despite being an Earl and not a higher-ranked Duke, had the more ancient family name, the older title, and the longer history with the Royal Family. His family home, Ellthrop Hall, was one of the oldest, largest, and grandest, with a portrait gallery rivaling that of the Royal Family itself and fifteen thousand acres of farmable land in Northamptonshire generating income for the Earl and his family. His daughters had wanted for nothing material. All they'd had to do was spend the useless years between their births and when they came of age doing three things: staying beautiful, learning a suitable hobby, and remaining virgins.

Alice, the eldest, had done two of the three. Tall and large-boned with a complexion that could turn flushed at any time and for any reason, she had been determined by her father not beautiful enough to attract an heir to a Dukedom, or even an Earldom, and he had signed her away to a low-ranking baronet as soon as she'd come of age. She'd born three sons in her young marriage, each one a plea for her father's affection and acceptance. He'd doted on his grandsons and continued to ignore their mother.

His second daughter, Emma, had approached Earl Kenfield one evening when she was sixteen and informed him that she was pregnant with a stable boy's child. She'd been thrown out of Ellthrop within the hour, with no money, and her sisters had been forbidden to try to contact her. The stable boy had also never been seen again. Marie, only twelve at the time, would forever remember the sound of her sister's footsteps on the gravel of the long drive. With Emma banished from the family, Alice married and in her own home, and their mother long in the grave, Marie had known deep in her immortal soul that she was going to be alone for the rest of her earthly life. And though it was a sin to do so, she'd prayed for a swift death.

But the Lord God did not hear her prayer, as usual. As soon as she turned eighteen, her father took her, his least-loved daughter, blushing and blonde and pale as a white rose petal, to London to be presented to Her Majesty Queen Federica, wife of His Majesty King Edward X, God Save the King. Queen Federica showed her favor to Marie, who was all done up in white with feathers and pearls in her hair. By the end of the week, Marie had attracted the attention of the most eligible man in England: James, Earl of Lincoln and only son of the Duke of Suffolk. They'd been married before Christmas, with Marie hiding under her veil as her father handed her over to her husband, whom she'd met only twelve times before that day. Her stepmother, Louise, had hissed at her to do her duty, and Alice had hardly met her eye from her seat in the eighth pew back from the altar.

Marie had brought to the marriage not only the prospect of an heir but also much-needed income for her new husband's ancestral home, Grayside, which was growing as decrepit as the old Duke himself. Within the year, the old Duke was dead, and James had inherited the Dukedom. Within three years, Marie had still not produced an heir. Her father stopped speaking to her altogether, and her husband did not speak to her any more than was strictly necessary.

For what was there to say to a third daughter of a mother who'd failed in her basic duty to her own husband? How long would it be before Marie's husband turned his eye to another woman? Marie spoke to the priest. She spoke to the doctor. She even spoke to the woman in the village who everyone called a witch. They gave her prayers, herbs, medicines, injections, bloodwork, new positions to try when her husband visited her bed. Nothing worked. Before long, Marie found telltale signs that her husband's eye was beginning to wander. A servant with a rumpled apron here, a tenant woman walking to the gatehouse there. At the shooting party, the wife of James's friend would disappear for a short period, then return, hair mussed and appetite ravenous, with her swollen lips and sharp teeth smiling at Marie as she devoured a tart.

Marie spent her days in the library, slowly and methodically making her way through the dusty old tomes that had been bought more as decoration than a thirst for knowledge. No one else read them; no one noticed that she took them. There was mobile phone reception at Grayside, but it was poor, and besides, the internet was not something ladies used. Her access was limited anyway by WifeLock, which prevented married women from doing or accessing anything on a phone that could betray their husbands in thought or deed. It was one of the many restrictions swiftly placed on phones once they had become available in England. Like everywhere else, they had represented a sharp break from the past and opened up a new avenue of clandestine conversation and research. This had led to women asking questions and learning about other parts of the world, two things that could never be permitted in England. So if Marie ever needed to use her phone, her husband or another approved man in the household used it for her. WifeLock kept her from using the more subversive parts of the phone, such as the internet or calling numbers that were not on a preapproved list.

She was one of the lucky ones—many husbands and fathers prohibited women from having access to any phone at all.

Books became her sole refuge. She'd open one and be transported away from this life. It was like going places. It might be what having friends was like. It taught her what it might be like to take a risk, to run away, to execute a plan—foolish things that people never did in real life.

Marie turned twenty-two. Twenty-three. By the time she was twenty-four, James hardly even looked at her anymore, and when he visited her bed, he was soaked in alcohol. The Dowager Duchess showed Marie the disdain that her husband couldn't be bothered to show himself.

Every look was a cold stare and a pinched mouth. Every turn about the garden was the discussion of what a wife should be and do. How a failure to produce multiple sons made a woman as useless as one of the mounted heads of animals that lined the walls of Grayside. Marie felt a kinship with them—they too had given their lives to be trophies.

Marie couldn't talk to anyone about any of this. Such things were simply not discussed. She hardly spoke to Alice, who avoided her assiduously. Marie knew Alice hated her because she had the husband that Alice, as the eldest, should have had. Alice could have given James the sons that he deserved, that he needed. Instead, Alice had three boys who would beg for the scraps leftover at the bottom of the peerage, all because she was taller than most men and her waistline was thicker than Marie's.

Marie thought of her mother often. Before she'd been carted off to London, she'd found a stack of letters and photographs that Charlotte had left behind before she'd died. They'd been left in their nanny Jane's care until she was dismissed just before Marie's wedding. Marie had not heard from Jane since then. The letters were then left in Alice's possession, and then in Emma's. Marie had found them in the rubbish heap after Emma left, and she had quickly stashed them away. At night, when she was alone, she'd read and reread the letters her mother had written. She'd trace her mother's profile in photographs, marveling at the same crease in the left ear that they shared, the same arch in the eyebrow, the same mole above the lip.

Another year ticked by. Marie turned twenty-five. She was as good as a spinster, wandering the cold, unfeeling halls of Grayside. She had read over one hundred books. She'd finished the poetry and was making her way through the histories and the geography books. When she cracked a new book open, she often wondered if she was the very first person in the house to open its pages and let it breathe. Books were the only things not suffocating in Grayside.

"You know, Your Grace," her maid Catherine told her in a whisper one evening as she brushed out Marie's hair. "I've heard that some ladies who are having trouble, they find some help from the men in the village, if you understand what I mean."

Marie slapped the girl for daring to speak the truth of her situation. And in the slap she concealed her fear. Of course she'd thought of that. But if her husband ever found out that she'd committed adultery . . . no. It was out of the question. Catherine was the closest thing Marie had ever had to a friend, and she ensured the girl was thrown out immediately with no reference.

Then, one morning, Marie huddled under a shawl as she walked the corridor near the garden, behind a tall hedge. She was so consumed with thoughts and worry that she nearly missed the Dowager Duchess whispering to her son. "No one will ask any questions," she was saying. "No one would even look."

She knew what they were saying. She had read about it in books that detailed the history of the English nobility. Wives of viscounts and earls and marquesses and dukes, after a few years of marriage that had produced no sons, had a habit of dying only to be replaced by more fecund women. Mistresses, or those who simply caught the eye of men. It hadn't been spelled out like that, of course. But it wasn't difficult to read between the lines.

Marie had heard it said at Ellthrop, and again at Grayside, that the estate was bigger than any one of them—that they were mere caretakers for something greater than themselves so that it could be passed on after they were gone. The succession was everything. Greater than any one wife who couldn't perform the one duty required of her.

Feet frozen to the garden ground, lungs full of cement, Marie knew that her time was up.

Now she was dead, and on her way to London.

Chapter Three

Marie had been cloistered inside Grayside for so many years that few people knew what she looked like—her wedding photo had been shared far and wide, but she was not that girl anymore, and had not been for a long time. She counted on that anonymity at the train station, where she knew she may attract unwanted attention as a woman traveling alone. She had once overheard her husband telling others that there was debate in the House of Lords in Parliament, where he held a hereditary seat, about restricting travel for women without a male chaperone. James had voiced his full-throated support for such a measure, while Marie had plastered a smile on her face and topped up his wine. So far, it had not happened. But Marie was certain that it was coming.

Women were seen and not heard, so men often forgot they were listening. Always listening.

It was so early that the conductor at the station was asleep at his post, a brown glass bottle dangling limply from his hand. From where she stood ten feet away, Marie could smell the alcohol and hear him snoring. She had a story prepared for if he woke up, but when the train roared into the station, he only snored louder. Marie hustled into the third-class carriage before he could wake up.

The carriage was packed shoulder to shoulder with people who had apparently been on the train all night, judging by the smell of bodies and general wrinkled appearance of everyone on board. Marie pulled her hat down farther, squeezed into the only available spot left, a gap on a bench between two sleeping men, and shut her eyes. The larger and sweatier of the two men grunted awake, took in his new seatmate, and gripped her thigh tightly with his hand. Marie froze, but decided not to make a fuss. Perhaps if she was quiet and still, he would remove it altogether. No matter who got on and off the train, he never did. But no one else bothered her, nor did anyone check for her ticket.

Marie wondered how long it had been since anyone cleaned this carriage. She guessed that it was rare, if ever. Train upkeep cost money, and none of the lords whose land it traversed were willing to pay for such upgrades. The King was the least willing. With only 2.6 percent of the population eligible to vote, and since the peerage and nobility never deigned to step in such things, Marie supposed that these same old carriages would be used until they fell apart, rusted and broken, the screws stripped and the wires exposed, the upholstery on the seats chewed into fodder by mice looking for nesting material.

The train was only supposed to take four hours to get to London, but it stopped twice to let sheep cross the tracks, so it was late morning before it pulled in to the city's sole station, Saint George's. This was the hub from which all railroad tracks branched out across England like a spiderweb. And as soon as the train pulled in, Marie tried to slither away from her seatmate's grasp. He briefly tightened his grip on her thigh, holding her down, asking where she was going in such a hurry. But when the man on Marie's other side told him to get his arse up because they were already late due to the delay, he grumbled and removed it. Marie waited for them to exit the train before she followed suit, lost in the crowd of alighting passengers, where she hoped no one else would take an interest in her.

London smelled of smoke, damp, and garbage. A thin layer of soot powdered every surface, and when Marie used a tissue to wipe her nose, the tissue was streaked black. The hem of her skirt was stained brown after stepping in a number of puddles on her way out of the station. The sound of the trains as they screeched to a halt was earsplitting, and the cacophony of voices, announcements, and young boys shoving newspapers in her face was overwhelming to Marie, who'd spent most of her life in the countryside ensconced in large houses that were built out of brick and stocked with servants whose professional dictum was to be neither seen nor heard as they tiptoed about on plush carpets.

Marie eventually made her way out to a small park that faced the entrance to the station. Looking up at the marbled gray sky, she thought about her next steps.

Buying a phone at a legitimate retailer was out of the question without a male relative providing written authorization; she remembered James's triumphant announcement of that law passing. But the city still had a number of phone booths, painted red with the crown atop, and she ducked inside the first one she saw. She nearly bolted outside as soon as she did—the smell of urine was so overwhelming she nearly choked on it. But she removed her scarf from her head and wrapped it over her nose and mouth, and with that small bit of help, she could tolerate the stench. She tapped the booth's digital screen so that she could run a search, but could not get the screen to switch on. She thought about finding another phone booth, but then she saw a moldy old phone book dangling from a chain, and she opened it up.

She searched the name of her sister, Emma Kenfield.

Marie had had no way of knowing for certain whether Emma was here in London, but it was as good a place as any to start. Discarded children were pulled here like planets to a dying star. Emma was strong, but even she would have been pulled in and eventually trapped by its gravity.

Marie's well-manicured index finger scanned the "K" page quickly, then stopped so suddenly she nearly tore a hole in the page. There she was. She had been living under her name openly all this time. It had an address associated with it. It listed her status as unmarried, which had probably limited her housing options.

Marie committed the address to memory and finally left the phone booth. London had a number of digital stations throughout the city with maps and directions on them, and so she visited the first one she saw. Mercifully, the display in this one worked when she tried it. She entered the address she had seen in the phone book. Emma's home was only a short walk from the train station, as if she had been waiting for someone to come for her all this time. And no one had come. For thirteen long years, no one had come. Marie memorized the directions, street names, and estimated amount of time. She whispered the address to herself several times, then decided to go for it.

To Earl Kenfield and his daughters, Emma was as dead as their mother, with no remembrance of her made anywhere. But Marie had remembered. She'd clutched the memories tight, cocooned them around her, taking comfort in remembering her sister's love and affection. Alice had always burned with so much jealousy toward her sisters that she'd withdrawn into herself. But Emma? Emma had smiled. Emma had laughed, which had been an alien sound in their home. Emma had had fun.

Even associating with Emma, as a fallen woman, would have created risk for Marie's own marriage prospects, so she'd buried Emma deep down in her heart where no one could find her. Now . . . now, none of that mattered. They were both as good as dead. There was freedom in that. Freedom to reconcile.

Marie thought of how she had evolved since she had last seen her sister, from daughter to wife to ghost, how much her perspective on the world had shifted, and she felt her entire body constrict. Thirteen years was a lot of time for Emma to be alone, waiting, hoping for someone to come. Marie wondered how much Emma had changed over that same period.

To focus on finding her destination, she resolutely ignored the rows of buildings; the town houses that bled one into the next; the cobbled and cracked streets; the music wafting out from the public houses; the squalling of children and babies from the soot-dusted windows of flats shared by multiple families; the statues of long-dead kings and their wives; the droppings of pigeons; and the posters and bills that were posted up and partially ripped down advertising concerts, plays, festivals, and church events. There would be time for all of that later. For now, Marie had to keep focused on the map in her mind as she superimposed it over the streets before her. She'd spent so many years looking at the maps in the books in the library, yet was still surprised at how simple it was for her to do this. It was not as if she'd had any practical experience navigating. She felt exposed without anyone with her, and yet also liberated.

Down south on Tottenham Court Road. Past Charing Cross. Left around the King's Mews. Straight down to the River Thames. Right to follow the river for about half a mile. The clean lines of the map were in her mind all the way.

She finally arrived at a three-story brick building built sometime in the last century. Granting herself the luxury of looking around, she saw that this building, like all the ones beside it and across the street, was showing its age. England and France had been at war on and off for a millennium. Every family who did not own land had at least one son, sometimes more, conscripted to hold on to patches of land in Calais and Brittany that were currently under English rule. The land had been ceded back and forth with France, volleying like a shuttlecock in an endless and bloody game of badminton. Because of this attempt to hold on to a few thousand square miles of land, there were fewer men available to keep up basic maintenance in London. There were cracks in foundations, paint peeling along the windowsills, broken windows that had been hastily patched up with tape, garbage piled up in the gutters, and weeds growing in the gaps between the bricks where the mortar had long since crumbled out. And, of course, there were the women and children who had to face the world alone. Women were, by both custom and law, paid less for their work than men. Married women were expected not to work, and it was not uncommon for a woman to be let go from her position once she got married. Many employers had policies, officially or otherwise, not to hire married women. From the remaining pool of unmarried women, there was a spectrum. Widows received the most money, never-married mothers the least, when they could find work at all. Many took to the streets to support their illegitimate babies.

The building facing Marie was a mixed-use structure, with a cobbler's shop on the ground floor and two floors of flats above it. The cobbler napped on his workbench inside his shop, snoring in his leather apron. Marie, suddenly attacked by a fit of nerves, watched him for a long while in order to avoid going to the black door next to his window, which presumably led to the stairs. She could see the buzzer on the door, a small patch of white amid the endless black. Staring at her like an unblinking eye, judging her for not lifting a finger to ring it. Judging her for not ringing it for over a decade. In the lintel above the door was the carved seal of the King: *EXR*. King Edward X, God Save the King. It was newer than the rest of the building. The old lintel would have been replaced just four years ago, following the passing of King Edward's father, King James IV. Whatever happened, whatever the labor shortage, whatever the poverty, the image of the current king was always promptly updated on every building in the kingdom.

Marie thought of all she'd left behind, and the weight of what she had stolen, and decided that enough was enough. She had so much to lose now, and even more to gain. She left the cobbler to his nap, stood before the door, squared her shoulders, and put her finger on the buzzer.

"Marie?"

With a start, Marie whirled around to find another woman standing behind her, wearing the same wide-eyed look of shock that she knew must appear on her own face. The woman was a couple of years older than Marie, but the faintest lines beginning to form around her light-blue eyes showed that she'd lived many more lifetimes than Marie herself had. Her hair was darker than Marie remembered—instead of the strawberry blonde it had been, it was now a deep red. More freckles across the cheeks than she remembered too. She must have spent time in the sun. Good for her.

She looked so much like their mother.

"Emma?" she breathed.

Emma nodded, looking both relieved and terrified to see her. Her face shifted through multiple other emotions before she finally appeared to settle on one.

"Excuse me," she said. And she brushed past her sister through the door, then slammed it shut behind her.

Marie pounded on the door over and over. She hadn't come this far to be left out in the cold and damp labyrinth of an unfamiliar city. "Emma!" she cried, not knowing whether she could even be heard. Emma probably lived one or two floors up, and maybe didn't even have a window to look down on her. Marie supposed Emma wouldn't even waste the steps to the window to watch her.

Long minutes passed. A quarter of an hour. A half an hour. Still no Emma. Marie blinked back tears. She couldn't do this without Emma. She needed to *tell* Emma everything. Even if she were dismissed again, she would be heard first. "Emma!" she cried out again, pounding with all of her might. It was unladylike and bound to attract the wrong sort of attention. Then again, no one passing by seemed to notice or care about her obvious distress, which both surprised and disturbed her.

She raised her fist to pound again, and the door flew open.

"You sound like a maniac," Emma said through clenched teeth.

Marie was so relieved that she forgot to be angry. "I'm sure," she said, choking on the hope swelling in her throat.

Emma stared at her for a long moment, then relented and stepped aside, opening the door wider. "Best not make any more of a scene," she said.

Marie nodded and, before her sister had a chance to change her mind, darted in.

They were shut inside a dark, narrow landing that smelled of dust and mold. A dim light flickered intermittently from a sconce on the wall. Power in London could go out from time to time, depending upon the coal supply and whether there was a labor dispute between the workers and the overseas businesses who controlled the mines. The country couldn't afford the same kinds of power generation systems commonly used abroad, including thermal or wind or solar or hydraulic energy. But coal? That they had plenty of, one of the few resources that *was* plentiful in England. So they burned it, even if it made the country an international pariah. It wasn't like they had much other choice. But, like many of its resources, the bulk went to the military. Wealthy businesses from Asia and Africa ran the mines, with many of the landed gentry and politicians benefiting from the arrangement. Marie's husband had no stake in these partnerships, but she was certain that her father, and now her brother, did.

Emma said nothing as she stomped up the stairs. Marie followed close behind. It was difficult to see; the stairs were wooden and slippery from years, possibly decades, of feet wearing on them without the benefit of a protective carpet. There was no handrail, so Marie held her balance by keeping her hand against the wall. The wallpaper felt rough beneath the soft skin of her fingertips and peeled away in large sections.

When they reached the second floor, Emma abruptly turned left down a corridor and passed three dark wooden doors until she reached one at the very end. Pulling a brass key from her pocket, she unlocked the door and entered without turning around, leaving it open for Marie to follow her, which she did.

The entire flat was smaller than Marie's bedroom at Grayside. The door opened into a small room with a threadbare couch and a table with two chairs. No television; the cost of a license was prohibitive to many, to the point that even at Grayside, they only had one. To the left was a door which presumably led to a bedroom; Marie could see the corner of what looked like a handmade quilt peeking out. To the right was another door leading to a small kitchen. Directly before them was a third door, shut. Must be the bathroom. She gave her sister a tentative smile. "It's very cozy," she said.

Emma shrugged and hung her coat on a hook on the wall. "It suits, I suppose."

Marie looked around some more. The flat was neat, tidy. Not what you'd expect for someone with a child who was now . . . twelve years old? Thirteen? She was ashamed that she did not know. Had never asked.

"Where is . . . ?" Marie's voice trailed off. She wasn't sure how to ask the question.

"Where is what?" Emma's tone was brisk.

"Your . . ." She could hardly bring herself to say it. She had no idea if it had been a boy or a girl.

Emma rolled her eyes. "My god," she said. Marie flinched minutely at the blasphemy. "Living in that manor has really stolen your voice, hasn't it? I'm so glad I escaped when I did."

Marie would never have described it as an escape. It was a disownment. Their father had even said that Emma was no longer a Kenfield, though obviously Emma had continued to use their family name. Her father had never bothered to take the necessary legal steps to strip her of it. Ironically, the two daughters who hadn't been disowned no longer used it. Alice was now Lady Penrhys-Evans, and Marie had been Duchess of Suffolk.

"I would give you the tour," Emma said archly, "but I think you've probably done so yourself already. And I'd offer you some coffee or tea, but I'm afraid those luxuries are out of my price range, though I'm sure I have some new beer, if you think you could choke it down."

Marie shook her head. "You needn't trouble yourself."

"I know," Emma spat. She threw herself down on the couch, arms folded, staring at the wall across from her. Marie stood awkwardly next to the coatrack, trying to become another item of furniture, before she slowly crossed the room and sat at one of the chairs at the table. She didn't dare join her sister on the couch. Not just yet.

The tick of the clock was thunderous, counting away the seconds and reminding them both of all the time that had passed. All the years that had been wasted.

"I was going to leave you out there."

Emma's whisper was almost drowned out by the sound of the clock.

"I was going to slam that door in your face and never look at you again," she continued. "You were the last person I wanted to see, ever. And especially looking the way you do now."

Marie looked down at herself. Still wrapped in the coat, with the simple dress and boots. The scarf was still tied around her hair. But Emma could see her. Always could.

When Marie had been eleven and Emma fifteen, they had often played in the picture gallery of Ellthrop, running past the priceless works of art that were merely wallpaper to the two girls who grew up oblivious to their privilege. Their mother had been gone for about a year, their stepmother had been busy with their new brother, and the two girls had often been left to their own devices. Alice had sometimes tried to corral them, but often gave up once she concluded that the worse they behaved, the better she looked by comparison. So Emma and Marie would run up and down the gallery, shrieking with delight, until they'd hit the end of the hall, where an enormous bust of their great-grandfather stood sternly surveying his property. Every time Marie saw it, she got scared, as if she knew how disappointed the Fifth Earl Kenfield had been in his heirs. Marie had always pretended she wasn't scared of him, because it was just a statue, and even she at this age knew that. But no matter how brave a face she'd put on, Emma would always put her arms around Marie and challenge her to a race to the opposite end of the hall. Marie had known that she was giving her an excuse to run away from the bust as fast as possible. She'd always taken the offer, and always appreciated her sister for it. But never once had she thanked her for it.

"Why didn't you?" Marie chanced asking now.

The clock ticked thirty-seven times before Emma finally answered.

"It was because of the way you look now," she said. "You, a Duchess, and you're here in very un-Duchess-like clothes, looking for me. Something went horribly wrong for you. And"—Emma sat up and dug out a phone from her pocket—"I was angry with you for scaring me." She tapped on it a few times and thrust it forward so Marie could see it. Marie overcame her shock at seeing her sister with her own phone to look at what Emma was showing her. It was a news article with a headline: **Duchess of Suffolk Missing, Feared Dead.**

There it was, officially. She knew it was in her husband's interest for her to be dead, but she hadn't expected it to go public so quickly. Hadn't expected them to give up searching for her within hours, rather than days.

She was committed now. This was real.

"Oh," she said.

"Yes," Emma said, shoving the phone back into a pocket of her dress. "So you can imagine my shock and relief and anger to find you here. Looking for me only an hour or so after I thought I'd lost you forever."

Marie thought Emma's lip just quivered when she said that. But Marie would never mention it.

"You didn't lose me," Marie said.

"Yes, I did," she responded. "I ensured it years ago."

"What do you mean?"

"But this time, this time it would have been final," Emma said, ignoring Marie's question. "I knew seeing you again was never really an option, but it was always there in the back of my mind. *I could see Marie again, if I really wanted.* Just the possibility gave me so much comfort over the years. And then I saw that article, and I thought it was gone."

Marie couldn't think of what to say in response to that. What could anyone say?

Emma made a sound that was a combination of a scoff and a laugh. "It never once occurred to me that you'd try what I did."

Marie was confused. "What you did? Father threw you out."

Emma eyed her. "Marie, do you *see* a child here?"

Relieved that she hadn't had to ask, Marie shook her head. But then she wondered. Had Emma . . . gotten rid of it?

"There was no child, never was."

Marie blew out a breath.

Emma continued. "I knew that the Earl would throw me out at the merest hint of impropriety. We were nothing more than liabilities to him anyway. I was certainly never going to marry the right sort of person, and I was staring down the barrel of my debutante year. So I told a lie that would be unforgivable, and got out of there."

Marie's jaw hung open.

It made sense. No one would have considered or discussed any other options for taking care of the situation, even whispered. All it would have taken to stain Emma's reputation was the suggestion of impropriety, and here Emma had flat-out admitted it, loudly saying what no one else would ever dare.

"I thought I had stumbled upon the perfect plan: ensure that I could never show my face in society again, and also be unencumbered by the scandal. If I was away from polite society, no one would know about the pregnancy. It never would have made the news, and in this rung of the social ladder, no one would care. Half the women I've met in the city had children outside of wedlock. I wasn't unemployable or shunned or anything like that. I was just . . . free. Or, rather, as close to free as anyone can be."

The poor women who'd had children out of wedlock could be seen beggaring in the streets with their waifs. It had relieved Marie to no end to see that her sister was not living that way, and she'd wondered how Emma had managed it.

But the relief she felt was now tarnished by the feeling of rejection. Emma had not been banished. Emma had abandoned her. And she hadn't been the first one to do so.

"I see," Marie said flatly.

"I had no chance of surviving in that life, but you? You could have thrived in it. I thought you *were* thriving in it. You were beautiful, obedient, a virgin. You were going to marry the best of the best, graduate from Earl Kenfield's daughter to duchess. And you did. It would have killed me to live that life, especially after seeing Alice married off the way she was. But you? You could do what the Earl always wanted, and that was worth it to me, to know you would be okay."

"I wasn't strong enough," Marie whispered. It was all she could say. She couldn't say what she really felt—it wasn't proper, and it was too hard. How could she tell her sister that losing her had been more difficult than losing their mother? That when she was at Grayside, dying inside a little more each day, she'd thought of Emma and wished she could talk to her? That she'd wondered about the child she believed Emma had been carrying? That she'd feared for Emma's safety and security, and how much she'd hated herself for never checking on her, seeking her out, or helping her? No, Marie did not say any of these things. At the same time, she suspected she didn't have to.

They sat in silence while the clock ticked another minute. Another three.

"Well," Emma said, finally. "It won't do to just sit around this flat together. I don't have much in the way of food in the kitchen. And I'm sure you don't know how to cook."

Marie couldn't help but laugh at that. She couldn't even say where the kitchen was at Grayside.

"So." Emma stood up. She gave her sister a look that was not quite a smile, but was less hostile than before. "Shall we go out?"

Chapter Four

Lady Alice Penrhys-Evans sat on the settee on the ground floor in her two-story home in the Devon countryside. Her husband was in town, doing something that Alice could not particularly remember. Her sons were off at school, not due home for several more months, and Alice was not going to visit until it was time. The day maid was upstairs doing Lord-knew-what, while the cook whistled as she worked in the kitchen, her melodic tunes floating out the open window onto the well-manicured grounds where the groundskeeper would enjoy listening to them.

In Alice's shaking hands was a printed copy of an email that had been sent from Grayside, delivered by personal courier that very morning, before it had gone public on the news.

> My Dear Lady Penrhys-Evans,
> It is with profound sadness that I inform you that your sister, Marie, Duchess of Suffolk, is missing and presumed dead from an apparent suicide.
> We will keep quiet the circumstances of the Duchess's death from the public so as not to inflame scandal.
> With our most sincere regrets,
> Francis Sharpe
> Estate Manager
> Grayside

Alice read and reread the missive multiple times, until she could quell the shaking in her body. She waited seventy-nine seconds, then stood up and went to the sideboard, where the maid left a pot of tea every day at ten o'clock sharp next to a fresh bouquet of flowers. Today, it was a collection of poppies and lilies. The tea was imported from China at great expense, and so a small pot each day was Alice's one indulgence. She poured the tea, spooned in the sugar, drizzled in a tiny bit of milk. Stirred. Stirred. Stirred. Then threw the cup at the wall, watching tears of milky brown liquid slide down the wallpaper.

She heard the maid come running and stalked out of the front door before she had to face the woman. She had just destroyed nearly a hundred pounds' worth of tea in her fit, and it wouldn't do to have someone silently judge her for such waste. That puddle of tea was worth more than the maid's monthly salary. The maid would sponge up the liquid, not daring to try a taste for herself. She knew her rank and position, unlike some. Good.

Alice continued walking until she reached the road. They didn't have a private drive, just a short driveway set back a few dozen yards from the road. Grayside had its own postbox and chapel. Back at Ellthrop, they'd also enjoyed their own brewhouse, mill, and equestrian grounds.

Taking a few short breaths to compose herself, Alice took her phone—the one her husband had permitted her to use, limited to calls only from an approved list of contacts—and placed a call to her brother. The housekeeper answered and agreed to take a message and have the ninth Earl Kenfield call her back forthwith. Alice thanked her politely, then stalked back toward the house; but rather than go inside, she walked around to a bench under two trees.

First Emma, now Marie.

Both of them drowned in their own scandals. Both of them indelibly staining the Kenfield family name. Both of them staining hers by reputation.

Emma, with her fornication and her bastard. Marie, with her sinful and selfish death, after the good marriage that their father had found for her. Those brats had never appreciated their advantages. They'd carelessly thrown away the lives that many would have killed to have.

It didn't matter what Sharpe said. Word would get out about how Marie had died. Alice remembered from her own mother's death that a suicide, even a suspected one, was too juicy of a rumor to be ignored, particularly among the pernicious society hens that always clucked around places like Grayside—a place Alice had longed to visit but to which she had never been invited. The funeral, if there even was one, would probably be there, and Alice would likely not be invited to that either. Though she supposed she wouldn't miss much; a suicide would not permit a service at the chapel, or any church.

Suicide. The most venal of sins, the coward's way out, as far as Alice was concerned. It was bad enough that their mother had done this. They'd been raised in the shadow of that shame. Alice had proved that she could do what neither of her sisters nor her mother could—produce sons. But to inherit what? Nothing much. And no one had ever appreciated her for it. She'd simply done what she was supposed to do, which was what Alice had always done. She had never once been thanked for it.

Alice pinched the bridge of her nose. Was there nothing that the women in her family would not fail at?

If only their father had been alive to see this. He would have had to admit that he'd ranked his daughters poorly, that of the three, Alice truly had been the one to show promise. She, of course, would never have said anything. But he would have known. And she would have known. And it would have been enough.

Alice continued stewing in the juices of her grievances until her phone rang.

◆ ◆ ◆

Arthur Kenfield, Ninth Earl Kenfield, listened to his eldest half sister for (he checked his watch) precisely forty-nine seconds before thanking her and hanging up the phone.

There would be much to sort out, now, with Marie's death, particularly of an apparent suicide. Despite the fact that he was not even twenty years old, he was the Earl, and the head of the family. While his married half sister's death was not his responsibility, it still affected him greatly. He'd have to clean up this mess. Messes were his job now. At least now he only had one sister left to manage.

He asked his private secretary to reach the Duke of Suffolk for him, who promptly took his call. After expressing his condolences, and receiving the same back from his brother-in-law, Earl Kenfield turned the subject to a more pressing concern, while ruffling his sandy hair with his free hand and catching his good looks in a nearby mirror.

"There is, of course, the matter of the Kenfield jewelry that she took to Suffolk with her. As she has no heirs, per the marriage contract, such jewelry is to be returned to Ellthrop forthwith."

The Duke immediately responded. "Yes, of course, it will be cataloged and sent to you by the week's end."

"I believe a list was provided for in the marriage contract," Earl Kenfield said. He had no idea if it was, but it sounded like the sort of thing his father would have done, and the hum of the Duke on the other end of the line affirmed his assumption. "If anything is missing, the monetary equivalent, per its last valuation, will be sufficient."

"Yes, I believe that will be agreeable. An inventory is being conducted as we speak."

The call ended without discussing the funeral, burial, or other arrangements. Such minor details were beneath their purview and would be arranged by others.

Earl Kenfield called Alice back and assured her that the jewelry would be returned and distributed as appropriate. Then he rang his private secretary again and asked her to notify him when lunch was ready, and to bring it to the verandah. The sun was shining today at Ellthrop, and he'd enjoy the weather while it lasted. His business for the morning done, he turned back to his chess game on the computer.

Chapter Five

"I have money," Marie said as they exited Emma's building. Emma turned sharply right in a practiced move.

"I'm sure you do," Emma replied. "More than you could ever hope to spend in a lifetime."

Marie thought about telling Emma about how her husband's income was down, how her share of the inheritance had been swallowed by the quicksand of Grayside, just like Marie herself had been. She had been subsumed entirely into her husband's family; neither she nor her money existed separately from him anymore. But she knew that what felt like a little money to her was likely a lot to Emma.

They crossed the street without waiting until they got to the intersection, with Emma stepping off the sidewalk without looking to her right or left. A car skidded to a stop with just a few feet to spare, laying on its horn, the driver gesturing wildly and shouting oaths. Emma didn't turn her head or slow her pace. Marie, frightened by the scene, scampered after her sister.

They were going down a part of the street that Marie had not covered on her earlier journey. A woman and three small children were crouched under a makeshift shelter in the gap between two buildings; there was a stack of cinderblocks with a sheet of plywood across the top and a heap of filthy blankets on the inside. Marie stumbled to a stop and looked at them. The children stared back at her with hollow eyes. One of them, a little boy of about four or five, had black soot scraped across his cheek and forehead, making his piercing blue eyes stand out as if they were electrified. Marie wanted to say something, but what could she say? There was nothing someone like her could say to someone like him. She'd never known want like that, even if she was now homeless as well.

Once upon a time, England had had more arable land than people. Then just enough land to support its people. And now it had ten times the population it once did—medical care wasn't as good here as it was in wealthier parts of the world, but it had made the death rate plunge while the birth rate continued unabated. Now too many families were living in poverty on too small a patch of land in the middle of the sea. Hence the constant warfare with France and the passing back and forth of the same land.

Emma flipped the children a coin without glancing at them and kept walking. With an apologetic look, Marie fumbled within her coat, found a coin, and tossed it to them as well. Not feeling better, she caught up with her sister.

"Not anymore," Marie whispered, referring to the money Emma had mentioned. "Not since, well . . ."

"That's right—you're supposed to be dead."

"Say it louder, will you?"

"Relax," Emma said. "Down here among the mere mortals, no one notices or cares about who you were. Most of us are dead, anyway. Our bodies just haven't caught up yet."

As if to punctuate Emma's point, a passing man yawned loudly and bumped into Marie's shoulder, then carried on without apologizing or stopping. He had done the unthinkable, touching a duchess, and hadn't even slowed his step. Marie couldn't decide whether it was because she no longer looked like a duchess, or because the idea of a duchess walking on this particular street was inconceivable to the average man. She supposed it was a little of both. It was liberating and insulting all at once.

"Your secret is safe here, which is why I suspect you have come all this way," Emma continued.

Marie thought about answering, then decided not to. While Emma hadn't embraced her with open arms, emotionally or physically, she hadn't thrown her out either. Being with her was a comfort, and Marie wrapped it around herself like a blanket. She didn't know where they were going but trusted Emma wasn't taking her someplace dangerous. If Emma had wanted to hurt her, she would have followed through on her initial instinct to leave her door closed and keep Marie out there in the street. There was hope yet.

London streets were notoriously narrow, uneven, and dirty. Feral cats slunk in and out of cracks in the buildings, no doubt living off the rats that came out at night. Dogs barked, and radios played from open windows. Street vendors sold chestnuts and sausages. A tattered Saint George's flag hung from a window. It was getting on toward afternoon. Children milled about everywhere, many selling newspapers or matches or candy, but none wore school uniforms. Just as in the countryside, education was available only to those who could afford to pay for it, making it largely out of reach for many. There were many mothers, very few fathers, and even fewer grandfathers. There were so few able-bodied men at all between ages eighteen and sixty, by Marie's reckoning, outside members of the landed gentry like her husband; titles kept you from being conscripted. Many returned from conscription with injuries both mental and physical, and with angry temperaments to match. It made finding a husband even more difficult, while the stigma of out-of-wedlock childbirth remained. A widow with two children was afforded much more respect than a mother who had never been married.

"Where are we going?" Marie finally asked.

"Dinner," Emma responded.

"Seems an awfully far way to walk."

"Far? We've been only five blocks. Still three to go."

Only five? Felt much longer. So much life was packed into such a small space here. Entire worlds were condensed into the crevices between buildings, and it was unknowable how much was happening behind each of the doors and windows they passed. Marie had only ever lived at Ellthrop and Grayside, where her family owned the land as far as the eye could see. She had spent scant time in London, where she was shuffled from one elite event to another, completely unaware of this other world that went on. Authors wrote about kings and emperors and heroes and villains and fantastical worlds and worlds inspired by the Scripture. No one wrote about the poor, the destitute, the huddled masses. They were only mentioned in passing in nonfiction texts, as vermin about whom nothing could be done. They were decried as immoral, irresponsible, and ignorant. But Marie saw that there was great humanity here, perhaps even more than there was in the world she had come from. The world that passed beneath notice—that's where she lived now.

Finally, after what seemed like an endless walk, Emma led Marie to stop before a building with a black-painted door and wide windows. A sign hanging above it read BAG OF NAILS.

"A public house?"

Emma nodded, then entered, not holding the door open for her sister.

Marie had never been inside a public house before. She'd heard that rough things could go on in such places, and that it was not a place for ladies to see. But she wasn't a lady anymore. And Emma didn't seem afraid. So Marie followed her.

The door opened to reveal a dimly lit but not unpleasant room full of mismatched tables and chairs. In the corner, several men played a game of darts; sharp objects, eyepatches, and alcohol did not seem like a smart combination to Marie, but she wasn't here to critique. Emma sat her at a table; it had a waxy, sticky feel to it caused by decades of being wiped down. Then Emma left to get their dinners from the bar.

"I can pay," Marie offered, raising the issue of money again.

"I know."

Emma returned a few minutes later, holding two large glasses full of dark, frothy beer.

"What's this?" Marie asked.

"Stout."

Marie sniffed it. "I'm not sure I can handle this."

"First rule of living incognito: change your eating and drinking habits. Who would ever expect the Duchess of Suffolk to drink something like this in a *place* like this?"

"That's the first rule? Not disguising your appearance and going into hiding?" Marie adjusted the scarf around her head for good measure.

"I'm sure it's up there somewhere," Emma said breezily. She offered her sister a mock toast, "To your health," and downed half the pint in five long swallows.

Marie sniffed at the stout again; she could smell the hops and the high alcoholic content. Her stomach turned. But she decided one sip wouldn't hurt. The beer was so thick she could chew it, and the taste was most disagreeable. But Emma had paid for it, and this was her life now. Emma was right; the Duchess of Suffolk would never have had such a drink. But Marie, newly anonymous? This could be her favorite drink.

She delicately dabbed at her upper lip when she was done.

The bubbles churned in her stomach. She felt the alcohol rising to her head. This wasn't new beer, nor was it wine. It was stronger stuff than she was used to. A few minutes later, a server dropped two plates of fried fish and a mixture of cooked carrots and cauliflower before them, along with a wooden condiment holder with five slots containing ketchup, mustard, vinegar, oil, and brown sauce.

Marie took a few moments to prepare herself to eat this unfamiliar food, but Emma dove right in, taking a big bite out of the fish and chewing in a most unladylike manner. Marie supposed that this was how her sister lived now. How she had lived for some time.

"So," Emma said, leaning forward. "Suppose you tell me why you're really here today."

Chapter Six

Marie sputtered. She wasn't used to people being so direct. It was like walking into a room and upending the nicely set table. You had to work your way up to these things.

Emma took another large bite out of her fish and talked with a full mouth. "You're supposed to be dead, so you can go anywhere you want. And yet you've come looking for me after thirteen years of estrangement. Surely you need something from me, or you'd never deign to come down to the gutter."

"I hardly believe you live in the gutter."

"Relative to where you've come from? Yes, I do."

"Do you like it?"

"I asked you a question first."

Emma took a bite of carrots this time. Even though it was late summer, vegetables could be hard to come by—so much of what was grown was shipped to the soldiers at the front lines. Most people grew them in their own small gardens. Grayside had had a large one, supplemented with the crops grown by the estate's tenants. Ellthrop had had an even more impressive garden, where such rare fruits as strawberries and grapes grew in abundance. Marie had never truly known how special a place it was until she'd gotten to Grayside and grapes had been a once-a-year decadence.

But for everyone else: Carrots. Onions. Cauliflower. Cabbage. Through an overseas aid program sponsored by the Inca Empire following a famine after several hard frosts in a row, potatoes were now plentiful in England and Wales. But most of those also went to the soldiers at the front. They were sturdy, hearty, grew quickly, and provided a lot of energy. It was said that potatoes were the engine of the English military. Marie thought that might be right. She'd never had one herself.

"I thought we might catch up first, since it's been so long," Marie said. "I don't even know what you do for a living."

"I clean houses. You're dead. There, we've all caught up. Now stop stalling and answer my question: What are you doing here?"

Marie used a grubby knife and fork to daintily cut a tiny piece of the fish. She ate it. It wasn't bad. She cut another, ate it, then took a deep breath and decided that if she was going to live among the likes of Emma now, she should start acting like her: direct and to the point. No matter how much it hurt.

Emma began taking a big swig of her stout and Marie answered her question.

"I think our mother is still alive."

Emma choked on her beer and spat some of it out as she coughed and tried to regain her breath. Marie calmly sliced up her carrot and took a bite. It needed more salt, which she added, before taking another bite. Yes, that was better.

"What?" Emma eventually choked out. Even in the dim light, Marie could see that her face was beet red with both shock and the effort of trying to breathe.

"You heard me. Clearly."

Emma took another sip of her stout and regained some of her composure. "I think you'd best start from the beginning."

"The beginning-beginning?" Marie asked.

"I need some context for this. And why you think what you think. Which is impossible."

"Not so impossible. I'm also supposed to be dead."

"Fair point." Emma considered for a moment then added, in reference to their eldest sister, "Does Alice know?"

"Of course not. She'll be all too happy to dance on my grave, if anyone even bothers to give me one. But I think everyone will consider it an unnecessary expense, given that my body won't have been found."

"Surely things were never that bad?"

"I never produced a son."

"You still had time."

"It had been seven years. I started to . . . hear things."

Emma arched an eyebrow. Marie looked around her and lowered her voice. "You can put two and two together on that one, can you not?"

"I'm not sure I know what you mean."

Marie gave Emma a brief rundown of everything that had transpired in the prior months, including what she'd heard the Dowager Duchess tell her son about how things could be handled discreetly, and no one would miss Marie.

"And there's, you know . . ." Marie looked around furtively before whispering, "Queen Matilda."

Matilda had been the wife of King Arthur III three hundred years earlier. After a decade of marriage, she had failed to produce a male heir—she'd borne only a single daughter and had multiple miscarriages after that. With a male heir less and less likely, and with King Arthur having no brothers, Queen Matilda had been suddenly tried on charges of adultery and treason, and beheaded. Arthur had married his pregnant mistress, the new Queen Margaret, only eleven days later. It was still forbidden today to suggest that Matilda had been innocent of the charges against her. Contradicting the word of a king, even a long-dead one, was illegal. But everyone knew what had really happened. And everyone knew that he had created a template for powerful men to rid themselves of troublesome wives.

"It all seems so beneath them," Emma said.

"Not really. Divorce is obviously not an option. But barren wives are expendable. Particularly when there are so many who are queuing up to take my place. They've already been road-tested, if you know what I mean."

"I'm sorry to hear that."

Marie waved off the concern. "Anyway, in the years I was the Duchess of Suffolk, I had lots of time alone. The estate more or less runs itself, and save for the social season, there just wasn't much for me to do. I had no friends, no profession. The Dowager Duchess never stepped aside. It's her house. Grayside is large and has a well-stocked library that no one ever visits. So I used it every day. They had every book imaginable, and no one wanted to read them. Can you imagine?"

Emma nodded. "Of course I can. You didn't really think that Ellthrop had a large picture gallery because our family were lovers of art, did you? It's about ownership of something unique. With books, it's about counting the number of spines on the shelves, the rarer the better, not what they might discover within the pages. It's just another way of showing off—hoarding beautiful things like art and knowledge just because you can."

"I wish there were libraries like this everywhere," Marie said. "I'm sure London has a couple, but I'm talking about big ones open to the masses. Think of what we could all accomplish if the whole country were literate and educated and curious."

"I never knew you to be so egalitarian," Emma said.

"I've had lots of time to think, and lots of time to read. I spent hours a day reading. I'd pop into the library, take a book, bring it back to my room, read it, and return it. I think I went through one book per day, sometimes more. Lots of the classics, of course, but also scholarly books—books about history and geography, like what they must have at universities. I read about the whole world, or at least Europe. There wasn't much about England except biographies of kings and copies of speeches made in Parliament. There were more books about China and the Islamic Empire, of course, and the nations across the ocean in the

New World, but I found a fair bit about other countries that are closer to home. They even had one on Ireland! And one on Scotland, by a Scottish author. It's all very different from the history we were taught. I could go on all day about that."

Marie was stalling, and she knew Emma knew. Emma was kind enough to let her ramble.

"Anyway, when I wasn't reading the books, I read and reread Mother's old letters. That was my other escape. I was so young when she died, and after you left, Alice didn't seem to want them, and so I took them."

There was so much more that Marie wanted to say. How Emma's departure had left a large hole in both her life and her heart. How she'd never felt loneliness like that before. How her life had become complete isolation, with neither beginning nor end. How marriage was her only hope for some sort of love and acceptance in her life. How desperately she'd wanted to follow her sister out the door, and how powerless she'd felt about all of it.

She couldn't tell her sister any of that. They were English, and the years between them were a chasm so wide that it seemed impossible that a bridge could be built. But she had to lay the first stone.

"I'm sure you remember reading them," Marie finished.

Emma shrugged. "I liked having them, but reading them hurt. I remember her more than you, and . . ." Emma sat taller and straighter. "Yes, it was best not to read them."

"And you didn't take them with you when you left?"

"I left them behind for you."

Marie suddenly felt herself blinking rapidly to stave off the swell of emotion that suddenly came upon her like a dam that had broken.

"For me?"

Emma nodded. "I knew that by leaving, I was abandoning you. I couldn't take anything of value with me. So I left the most valuable thing behind—her words. It was all I could give you."

They sat in silence. While Emma had left behind the most valuable things at Ellthrop, Marie had taken the most valuable thing with her from Grayside. She prayed her husband would never know. Marie sliced up another carrot, which was now growing cold.

"Since you haven't read them, perhaps this will summarize where I am going with all of this." Marie wiped her hands on a napkin and took the folded and refolded letter from her cloak. She held it out to Emma.

"I haven't shown it to anyone."

Emma hesitated, but then accepted the letter.

"If you still aren't ready to read it . . ."

Emma shook her head. "No, I'll do it." She unfolded the paper and read the missive in her mother's faded handwriting with tears in her eyes. The letter was to the sisters' nanny, Jane. It was dated a mere eight days before Charlotte had died.

14 April 1999

Dear Jane,
Springtime in London is the one season in which it is tolerable. I am always sure to spend a bit of time along the banks of the river Thames. This time of year, it actually appears blue and smells of sunshine, despite all the boats traversing up and down as if it were a canal. People call out from one to the other, and business is exchanged between the boats. People sell the most unusual things from boat to boat. It appears even some people hire boats simply to do their shopping on the water.

The wind here is cooler than usual, though it is not affecting the weather at all. It blows North to South, rather than South to North, and certainly not East to West. It allows me to smell the bread from the bakeries that are just behind me. Perhaps I will buy a bun once I finish writing.

Please give all my love to the girls. The Earl and I shall return in a few days.

Fondly,

Charlotte

Emma set it down. "She wrote so formally," she said, her voice shaking. "She never spoke like that with us. It's not how I remember her speaking. But I do remember how much she liked the water," she said, her voice so low it could barely be heard above the din of the people in the pub.

The men playing darts began shouting at one another, accusing one man of cheating, and within a few short moments the offender had been tossed out onto the street by his companions. The rest then sidled up the bar to buy another round of drinks, and the room settled back into its prior equilibrium.

"I didn't know that," Marie said. "I thought maybe there was something special about the Thames."

"Not really," Emma said. "It's usually clogged with ships and too dirty to be able to eat any of the fish you might catch. It would feed a lot of hungry people if that weren't the case. Some try anyway."

"I believe it."

"Well, anyway, what about this particular letter struck you?"

"By itself, nothing in particular. I never sought it out specifically, and only read it if I were going through her letters in chronological order. Which I did pretty often. At least once per year. This was always the last one, the punctuation on the sentence of her life, so I always lingered on it long after it was done. Point is, this letter was always one that I knew, but it was never significant beyond the fact that it was the last one.

"Anyway, as I mentioned, I spent a lot of time in the library. I made my way through the history and geography books in recent months.

And I happened to read one about Flanders." She withdrew the book from her coat as well—small enough to fit comfortably in a pocket and insignificant enough not to be missed from the library. "There was an entire chapter on Zeebrugge, a city in the north that's rather a large port that connects to the city of Brugge just south of it. Never thought much about it otherwise. But I continued reading, and it discussed its system of canals. And the commerce transacted on those canals. And I made the connection with this letter."

Marie opened the book to the page in question, and pointed to a picture of the bustling canal at Brugge.

"I think Mother was sharing a plan with Jane. I don't think she died. I think she escaped."

A few moments passed while Marie let the information sink in with her sister, who when she finally responded said, "That seems like quite the leap to me."

"I know," Marie agreed. "I thought it was insane, too, when I first had the thought. But look at the letter. It's such a bizarre thing to write to Jane. Mother's language is so stilted and formal, like you said. Exactly the sort of letter designed to be overlooked or ignored. I know she and Jane got along, but you wouldn't waste ink and paper on something this banal. The directions of the wind? Who cares? Commerce on the Thames? Everyone knows about that. Unless these were clues to her plan."

Marie took the letter from her sister and pointed to some of the language.

"'The wind here is cooler than usual, though it is not affecting the weather at all. It blows North to South, rather than South to North, and certainly not East to West.' She's telling Jane that she's going to leave the country and go south, to Europe, rather than north to Scotland. And she's going to southern Europe, rather than to Scandinavia. These must have been other possibilities that were considered. And then she narrows it down further: 'All the boats traversing up and down as if it were a canal.' Why compare it to a canal? Boats transact business on lakes, rivers, the ocean, docks. She's telling Jane where in Europe she's going to go. And it makes sense that she'd go here. She obviously can't go to France, and Flanders is reasonably close if that isn't an option. You can catch a ferry to Zeebrugge directly, and from there it's a short hop to Brugge.

"I think this is the final plan, and she was telling Jane so that she would have someone who knew where she was headed. And she had to bury it in a letter full of other banal nonsense so that no one would think twice about it. If you didn't know what you were looking for, you would dismiss this immediately. Jane would have dismissed it immediately—thrown it out immediately, not kept it for eight days, let alone longer."

"And Jane left it to us with the other letters," Emma said. "I always assumed she just bundled up all of them and gave them to us."

"But what if it wasn't Mother's last letter? What if she wrote other correspondence? She was the Countess Kenfield—of course she'd have written other letters between this and the day she died. Probably wrote many more that same day. To finish off the pile with this letter, it has significance. Jane put this particular letter at the end for a reason, so that we'd pay attention to it.

"It's a message in more ways than one, Emma. Mother lived. She escaped our father and went to Flanders. Mother went to Brugge."

Chapter Seven

Marie stared expectantly at Emma. Emma stared back at Marie with an inscrutable expression.

"What do you think?" Marie asked, when she could bear the wait no longer.

"What do *I* think?" Emma asked.

Marie nodded.

"You want my honest opinion?"

"I would never ask you for anything else."

"Very well." Emma set down her fork. "I think you're mad."

Marie had deliberately not kept her hopes up about this, but felt deflated nonetheless.

"Maybe," she said.

"It's just . . . I think you're making connections that aren't there. These things that you're saying? Pointing to words in our mother's final letter and convincing yourself that they're tied to something you read in a book? Not only that, you reach the conclusion that she faked her death, the very thing you just did in your own life? That's madness. Madness born out of loneliness and rejection and a yearning for a time when life was better for you—for when both I and our mother were still in your life. It's grasping for a connection that isn't there. You were under so much stress, desperate to conceive, and your husband's head was starting to turn. Of course you'd start to believe in outlandish things, like thinking our mother were still alive or hearing what you thought was your mother-in-law plotting to have you killed. And I understand it. I do. That life we were raised in, the one you just escaped, it's enough to break anyone. I had to escape it too." Emma gave Marie a look that seemed like pity. She reached out and took Marie's hand. "It would break anyone."

Marie snatched her hand away. "I'm not broken."

"No, no, no," Emma rushed to say. "Of course you're not broken. I'm just saying: the pressure that you were under, it would make anyone start to believe in things that weren't there. And there's nothing wrong with it. It happens to everyone eventually. Especially women in your position. A life of pressure wrapped in a life of boredom. I knew I'd never be able to handle it. That you managed to do so for this long is a testament to your character."

"Should I say thank you to that?"

"You're here now, and away from all of that, and I think I can help you. Doctors cost money, but we'll figure something out. Get you the care that you need."

Marie shook her head. "I can't do that. I'm supposed to be dead. The longer I'm here, the more services I use, the more likely I am to be found out. And if I am found, I'll be dead for real. There's no way they'll let me out of Grayside after that; I'll be kept under lock and key. And as the Dowager Duchess said, I'll not be missed if anything happens to me."

"That isn't true. You're the Duchess of Suffolk. People have already noticed that you're gone."

"I'm 'dead' now, and very few have noticed or cared!"

"It made the news."

"And yet no one, including our brother or our sister, called you about it."

"I'm sure they would but they don't know where I am."

"If I could find you, they could find you faster. If they wanted."

Emma didn't seem to have a comeback to that.

"If you don't want to come with me, that's fine," Marie went on. "I didn't really expect it, and I know it sounds outlandish. But I'm going to find Mother, whether you want to come with me or not. And when I find her—*if* I find her—I'll let you know. You can decide what to do then. But this can be a quick reconnection with me, so many years after we were separated. It doesn't need to be anything more than that. It's more than enough for me."

Civility be damned. She needed to just say the words out loud, painful as they might be.

"I understand if you can never forgive me for not coming after you. But I've missed you terribly, and I'm so happy to see you again." Marie let her lip quiver for just a heartbeat before collecting herself. She'd already shared so much emotion; it felt like she'd had her chest cracked open and her insides splayed out. "Thank you for that."

She felt the oil of the fish churning in her stomach, mixing with the stout, and decided that was enough eating and drinking for the day. She laid her fork and knife down parallel to each other, prongs of the fork facing up.

"They won't come and collect that from you," Emma said, nodding at Marie's plate.

"I'll handle it," Marie said. It would be a first, clearing her own dishes.

They sat in silence for a long time.

"I've missed you too," Emma said. "I didn't miss that life. But my God, I missed you."

They didn't look at each other. They didn't clasp hands or embrace. The words were enough.

"And that's why it pains me to see you this way," Emma continued. "I see what it's done to you, that life. And I want to help you, before this goes any further."

Marie shook her head. "I'm not mad, and I'm not changing my mind. I can't stay in England; they'll kill me. If I leave, then at worst,

I get a holiday out of it, and perhaps a new life abroad. I can live with that. It's hardly a poor consolation prize. I can't lose anything more than I have now. I've already lost everything. I have to do this."

Emma sighed. "If you insist upon doing this," she asked, "can you at least tell me what your plan is?"

Marie shrugged. "I go to Brugge. I look for Mother."

"That's your entire plan?"

"It's a work in progress."

"Doesn't seem conducive to finding her."

"I didn't have more of a plan than that when I came looking for you. And I found you almost instantly."

Neither of them said that it had been this easy all along, that Marie could have found Emma if she'd tried. Anyone in their family could have. They both heard it nonetheless.

"It's not like it's the Middle Ages," Marie continued. "I bet there are ways to get a phone. There are maps. There are ways to find people. Even those who don't want to be found."

"No one will sell a phone to a single woman," Emma said. "Unless, of course, you know where to look."

"Will you tell me where to look?"

"What makes you think I know anything like it?" Emma said, sounding affronted. She gave her sister a look that told her *don't say things like that so loudly.*

"Well, I'll figure this out. With or without you."

Emma looked at Marie, her eyes imploring. She looked so much like their mother. "Will you at least stay with me tonight? Start your adventure in the morning?"

Marie hesitated. "I couldn't inconvenience you like that."

"It's no inconvenience at all. You're my sister." She folded her hands in her lap. "Please."

Emma fussed about the flat to make sure that Marie was comfortable. *I can turn on the woodstove, but it gets very hot. Here's a blanket, it's not much, but it'll be better than nothing. Are you sure I can't get you something to drink? Please, take some of my sleep clothes.* It took forever to get Emma to stop fussing. Marie could sleep in her own clothes just fine, thank you, and the temperature is just fine as is, but yes, she'd take the blanket, and no, she did not need an extra pillow. Please go to bed.

It wasn't the luxurious bed at Grayside, but it was better than the grave. Marie settled onto the sofa, turned her back to the room, and did not sleep.

She heard Emma quietly get ready for bed. She heard her tapping on her phone. She heard the discreet phone call to the hospital, inquiring about whether she might have her sister admitted for nervous exhaustion, hallucinations, and stress, and what the cost would be.

Marie chose to see it as concern, rather than betrayal. She wasn't stupid. She knew how this probably sounded to Emma. But Marie knew in her heart that this was worth pursuing. And she knew what she'd heard at Grayside. She hadn't imagined it, not by a long shot.

And if she was wrong and her mother was dead, well. No one would ever know except her. And she could forget. If she had to.

But she certainly wasn't going to be stopped.

She waited until she was sure Emma was asleep, and then waited a little longer.

When she heard the church bells strike two in the morning, Marie got up, silently folded the blankets on the sofa. Smoothed down the couch cushions with her hand so that no indent from her body was left. There. As if she had never been there.

Stepping out into the foggy night, she took one look back at her sister's building, and then vanished into the city.

Chapter Eight

Emma slept quite deeply, considering all that had happened that day. It took her a long time to quiet her mind. Marie had been both dead and resurrected within the span of a day. Her sister had said some truly outrageous and frankly unbelievable things. Things Emma could not bring herself to believe.

And yet.

And yet they were all at least *plausible*.

Emma, for her part, had never once believed that their mother had killed herself. She'd always believed that something more sinister had happened: that Earl Kenfield had murdered their mother.

It was all too convenient. He could have demanded an annulment on the grounds of a failure to produce an heir. It would have dragged the Kenfield name through the mud, something that the old Earl could not have afforded before he died. Uncle Edmund would have seized upon that as a reason to claim the estate—and while Emma had never met her uncle, she'd heard Earl Kenfield curse his brother enough to know that he was not worthy of the estate, and why. She'd internalized that her whole life. Earl Kenfield would rather have burned Ellthrop to the ground and salted the earth itself than let Uncle Edmund take possession of it.

So he'd subjected his wife to a parade of humiliations, one after the next. Mistresses. Illegitimate children. Deliberately taking her to social occasions where his infidelities were widely known. And still, his wife had stayed with him. What choice did she have? She belonged to him.

What were the odds that she would have taken her own life, something that was too convenient for him and solved all of his problems? He hadn't even had to worry about securing a church or a Christian burial.

Emma hadn't believed it then, and she didn't believe it now. Their mother, the beautiful, sweet redheaded woman with piercing blue eyes, would never have taken her own life and left her daughters behind to fend for themselves. Not Alice, so insecure. Not Emma, so trapped. And certainly not Marie, so small.

Never.

No, Emma was certain that Earl Kenfield had blood on his hands. (He was always Earl Kenfield in her mind. She had no father anymore—he'd told her that directly. So just as he had stripped her of the family name, she had stripped him of that most sacred and exclusive title: Father.) And when Emma had been old enough, she'd said the worst thing she could possibly have said to him. Made sure that enough people heard it so that the family name would be sullied. And she'd shut the door on that life forever. Saved herself from being a burden on their half brother, whose existence was a mockery of their mother and all she'd been to them. And her belief that Earl Kenfield had murdered her mother was better than the alternative—that Marie was correct and their mother had been alive all this time. The idea that their mother could have just abandoned them to that life was completely unthinkable.

Noblewomen didn't raise their own children. They loved them the way they loved a painting—at arm's length, aesthetically, and with appreciation rather than true feeling. Not Charlotte Kenfield. She woke her children up each morning. Took her breakfast with them. Dressed them for the day. Spent her afternoons with them, talking about everything and nothing. Took them for long walks on the immaculate Ellthrop grounds. Gave them their baths at night. Sang with them.

Listened to Evensong with them. Read books with them. Taught them everything they needed to know in order to secure good marriages—the only available occupation for young women. Warned them about the sorts of things that made a good marriage on paper versus a good marriage in practice. Things that did not matter, she told them, were titles, looks, or professions. Things that did matter were character, values, and whether the person made you laugh. "Look at me," she'd implored them. "Consider the factors that I weighed most heavily. And look at what's become of me. I live in a beautiful house, but it's a mausoleum, not a home."

Love and security need not be mutually exclusive. In their position, in their circle, there would be no shortage of men among whom a husband could be found. Some women were even given the illusion of choice. *Choose wisely. Because we don't get a do-over.* Then they were married to the man their fathers chose.

Charlotte's daughters had all been too young to fully appreciate what she was trying to warn them about. And by the time they'd been ready to be married themselves, they'd been under their father's thumb for too long. Their stepmother had not seen any reason to bond with her husband's children from his first marriage, particularly when none of them were going to be heirs or threaten her son's position in any way. They'd been nothing more than an afterthought—an extra three mouths to add to the food budget, plus the cost of their trousseaus. They had not been so much as a rounding error in Ellthrop's budget.

So no; as far as Emma was concerned, their mother was dead, and not of her own accord.

That's what made her so frightened for Marie. Marie's experience was too similar to their mother's. And while she'd assured Marie that what she'd overheard could not have been true, the truth was that Emma believed her.

Emma was sure that Marie had heard correctly, and that murder had been the plan. Wives who couldn't produce sons and heirs were deadweight. What mattered was the survival of the estate, and a woman had to provide an heir (and, if possible, a spare) to keep the property in the family.

That didn't mean that Marie hadn't started to crack under the pressure. Who wouldn't? And who wouldn't have drawn a parallel with her own mother, who had become similarly useless to their father? Of course her sister was grasping at straws, trying to find a connection back to the mother they had lost. Marie needed help, and in her frenzied state had sought out Emma. And when Emma had seen her standing there on the street, it had been as if every prayer she'd ever secretly made for the last thirteen years had been answered. Emma had seen in Marie the same haunted look that she'd seen in their mother. At the same time, though, there had been a fierceness and determination that had never been in their mother's face. Unlike their mother, who'd lain back and accepted what her husband did to her, Marie had taken matters into her own hands. It was mad—she'd faked her own death and come to London talking about something that more or less amounted to hallucinations and fantasies. But she'd gotten out, which is more than their mother had been able to do.

If that mistaken belief had pushed Marie to take a step that saved her life—if the idea that their mother had done the same had become the life raft that she'd used to save herself—who was Emma to begrudge her? But false beliefs were worth clinging to for only so long; they may buoy you for a short while, but their holes would eventually cause hope to sink and drag you down with it. She had to keep Marie safe, and if that meant sending her to the hospital for the help, then Emma would. There would be the matter of having to give them a name and show identification, but Emma figured she could rectify that. Mr. Davis could help. Lord knew he owed her.

Emma lifted her head from the thin pillow. London in the morning did not wake quietly and slowly, particularly not in her part of town. The horns blared, and the shouting began long before the misty break of dawn. Emma had largely learned to tune it out, so it didn't bother her. But she figured it likely would have bothered Marie, who'd lived her entire life in near silence. She sighed and pulled herself out of bed, fully expecting Marie to be on the sofa or seated in one of the chairs, ready to press her case more.

But she wasn't.

Emma rushed around, calling her sister's name, but the flat was small, and it was clear within a few seconds that Marie had left.

Emma sat down on the couch that Marie had slept on. Marie was gone from her life, as fully and completely as she had been as recently as yesterday. She had not even left an indentation on the sofa cushions.

Emma heard the tick of the clock. Just twenty-four hours ago, this flat had been empty like this. And yet now, it felt like something was missing.

Emma steeled herself. This would not do. She had made the decision years ago to leave her family behind—it had been a good decision, the right decision, the only decision for her. A life spent in a gilded cage of a great house, nothing but a broodmare to provide sons for her husband? It was worse than death. It was a life that had destroyed their mother. Its expectations had crushed their eldest sister until nothing was left but resentment and bitterness. And it had driven her younger sister mad. Her younger sister, who was now presumably roaming the streets of London on her own, trying to launch her ridiculous plan. And who was probably lost, or being so obvious in her quest that she'd attract the wrong sort of attention.

Emma shook her head. Marie had successfully faked her own death and come all this way undetected. She'd found Emma quickly. She had, so far, proven herself surprisingly resourceful and competent. Even if she was starting to crack up, Marie would survive. Emma would survive. It was better this way. No attachments to the old life. That way just led to heartbreak and regret and rejection. It was good to see Marie had escaped it too. That was enough for her. It was time to move on, again.

She returned to her bed. She lay down. She closed her eyes.

She lasted thirty-four seconds before she was up, pulling on a coat, and going out to the street to find Marie.

Chapter Nine

Marie had quite literally looked up to her two older sisters while they were growing up. Alice and Emma had been born in quick succession, one right after the other; their mother had barely recovered from the birth of Alice before she found herself pregnant with Emma. But then there had been an unwanted pause as her parents tried for the son they so desperately needed. It took them four years to have another child, and the long wait had only amplified the disappointment they both felt when Marie arrived.

After their mother was gone and their father had swiftly remarried, Marie had shuffled around Ellthrop in the shadow of her sisters, the only two family members she had left who at least acknowledged her existence. She had known from birth that she was a disappointment, and time with her sisters was her only chance at being loved.

Alice had been shipped off to boarding school not long after their mother's death. She became Marie's "holiday sister"—the one who appeared for certain Feast Days and summer holidays but otherwise was packed off to a school run out of a convent for most of the year. Alice, with her large bones and wide-set shoulders, her long torso, and legs like tree trunks, had been ridiculed for her build. Alice had wound up with the worst features of each parent in her face: the nose too big, the lips too thin, the face too long. "She'll never fetch a good husband," Marie overheard their stepmother say to their father once, in a rare display of recognition that he had three other children.

"Poor Alice," Marie had repeated to Emma later that evening. Marie had been seven, seated on the carpet on the floor of Emma's bedroom, idly reading through one of the books that Emma kept hidden under her bed. They were not dangerous books, but these were two well-bred daughters of an Earl. For girls at such an impressionable age, and especially according to their father, all books were dangerous. Ellthrop had a library that served more as a status symbol than a source of knowledge, but Marie had found more than a few books in there to catch her eye. No one had ever seemed to notice that they were missing.

Emma, who had been eleven, had been on the bed above her. The curtains had been shut. The light in the room had been low. Her room was often forgotten by the rest of the house, which suited Emma just fine.

"What did you say?" Emma had looked up from a notebook where she'd been scratching out a drawing or a script or a diary entry—Marie never knew, and though she was always desperate to, she never dared try to find out.

Where Alice was absent and their stepmother indifferent, Emma had become Marie's whole world. She worshipped Emma. Emma, with her red hair and bright-blue eyes, fair skin, frequently eclipsed any other woman in the room. Marie always ignored it when their stepmother said that she was too similar to pictures of the whore Mary Magdalene.

"Poor Alice," Marie had repeated. She'd meant it too.

"Why 'poor Alice'?"

"Well, you know, she's going to have trouble finding a husband."

"Alice is only twelve," Emma had said.

"Some girls in her year are already engaged," Marie had replied.

"Promised," Emma had corrected. "Like a pig being fattened for slaughter—waiting for them to grow to just the right size. But they had no choice in the matter. Most have never even met their fiancés."

"Alice told me that some of them have phones, and they can exchange texts and photographs with their intended."

Emma had snorted derisively. "I doubt it. First, the convent doesn't allow phones. No convent does. Second, even if you could smuggle one in, it would destroy any engagement before it could be fulfilled. The girls would be seen as fallen. If they could text their betrothed, who's to say they couldn't text some other young man? Lies, all of it." She'd gone back to her scratching.

"I don't understand," Marie had said.

"Don't understand what?"

"Why would they lie about that to Alice?"

"They're not lying to Alice. Well, they are, but not really to Alice. Alice is just the audience. They're really lying to themselves."

"What do you mean?"

Emma had sighed with exasperation as she threw down her pencil and gave her little sister a scathing look, as if Marie were the dumbest creature in England. "Marie, imagine that the biggest decision of your life, who you will marry, has been made for you. Before you were even born, or when you were a young infant, the man was chosen for you. He might be your age, he might be your father's age. You have no say in the matter. They are just waiting until you are old enough to be bedded, and then they take you to the church and make it official. Like purchasing a car; the title is transferred from your prior owner, your father, to your new owner, your husband. And just like that, your life is over."

"Oh no," Marie had said with great authority. "That's when your life is truly beginning!"

"Why do you think the fairy tales end with the wedding?" Emma had retorted. "What comes after isn't worth spilling ink on a page."

"I'm looking forward to my wedding," Marie had decided. She was an Earl's daughter. She was going to have a good husband. She and Emma both would. Not Alice, though. Poor Alice.

"I'm not having one," Emma had declared.

Marie had looked up at her in shock. Not getting married was unthinkable. Not in the sense that it was horrifying or scandalous, though it was, but because Marie could not conceive of what a woman would do with her life if she had no husband or children. It was like an unformed shadow, unknowable and sparking fear.

"It's true," Emma had continued. "I'll never marry. I'll die before I do."

"Shush!" Marie had cried.

"Oh, you shush," Emma had said casually.

"Father will never let you do that," Marie had said.

"Father is going to marry us off as soon as possible," Emma had told her. "You're right to say 'poor Alice,' because they aren't going to try to find her a good husband. They haven't found her one yet, which tells me they're putting it off or they haven't received any offers for her. Her body won't help with that, nor her face." Emma had made a face of her own. "Or her attitude."

"Alice isn't mean."

"Maybe not to you," Emma had said. "You aren't worth her time to be mean to. But me? Oh, the things she says to me."

"What does she say to you?"

Emma had shaken her head. "Nothing you need to worry about. But she's afraid I'll get a husband before her, and that it'll be a better one than she gets, if she even gets one at all. Don't worry, she'll turn on you too. You're beautiful, and when you get a bit older you'll have options that Alice does not. And she'll hate you for it the way she hates me for it. And when she finds out that I'm not going to get married, that I'll throw that opportunity away . . . well, she'll hate me even more."

"You can't just not get married," Marie had insisted.

Emma had smiled like a cat. "Watch me."

"You're wrong."

"If you say so."

"And Alice will have a husband someday—a good husband. And so will I. And so will you." It had been more a prayer than a statement of fact, though Marie had pretended it was the latter.

"Hmmm," Emma had murmured.

The next five years had passed. Emma had joined the boarding school at the convent. Marie had stayed home, counting down the days until Emma could return, hoping that Emma was happy at school and knowing she was not. Alice had been in her final year there, and as the two had predicted, she was still without a husband awaiting her.

"I got you something," Emma had said on her first visit back. She'd handed Marie a small object wrapped with brown paper.

"What is it?"

"You'll see."

It was a mobile phone. "Where did you get this?"

Emma had just smirked. "Keep it hidden," she'd said. "But keep it close. This way, we can stay in touch."

"So the girls do have phones there after all?"

Emma had laughed. "Not the good girls."

Marie had dropped the phone as if it had scalded her. "I can't take this," she'd said. She'd wondered if she needed to wipe her fingerprints off the thing. Whatever Emma was doing, Marie did not want to have any part in it.

"Take it," Emma had replied. "A phone never hurt anybody."

"I can't ruin my reputation," Marie had persisted.

"You're only twelve!"

"Exactly. And I don't want to end up like Alice."

"End up like Alice?"

"No husband, no offers, nothing. This is the best she'll ever look, and she can't attract a man."

"That may be the best thing that ever happens to her," Emma had said. She'd shrugged. "Keep the phone, don't keep the phone, your decision."

"Ruining your reputation will ruin mine as well," Marie had reminded her.

"Well then," Emma had rejoined, "I'll have to ruin mine so spectacularly that I'll be erased from the family."

True to her word, she had. Before she'd been due to return to school, she'd informed her father that she was pregnant. He'd slapped her so hard that the sound had echoed through the corridors and against the centuries-old portraits on the walls of the picture gallery.

Emma had only smiled back at him, satisfied with what she had done.

She'd strutted out of the house, waiting for Marie to call her on the phone she'd given her.

The next morning, Marie had gone out to the pond on the grounds at Ellthrop, one of her favorite places in the world. She'd chucked the phone into the water.

Chapter Ten

Green's Lane was known for being a place where anyone could buy or sell anything, legitimate or illegitimate, real or fake, no questions asked about where it came from. Marie found this to be true as she became immediately lost in the packed, crowded street full of vendors and shoppers squeezed shoulder-to-shoulder, shouting over and shoving into each other. Paintings that were purported to be done by the masters were stacked four thick on rickety shelves. Canaries chirped from cages; geese and pheasants clucked from pens; and the smell of meat pies and ale wafted up everywhere. It almost covered the smell of the dog shit that Marie had to try to avoid stepping on. Livestock lowed and bleated from the auction block. People barked at Marie to come inspect their wares, giving her their full attention for just a second or two before moving on to the next potential patron. Children hawked newspapers that they themselves could not read. Some people looked at their phones, but many more did not, as they did not have them. People carried wicker baskets full of flowers and clutched paper bags full of buns. In a basket, commemorative coins from the wedding of a duchess to one of the king's children a few years back twinkled in the sunlight. Marie remembered they had once been all the rage, before everyone moved on to the next royal bride. She wondered what had happened to that duchess. Marie realized she hadn't seen her in years.

Marie felt strangely safe. There was anonymity in crowds. When everyone looked at you, no one looked at you, and you could blend in and disappear. This was a new sensation for her. At Grayside and Ellthrop, everyone knew who she was. Maids and servants stopped and bowed to her when she walked past them. In town, people knew who she was—the wife of the man who owned the land they lived on, the woman whose sheets they changed and whose clothes they washed, whose jewels were paid for by their farming labor. There was a necessary separation between them that Marie had never questioned. Here? People bumped into her and stepped on her toe. They didn't care who she was. She was nobody to them, invisible. Anonymity, that was true freedom. She rather liked it.

Marie didn't know everything she would need, but knew at the very least that she wanted to try to get a phone of her own, which she figured could not be sold to her in the open. In such a bustling bazaar that operated in full view of everyone, there had to be some sort of black market here. If one knew where to look. They were often mentioned in the stories Marie had read back in Grayside's library. Maybe they were based on fact. She'd spent so much time absorbed in books over the last few years. Maybe Emma was right; maybe she was extrapolating some of the more fanciful plots into her own life.

But Marie hadn't imagined the real threat to her. And now she was out. And she'd taken from James the thing he valued most. She hoped she could get out of the country before he or anyone else realized it was missing. Which is why she was here today.

"Can I help you, Madam?"

Marie turned at the sound of a young man's voice. She pulled her scarf more tightly around her head and took a step back. The young man appeared well-dressed, with his hair gelled back. He wore mostly black, and he had spectacles. Speaking with strange men was completely against everything she knew and had been raised to do. She turned her head away.

"Don't be afraid," the man said. "Are you looking for anything in particular this morning?"

Marie hesitated. How did one go about asking where the black market was? It obviously wasn't advertised anywhere. And you needed to talk to people, but who did you even talk to? The books never addressed this part. Perhaps being subtle would work.

"I'm not quite sure what I'm looking for can be found here," she said, hoping that her meaning was clear.

The young man nodded. "I see," he said. "Well, here you can see we have nice napkins. Tablecloths. All the linens you might need. If you're looking for things for the home, this is the place. Are you looking for things for the home?"

Was this code? It was too difficult to work this out. "I'm not sure I can afford it," she said. "I don't think I have the right currency."

"We take more than Sterling, Madam," the man said. "However you wish to pay, we can accommodate you."

Well, that was at least a bit more helpful. "What sorts of payment do you take?"

The man made a point of looking her up and down slowly. Surely he was considering how much money she might have.

"I'm sure we can arrange something," he said.

Good, a man she could do business with. This was perfect. What luck that she had found him so quickly.

"Just tell me what you need," he continued. "And I'll tell you what I need."

Marie nodded and opened her mouth to speak, when she felt a jerk on her elbow.

"You leave her alone!" a voice hissed. Marie turned at what she hoped was a familiar voice, but it was an older woman wearing a purple dress and a hat under which waves of gray hair were pinned perfectly. "Be off with you!" The lady unhooked her parasol from where it perched on her arm and started beating the man with it.

"Stop it!" Marie cried.

"Vermin!" the lady cried. "Rat!" She used a new insult with each strike. The man cowered. No one even stopped to spare them a glance.

"What are you doing to him?" Marie asked.

"Come with me," the lady said, grabbing Marie by the arm and hauling her away through the crowd. Her attack on the man had not caused a single hair on her head to slip out of place.

"Let me go!" Marie said, struggling out of the lady's grip, which was as tight as iron clamps. "I don't know you!"

"You can't go talking to men like that," the lady said.

"He was going to help me!" Marie turned around. "Oh, and now he's gone!"

"Of course he's gone," the lady said, continuing to pull her forward. "That type never stick around for the constables to show up. Do you know what he wanted to do? He was going to tell you that he could help you, but would demand payment first. And such payment, if you know what I mean, was not going to be in Sterling, or gold, or Francs, or any other form of money. Do you understand?"

Marie gulped.

"So don't you mind him," the lady said. She spoke quickly as she weaved them through the crowd like the needle on a sewing machine. "He's going to find his next victim in no time, you can rest assured about that." The old lady clucked her tongue. "This is why young ladies must never go to such places alone. It's simply not safe without a chaperone. Though by the looks of you, perhaps you were never taught that. You must guard your virtue with all that you have. For once it is lost, there is nothing to take it back, and there will forever be a ceiling on your ability to secure a good home. Do you have a good home?"

The lady had been speaking rapidly, not pausing for breath or to allow Marie to answer, but to this question, she seemed to require a response.

"Um, no, I don't," Marie said. It was true now.

The lady nodded. "Don't you worry then, my dear." She hooked her parasol over her arm again and patted Marie on the forearm. "I've got a place I can take you. It's for wayward young ladies like yourself, who have been lost in the world and need someone to look after them."

"Oh, no thank you," Marie said, trying to pull her arm out of the lady's grip; but the woman's grip tightened.

"Oh, but I insist," the lady said. "I couldn't possibly let a young lady like you fall into the clutches of that young man again. Particularly when at my house, we would screen out such men before they were even permitted to look at you."

A trickle of ice ran down Marie's back. "Let me go!" she cried, trying to pull harder. The lady was leading her away from the market now, to a small alleyway between buildings.

The lady gave her a tight smile, but did not let go or stop walking.

Panicking, Marie snatched the parasol from the lady's arm and whacked her on the head. The hat fell off, and a few strands of gray hair fell from their pins. Marie felt a small surge of victory. She hit her again, and the lady's grip loosened. Marie jerked her arm away and, parasol in hand, began running back to the market.

"Thief!" the lady cried. "That woman has my parasol, stop her!"

But by now, Marie had disappeared back into the crowd, and no one turned their heads. If anyone was inclined to help the lady, no one had seen Marie. Marie bobbed and weaved through the crowd until she came into a market stall selling vegetables. She slipped inside and ducked down behind a pile of cabbages.

"Madam?"

Marie turned up to see the shopkeeper looking at her quizzically.

She peeked over the pile and then ducked back down. "Please," she whispered.

The man looked around at the commotion and then bent down and whispered, "What do I get in return?"

Marie held up the parasol threateningly. The man shrugged and went back to his work. Marie breathed a sigh of relief.

"Marie!"

Marie startled and crouched even lower behind the cabbages.

"Marie!"

Suddenly a shock of red hair, electric blue eyes, and a furious expression forced its way into her vision. "What are you doing here?"

Marie nearly fainted with relief. "Emma!"

Emma grabbed Marie by the arm and pulled her up. "I saw you come back here like a lunatic. Come on, it's not safe here." She led Marie out, and in the process knocked over a few of the vegetables.

"My cabbages!" cried the shopkeeper.

Emma shrugged an apology while Marie held up her parasol again, and the man simply knelt down to pick them up.

"I thought so," Marie said.

"What were you doing back there?"

"Oh, the most horrible things happened!" Marie related the tales of the man, the lady, and the shopkeeper.

Emma rolled her eyes. "Of course that was going to happen," she said. "You came to Green's Lane alone, like a crazy person. It's amazing nothing worse happened to you."

"Don't call me that; I'm not crazy! No matter what you think."

"Forgive me, it was a bad choice of words. But it was unwise to come here alone."

"Alone? There are people everywhere."

"Not women alone. Look around you!"

Marie did, and saw that women were walking in clusters of two or three, or on the arm of a man. None were walking alone as she had been.

"Oh," she said. She felt deflated. "I guess I thought it might be different here."

"What do you mean?"

"Well, back in our old life, everything is so packaged, you know? We're beautiful things set on shelves or pedestals to be admired, but never touched or used. We're locked away in these gorgeous country houses, occasionally paraded into the city, but we're always under lock and key and removed. Food came fully prepared, but we never thought about where the ingredients came from; they just appeared after someone else bought them with our money. At least I never did. Books don't cover it, and people never talk about it. But the people in these classes, well, they aren't locked away, are they? They're free to walk around and interact. Like we did yesterday."

"You think any of us are free?" Emma asked. "Women? Girls? In any class, we're not people. We're commodities. We're investments—get one woman and get any number of children. We're painted and dressed up like dolls to show off. We're traded for land, or money, or political access. We're only as valuable as our bodies—and we're never more valuable than when we're untouched by a man. Because once one of them have had us, all of them may as well have had us. It's the exclusivity that makes us valuable. For once you've been used and discarded aside, you become open for any man. That's why no matter the class you're in, there's only so much you're allowed to do. Mobile phones? Perhaps, with a husband or father or brother there to sign up for you and put WifeLock on it, because otherwise we might use them for illicit activities. We can't get our own bank accounts because we might run off with the money. You see what they fear about us? The idea of independence. So of course we're not free, because if we're free, then we can't be their commodities anymore."

Marie felt tears well in her eyes. "It's better in other countries, isn't it? Women's rights aren't tied to their relationships to men. Women can travel, earn their own money. Vote."

Emma shrugged. "Maybe. Maybe not. It's a big world out there. No sense in pining over it. And it's not like we can go."

"We can," Marie said. "And I'm going to. That's why I came here. I needed to find a place where I can buy what I need to truly escape."

"Like what?"

"Like a phone, one without WifeLock. And if I'm going to follow Mother, I will need a passport with a different name."

"You had the presence of mind to think that far ahead, but not to go to Green's Lane alone?"

"I needed to find the black market! I thought for sure this would be the place to start."

"That if you went to a regular market, there would be a black market here too?"

Marie shrugged. "It made sense at the time."

Emma stood there, considering. Then she sighed. "I know where to take you," she said. "And it's a lot safer than it is here."

Marie felt an ember of hope begin to glow just as she thought it had been dying out. "You do?"

Emma nodded. "Yes."

"How?"

Emma shifted uneasily. "Do you really want to know?"

Marie nodded.

"I'll tell you when we get there."

"And you won't make me go to a hospital?"

Emma shook her head. "No." She hesitated, then added, with her head turned to the marbled gray heavens, "May the Lord God have mercy on my soul for this, but I'm going to help you."

Chapter Eleven

Emma led Marie through several streets and onto a streetcar, where she paid with two coins and then directed Marie to the ladies-only section in the back. The city passed outside the window in a gray blur through the greasy window. Emma suddenly stood up at one point and yanked on the cord, and the streetcar screeched to a stop. Then, following a few more twists and turns after they had alighted onto the street, Emma and Marie arrived at their destination. Marie stopped short as her sister passed through the door before her. Emma glanced over her shoulder, then came back to the doorway. "What's the matter?"

Marie gestured at the building. "This is the right place?"

Emma nodded. "Of course."

"But . . ." Marie looked to either side quickly, then whispered, "But this is a supermarket."

"Indeed."

"But . . . we don't need to buy food."

"You'll see," Emma said, plastering a benign smile on her face that Marie immediately recognized as the fake one she had worn whenever they had been around their father. Emma took Marie by the arm and tugged her hard through the doorway. Marie stumbled only slightly, but she quickly regained her composure as they entered the building.

The supermarket was practically empty, at least compared to Green's Lane. A cat meowed and hopped down from behind the counter of the checkout station, then pounced on a mouse that was scurrying across the floor. Marie squeaked along with the mouse, but Emma pulled her along. They passed shelves that were largely empty save for a few bags of flour and sugar and salt, and the only vegetables available were limp rutabagas and turnips. More had been available in Green's Lane in the market stall where Marie had hidden, and she wondered why that was. Perhaps it was always like this. She'd never been in a supermarket before. She'd never had to do her own shopping.

The fan above them squeaked, and the light flickered. An old woman pushing a cart spared them no glance as she argued with the shopkeeper about why there was no dried fish available, who argued right back that she was free to go elsewhere with her complaints.

Emma led her toward a door in the back that was covered with a layer of grease and dust. A rush of cold from a humming refrigeration unit blasted them when they opened the door. Marie pulled her coat tight around herself. A couple of employees wandered about beyond, neither one paying the sisters any notice. Clearly visitors were not unusual back here.

"What are we doing in here?" Marie asked.

Emma shushed her and led her behind some empty shopping trolleys. There was a half-open door past that, and inside was a man with stringy black hair sitting at a desk in a dingy office, playing solitaire with a pack of well-worn playing cards. He looked up disinterestedly at Emma and nodded once in greeting, as if he had been expecting her.

"Mr. Davis," Emma said.

"Mrs. Phillips."

Marie's eyes snapped to her sister, but even she knew better than to ask questions or offer corrections in this moment. Was it a fake name? Had Emma gotten married? She'd found Emma under her real name, and found her quickly. Did Emma have some presence in this underground world?

"What will it be today?" he asked.

"My friend requires a phone."

"Phones can be arranged."

"And a new name."

Mr. Davis nodded, dealt out three more cards, did not look up. "Just a name?"

"A passport. One that works."

Mr. Davis clicked his tongue. Laid down an ace. "Those are difficult to come by. Expensive."

"I believe we can pay what you require."

"It's a risky business. Questions get asked. You plan to actually use the passport?"

"She'd like the option," Emma said.

"You need to use it soon, I presume?" Mr. Davis said, flipping over three more cards and then, shaking his head at those three, dealing out three more.

"She'd like the option," Emma repeated.

At this, Mr. Davis looked up from his game for the first time. The overhead light shone brightly on his greasy forehead, peeking out between strands of hair. "Options are hard to come by," he said. "Rare things, options."

Emma looked uneasily at Marie, then nodded her head. "We understand." She turned to Marie and whispered in her ear, "Let's step outside for a moment." To Mr. Davis, she said, "May we use your toilet?"

He jerked his head in the right direction, then returned to his card game. Emma led Marie to the toilet next door. Marie put her hand to her nose at the smell.

"My goodness," she said, making every effort to breathe through her mouth.

"Wait a moment," Emma told her. She went to the wall next to Mr. Davis's office and, when she found a small hole there, slapped her hand over it. They heard a muffled chuckle from the next room, and the sound of Mr. Davis's chair scraping along the floor away from the wall.

"Are they all like this?" Marie whispered.

"Who?"

"Men! Women! He's, what, the fourth person today to do something inappropriate."

"Yes, out here in the real world, people are real assholes to one another."

"Language!"

"It's the truth, isn't it? Like I said, we're commodities out here. We were in that world as well, but more along the lines of a rare and expensive vase: look but don't touch, appreciate but don't use. Here, it's use or be used."

Marie hated it being put in such stark terms. She'd been hoping that her sister might give her some comfort. "I suppose."

"Dearly bought knowledge," Emma said, with a darkness in her voice, and Marie wondered what it had been like for her all these years. "But freely given."

"Mrs. Phillips?" Marie asked, deciding a change of subject was necessary before she completely lost hope.

"Only when I do business with him," Emma said.

"Do you do business with him often?"

Emma seemed to consider a bit before answering. "Yes."

"I see."

"And so in this line of work, a husband, even a dead or fake one, provides a great deal of protection. They'll honor the property of an absent man rather than listen to the woman herself."

"I suppose that is the way of things."

Emma nudged Marie away from the wall. "Now, this is going to get expensive, to get you a passport that you can actually use to leave the country fairly quickly. You said you had money with you. I need to know how much."

"Five thousand pounds," Marie said.

Emma blew out a breath. "That won't be enough."

"Really? I didn't know how much I'd need. It was the most I risked taking with me." She had worried that the estate would notice any amount larger than that, particularly since it had had so many financial troubles over the years. "It sounded like a lot." She felt ice crystallize in her stomach as it occurred to her just how unprepared she truly was to survive in the real world. She cursed herself and wished she had researched this more thoroughly.

"I'll put it this way," Emma said. "It's a lot to owe someone, but it's not much to own."

"I have some jewelry too." Marie reached into a hidden pocket inside her coat and removed the pouch that had been weighing against her, literally and figuratively, since she'd left. "Would that work?"

"Maybe. What do you have?"

There was a small shelf over the sink. Marie took a paper towel and lay it across the top. She then began emptying the pouch. Her sapphire engagement ring. A ruby pendant. An emerald-encrusted necklace, each one surrounded by tiny diamonds.

"My lord!" Emma gasped, picking up the jewelry and examining it.

"What? Is it not enough? I have more." She reached into the pouch again.

"Let me see!" Emma snatched the pouch from Marie's hands. She pulled out and unrolled a string of pearls.

"Were these Mother's?" she asked. Her voice was thick.

Marie nodded. "Yes."

It took many long moments for Emma to respond. She rubbed a thumb over one of the pearls. "I remember her wearing them."

"I wasn't planning to sell those, if I could help it. I was hoping to return them to her."

Emma stared at the pearls for a long time, then shook her head. Marie thought for a moment that the shine in Emma's eyes might be unshed tears. "No," she said. "No, let's not sell them. If we can help it." She returned to her inspection. She found a pair of ruby earrings, which were part of a set to go with the pendant. And finally, she dug out a diamond ring surrounded by pink sapphires.

"So," Marie said. "What do you think?"

Emma considered the items before her. "I think we'll be just fine." She helped Marie load everything back into the pouch, but kept out the sapphire ring. "We'll use this to buy our freedom to go abroad," she said. "This will cover the cost of usable passports." A beat. "For both of us."

Marie felt her heart rate rise along with her sense of hope. "Both of us?"

Emma nodded. "Yes."

"You're coming with me?"

Emma nodded again, this time with a grimace. "Yes, I'm coming with you. There's nothing here for either of us. I still think you're wrong about Mother. I don't think we're going to find her. But I'll come with you either way on the journey. At the very least, there's a new life out there waiting for us."

Marie threw her arms around her elder sister, and the two hugged for a long time, both holding back tears. They may have been in the gutter now, with only a handful of stones to the names they were about to abandon. But they were still upper-class enough to not show emotions. They could blame the watery eyes on the smell.

"It doesn't mean I forgive you," Emma said.

Marie sniffed. "I'm sure you won't."

"But I've missed you, and I want to stay with you."

"I hope you will."

Emma pocketed the ring. Quite enough emotional confessions for one day. "Let's go make Mr. Davis a very happy man."

They strode back into Mr. Davis's office. He was shuffling the cards, preparing for a new game. Emma shut the door behind them this time, ready to talk business.

"We'll need two phones," she said. "And two passports. Usable ones. Widows, so we can go unmolested. And we'll need to be able to leave soon."

Mr. Davis looked up from his cards. "I take it that I shall not be able to count on your continued services?"

"Consider this my notice."

"Hmm. Well, expect no quarter from me. Everything I said before still goes. And double, for two of you."

Emma proffered the ring. "What can you do with this?"

Mr. Davis dropped the cards.

"A fair bit, I'd imagine?" Emma asked again.

He reached for the ring, but Emma drew her hand away.

"Maybe even book us passage across the channel?"

"I'm not a bloody travel agent."

"No, but I imagine you could find us room on an otherwise fully booked vessel. One going to Zeebrugge."

"Antwerp is easier," he said.

"But more dangerous," said Emma. "And we want no hassles with customs officials. Or immigration. Passports that work. A quick look and a stamp of entry. No questions asked."

"I'll need my man to look at it," said Mr. Davis, nodding at the ring.

"Provided we can attend, so we know that we'll see the ring again," said Emma.

"I'm a businessman, Mrs. Phillips, not a common thief."

"That's what they all say, and I've been bilked enough times to know what not to do."

"And I don't stay in business when folks feel cheated by me."

"You stay in business because you can procure what others can't."

"I rely on referral business and repeat customers. That doesn't work if people think you're going to do them wrong."

Emma and Mr. Davis were locked in a staring contest. Finally, Marie piped up.

"It's fine, Emma. I trust him."

"You trust everyone," Emma hissed.

"When you can't trust anyone, you have to trust everyone," she said.

"How soon can your man look at it?" Emma asked.

Mr. Davis stood up. "For this piece? He'll drop what he's doing." He took his coat from a nail on the wall and donned his hat. "If you'll follow me, ladies, I'll take you to him now."

Chapter Twelve

"This isn't what I thought the black market would be like," Marie whispered to Emma as they followed several steps behind Mr. Davis. He was leading them down the street, out in the open, as if they were simply walking to do some shopping or to meet someone for an appointment.

"What were you expecting?"

"An actual, you know, *market*."

"You thought there would be market stalls selling things like organs, abortion pills, and pro-republican literature?"

"Alongside illegal weapons, French champagne, and contraception. Yes."

Emma laughed. Marie didn't. "You were serious?" Emma asked.

Marie shrugged.

Emma laughed. "Seems like an easy way to get caught, having all of that in one place. Especially if operating hours are posted."

Marie felt her face flush with embarrassment. She'd been trained her whole life how to hide her emotions, but she'd never been able to hide this one. She changed the subject. "How did you learn about this man?"

Emma patted Marie's hand. "Do you remember how I told you that I support myself by cleaning houses?"

Marie nodded.

"Well, it doesn't pay well enough to afford my own flat. Even the small one you see. So I've had to supplement my income to afford a place as nice as that."

"*That* is a nice flat?"

"You should see where I was living before."

"So what do you do to supplement?"

"I told you, I bring customers to Mr. Davis. People who need things. Abortion pills and contraception are big business. So are items made in France. Those who are against the Church want the subversive literature that can be more easily found elsewhere. I made myself a part of that supply chain. I am the go-between for Mr. Davis and wherever he obtains whatever he needs to obtain for the customer. And I get a small fee from that as the broker."

Marie was impressed, and told her sister so.

"We all have to do what we all have to do to survive," she said. "As you well know."

"So you can't operate under your own name for this."

"No. And Mrs. Phillips's bank account is secure."

"You have a bank account?"

"Widows don't need husbands to open one."

"Widows get to do a lot of things."

"Now you see why so many men die of indigestion or choking."

"What does that mean?"

"Think about it."

Marie did. After she did, her stomach dropped. "Really?"

Emma nodded.

"Wow."

"Just in case you need to know for the future," Emma said.

"I'd be even more useless as a barren widow," she said. "Widows who failed to produce heirs aren't provided for in the will. Only their sons are."

"I guess you killed the right person, then."

Mr. Davis led them into a jeweler's store with iron bars over the windows and a burly security guard who eyed all three of them suspiciously while they waited for someone inside to buzz them in. Marie tried giving him a weak smile, but she immediately ducked her head back down when he scowled at her in return. The wait was agonizing; Marie was paranoid that they'd be seen by . . . someone . . . for doing . . . something. She felt like a cloud of illegality was over them and attention would be drawn, or that she was already in the crosshairs of a hunter's rifle.

Once the door buzzed, Mr. Davis led them past the rows and rows of sparkling jewels winking at them from blue velvet displays and toward the back room, which was far less grand and sparkly than the front. Mr. Davis breezed through as if he owned the place. Maybe he did. No one paid them any attention as they slipped into the nonpublic area of the shop. Marie got the sense that back rooms were where she'd be living much of her life these days. She didn't dislike the idea. She'd been on display enough in her time.

Emma provided the ring to the jeweler, an old man with hair like the head of a dandelion who looked at her skeptically before inspecting the ring with a magnifying glass held between fingers that were crooked with arthritis. After a moment or two of close scrutiny, he nearly dropped it in surprise. "This is real!" he exclaimed.

"Of course it is," Emma replied, sounding bored. She turned to Mr. Davis. "Have we got a deal?"

"Only if Mr. Harrison agrees," said Mr. Davis.

Mr. Harrison was still gaping at the stone, before finally removing his magnifying glass with a trembling hand. He seemed reluctant to part with the stone, but eventually placed it back into Emma's waiting hand after catching her withering stare.

"I cannot sell this," he said.

"What?" Marie cried out before she could remember herself.

"I don't understand," said Emma in a cool tone.

The old jeweler gazed longingly at the ring as Emma returned it to her pocket.

"Madam, there are no buyers for a jewel such as this."

"How do you mean?"

"I mean that no one, short of a Duke, could afford such a piece of jewelry. Not only that, such a stone is so rare as to already be known among any potential buyers, so I cannot remove it and attach it to another piece of jewelry. A sapphire the size of an olive is going to be noticed. Selling a stone like this is far too dangerous. It is likely to be an heirloom piece. Which means it is also likely to be stolen."

"Since when has that mattered?" Emma asked.

"Since the rightful owner is likely to be a member of the peerage," Mr. Harrison replied placidly.

"So?"

"So they like to inventory their jewelry," he said. "And they send their people to retrieve them."

"There has to be a buyer," countered Emma. "Anything that special and rare has a buyer."

"There are people abroad who would pay well for it," said Mr. Davis. "I have a contact in Fanteland. He is always seeking jewels like this."

The jeweler considered. "Fanteland is one of the few places with buyers who could afford this. You can vouch that the jewel will be purchased?"

"I don't believe I'll have much difficulty," said Mr. Davis.

"Very well," said Mr. Harrison.

"I should have the sale confirmed in a few weeks."

"No," Emma said. "This can't wait that long. We have to move it now."

They began debating back and forth, when Marie turned around and blindly fished another piece of jewelry out of her coat. "What about this one?"

She held it out without looking. It was their mother's strand of pearls.

"Marie," Emma breathed. "No."

Marie shook her head. "She would agree." She held them out farther. "These cannot be tied back to any noble house. No one will miss them."

"May I?" Mr. Harrison asked. Marie's fingers clenched tighter around the pearls for a moment, then released them. She swallowed down her upset. Mr. Harrison took the pearls and examined them. "Good quality. Imported, I should think."

"You could sell those now?" Marie asked.

"Rather easily," he confirmed.

"Please don't!"

All heads swiveled to look at Emma. "Not those," Emma whispered. "Something else. Anything else."

Marie nodded. She replaced the pearls in her pocket and withdrew the diamond ring. "What about this?"

"A diamond won't get you anywhere near what pearls will."

"But you could sell it?"

Mr. Harrison nodded.

"For how much?"

Mr. Davis and Mr. Harrison conferred, and gave an amount. "That should cover your necessities that we discussed earlier," said Mr. Davis.

"So we'll take it in trade?" Emma asked.

Mr. Davis nodded.

"If you will kindly exit out the back," said Mr. Harrison. "We don't want this attracting attention. Mr. Davis, you shall receive my bill."

They exited out the back, finding themselves in the damp alley behind the shop. It had rained while they were inside, and drizzle still filled the air. Marie's blood ran slightly cold, though she could not tell why.

"How long until you can have the passports?" Emma asked.

"Four days, give or take," said Mr. Davis.

"Excellent," said Emma. "We will meet you then." She started to lead Marie back, when a hand clasped Marie's shoulder and gripped it hard, like a falcon's talons.

"I'll take the rest of the jewelry you have hidden in there," Mr. Davis said, whipping Marie around and groping about her, looking for her stash.

"You take your hands off me!" Marie cried.

"I'm a businessman, and if you think for a moment that I didn't creep back over to the wall and see what else you've got hidden in there, you've got another thing coming. I didn't last in this business by being stupid. I just had to confirm that it was real, and now that it is, well, that's all I need to know. I can retire now." He twisted Marie's arm. She cried out in pain and tried to pull away from him, but he was too strong. She slackened as the truth of her powerlessness washed over her. There was no point in fighting when you had no hope of besting your opponent. She might strike a blow or two, but the only person who was going to be hurt was her. She averted her eyes from whatever it was he was planning to do to her.

He stilled. Marie braced herself. Mr. Davis still held her tightly, but he was no longer hurting her. Marie unclenched her eyes and chanced a look at him. Emma had a knife held to his throat.

Her big sister, saving her again.

"Really, Mr. Davis, must we go through this again?" Emma sounded dispassionate, almost bored.

Mr. Davis sighed, then let go of Marie. She scuttled over to stand behind Emma.

"You know I could pull my knife on you, and have you both killed in a matter of seconds, and no one would even pause to look at you?" he asked.

"What a disappointment you don't recognize that it's your own knife at your throat."

Mr. Davis patted his clothes. "Well done," he said. "But if you think I stopped at just one weapon—"

"That would be exceedingly naive of me," Emma agreed. She twirled a second knife in her other hand. "Now, I'd hate to stop doing business with you."

"And I you," Mr. Davis admitted. "You shall have your passports in four days. Come to my office." He held out his hand for his weapons.

"You get these back," Emma said, making a show of pocketing them, "when you hand over the passports."

Mr. Davis tipped his hat to her, and turned and left.

Marie grabbed Emma's shoulder and turned her back around. She looked at her sister, both recognizing and not recognizing her. This was like meeting one of the heroes from her books in the flesh. Except it was her sister, and she was a woman, and it seemed impossible that a real person could be so incredible. "What was that? How did you do that? Why did you just walk away? You don't really trust him to get us usable passports, do you?"

Emma laughed and tied her scarf tighter around her head. "Honor among thieves," she said. "You're one of us now, so you need to learn. When you whipped out that jewelry, he had no choice but to try to take it. Don't ever do that again, by the way. The next one may not be so accommodating."

"But how did you learn to do that?" Marie couldn't hide how impressed she was. Nor would she. It had been incredible, and Emma should know that. "Find his knife, take it, and threaten him with it—all without him knowing?" Marie left unsaid the last part: *Can you teach me how?*

"Marie," Emma said. "I've been a woman living alone in London for over a decade. I've managed by doing all manner of things I never wanted to do. It was all done in the name of one thing: survival. If I know how to find the black market, it was because I needed things from it. If I know how to find buyers of illicit objects and connect them with sellers who have procured them by extra-legal means, it's because I found myself at that nexus more than once. If I know how to go under an assumed name, it's because I learned the hard way what the value of your real name is once it's put at risk. And if I know exactly where Mr. Davis keeps his knives, how to get them in a hurry, and where to press them to make him leave you alone? Well, it's because it's hardly the first time I've been in this position."

She smoothed down her skirt. "You see, then, what you're in for in this life? It's freedom, but that freedom comes with a terrible price: danger. There is danger everywhere in London for an unmarried, unescorted lady. I can't even fathom what it might be like elsewhere, but I'd like to come with you and find out."

Marie grinned. "I've read about adventure my entire life," she said. "I've lived a long time, but like a museum exhibit: to be looked at from a distance but never touched. I want to be touched. Handled. Thrown around. Taken out to see things. And I'm going to find our mother. She's out there, in Zeebrugge, waiting for us."

"I just don't want you to be disappointed."

"I won't be," Marie said with confidence. "I'll be with you."

Chapter Thirteen

The Dowager Duchess of Suffolk delicately set down her cup of tea. She winced at its slight bitterness. The maid had once again failed to put in just the right amount of sugar. She supposed it was an overcorrection from last time, when the girl had put in too much. It really wasn't difficult to measure out sugar, was it? Didn't they have special spoons for it? Perhaps the girl would have to be let go. Basic competence was essential in this home, particularly when something as expensive and rare as tea was at stake. Even if it was something they could procure with relative ease.

She considered the cup before her. This porcelain cup had been part of Grayside for generations. Her husband's mother had inherited it from her own mother-in-law, and so on and so forth from there. And it had gone to her son's wife, the now-late Duchess of Suffolk. Thrown herself from the cliff into the sea below. Her body had not been found yet, nor was it expected to be. They hadn't really looked. The Dowager Duchess grudgingly appreciated what Marie had done. Best for all concerned for her to step out of the way. The Dowager Duchess only wished that Marie had had the good sense to do it sooner. It's not as if there were anything that she could have done to help herself by that point. Her husband certainly wasn't going to fall in love with her. And she'd proven herself incapable of her one duty as a wife. The Dowager Duchess almost admired her daughter-in-law for having done it. Almost.

The bell rang, and in came John Hart, who gave a deep bow at the waist upon his arrival. The Dowager Duchess did not smile outwardly, but she was always glad to see him. He was the one she could trust above all others.

"Good, you're here," she said. She picked up the cup for another sip of the tea, and then decided against it.

"The inventory of the late Duchess's jewelry has been completed, and we have found some items missing," John reported.

"Oh?"

"Yes. There is, in particular, a sapphire ring that the Duke wishes to give to his new betrothed. It may have been on the Duchess's finger when she fell into the sea."

"How inconsiderate. And now that we've canceled her . . ." Her voice trailed off, but she quickly recovered. "We'll have to search for the body after all."

"Indeed. That said, it's also possible that it could have been lifted by a member of the staff in all the commotion after the Duchess's death. The Earl Kenfield has also inquired about some of the personal jewelry belonging to his family that he would like returned. As it was not the property of the Duke upon the marriage, it has not been cataloged, so we are still looking for it. When we check for the ring, we will look for those items as well."

"Very good," said the Dowager Duchess. Then she added, with deliberate casualness, "Was all the other jewelry accounted for? There was a pair of ruby earrings that I have not been able to find, though I admit that I have not looked very hard for them."

"I will ensure that they are found."

The Dowager Duchess nodded, knowing that if any of their missing property was still on the estate, he would find it. And if it was not, he would still find it.

"And," John Hart continued in a lower voice, "that one other item you suspected may be missing?"

The Dowager Duchess froze, like a deer who had been caught in the sight of a hunter's rifle.

John Hart nodded.

She sat for a long moment. "I see." She then looked at him. "Can you get it back?"

"I won't rest until I do."

The Dowager Duchess nodded. "Very good. Use all available tools at your disposal."

John Hart bowed and turned to leave.

"Oh, and one other thing?" the Dowager Duchess called out.

He turned back around. "Yes?"

"Don't tell her husband."

Chapter Fourteen

They had paid Mr. Davis dearly for his services. And he'd gotten them the passports he had promised. But he had never promised them that they would be able to pass the fingerprint scanners at the border checkpoint at Ramsgate. In hindsight, they had only asked for valid and usable passports, not for safe passage out of the country. Marie had assumed they were one and the same. Emma apparently had too.

Marie gulped and let Emma do the talking.

"This is completely unacceptable," Emma said smoothly, speaking in the crisp accent used only by people who could afford it. It automatically conveyed imperiousness. It required the other party to pay attention and obey. "My late husband and I were never subjected to this nonsense, and—"

"And, as I said, Madam, this is required of all women traveling alone." The border agent spoke just as crisply, though the fact that he was working for pay at all suggested that he belonged to a once wealthy family who had fallen on hard times. "If you had a male chaperone with you, then we could let you cross the border without this additional check."

Emma huffed and raised her voice, in full authority as a relative of the Earl Kenfield. "I have never, in my life—"

"It's the only way to ensure that women who are authorized to travel alone are actually traveling alone. I do apologize for this inconvenience, but I have no authority here to change it. If you please." He gestured to the fingerprint scanner.

Marie tried to quiet the screaming in her head. If she used that scanner, their real identities would be known, and she in particular would be in trouble. A married woman trying to leave the country without her husband's permission . . . well, she supposed that was why they had this additional security. Even though most of Europe was subject to Church Law, England's interpretation of it was particularly severe and restrictive in how it treated women. As a result, women tried to escape England all the time.

Emma stomped her foot and held up a gloved hand. "I will not be dictated to," she said.

The border agent drew up to his full height and took two steps toward her. "Madam," he said in a voice that could cut glass, "you either submit to the scanning, or you travel with your male chaperone."

"Very well!" Marie spoke up. She dashed over and took Emma by the hand. "Our brother is traveling with us, but we had hoped to go through ahead of time as he is occupied with business concerns. We will have to interrupt his work so that we are not unnecessarily delayed. He will not be pleased." Ducking her head down, she led Emma away. She saw her sister struggle to suppress a smirk, and Marie momentarily basked in the glory of having impressed her big sister.

"Nice thinking," Emma whispered.

"Where are we going to find a brother?" Marie whispered back, an octave higher than she meant to. She knew this was no time to panic, but she hadn't planned for what to do after she'd finished speaking. There was no planning in any of this, just survival and instinct. No one planned; they just did. She hated it.

"It's a busy port," Emma replied. "And any brother we might find here will be far superior to the one we have."

Three hours and one set of ruby earrings later, Marie staggered down the deck of the ferry as it pulled into Zeebrugge. The channel's choppy water had turned her stomach the entire time, and she'd had to lie down for most of the journey. Though that hadn't been the only thing to turn her stomach. Even though they had paid the man they'd found in the terminal to pretend to be their brother, he had insisted on accompanying them throughout the journey. When Marie laid her head down, he had forced it into his lap, and it had been a struggle to keep her head facing away from him. That did not prevent him from groping her, despite Emma's repeated threats of violence. But in that moment, he had the power over her: one word, and she and Emma could be hauled into the brig and swiftly returned to England. And returning to England was not an option. He knew it too. She saw it reflected in Emma's expression of disgust, and when she darted her eyes up at the man, she could see the smirk written on his face. *What are you going to do, tell me no?*

So she bore the discomfort as bravely as she could, humiliation after humiliation, as the ferry crept across the channel one wave at a time.

As she stepped onto the ground of a new country for the first time, she half expected that the very ground itself would feel different—maybe less solid, or off-kilter in some way, as if she were literally stepping onto another world, as that multinational team had done on Mars a few years earlier. But no. It was still the Earth, still unyielding, still flat. It was paved, as England had been when she'd left it. She wondered if she'd ever walk on English soil again. She prayed not. England was her past. Zeebrugge, where she knew their mother was waiting, was her future.

In contrast with Marie's cautious tip-toeing into Flanders, Emma walked briskly off the deck as if she'd done it a hundred times before. As soon as they were waved through into the city, their "brother" caught up to them and wrapped his arm tightly around Marie. "Where are we headed next, dear sisters?"

Emma whipped around and punched him in the face. He staggered backward and fell to the ground. A passing man in a well-tailored suit talking on a phone merely stepped over him without pausing his conversation. Before he could get up, the sisters disappeared into the crowd.

The port of Zeebrugge was more impressive than either had expected. Cranes as tall as cathedrals lifted and lowered shipping containers the size of railway carriages. People shouted in just about every language imaginable. Ships of every size and purpose lined up: cruise ships, ferries, container ships half a mile long, tugboats, and yachts owned by the wealthiest families in the world—Marie recognized one that looked like it belonged to the Duke of Marlborough. People movers rolled about carrying luggage and passengers from the dock to the terminal, or from one ship to a connecting one. The sisters opted to walk, hoping to blend in with the crowd, but this proved somewhat daunting when they saw that the entire port was under video surveillance and projected on huge screens all around them. They ducked their heads down and hoped no one would notice them in particular.

There were signs in both English and Dutch here at the port, but they knew that once they got into the heart of the city, it would be all Dutch. English was one of the least-spoken languages in the world. Fortunately, Dutch sounded near enough to English that Marie hoped that they'd be able to make their way through.

There were three ways to get to Brugge from Zeebrugge: a road taxi, a sky tram, or a hired boat on the canals. All three would deliver them into the very heart of the city. They opted for the canal boat. It was the cheapest option and granted the greatest amount of anonymity, even if it was the slowest. But at least it gave them sufficient time to take in the grandeur and beauty of their surroundings.

According to the books in the library at Grayside, Brugge had grown from a small, walled medieval village to expand all the way to the ocean as one of the busiest ports in the world as it became the destination of choice for exports intended to reach the markets of England and France. Since any shipment bound for either country was liable to be searched or even attacked, and since the Islamic Empire controlled both sides of the Strait of Gibraltar, Zeebrugge was the remaining point of entry to Europe, and for France and England in particular. Neither country was particularly wealthy, nor were they rich in natural resources, which made international imports essential to their survival. The need for all goods to enter via Flanders made their costs skyrocket in both England and France, making it difficult for many to pay for basic needs. But nationalism had trumped economics.

Maire had never had to worry about where her next meal, dress, or book was coming from, or whether it was coming at all. It had all been assumed. Now, she thought about it a great deal. How many of the goods that she'd owned over the years had passed through this very port? On which canals, riverways, airways, and railways had it traveled? Had the fabric of every pair of shoes she'd ever owned traveled to more countries than she could identify on a map? Had her shoes traveled more miles than she had? Had every banana she'd eaten seen more of the world than she ever would? It was humbling to see how much trade crisscrossed the globe while she had sat in one great house after another, reading books printed on paper made from trees that had been felled half a world away, making a book one of the most expensive and valuable things a person could own—particularly ones printed in such an obscure language as English.

Traveling down the canal was like traveling backward through time at least eight hundred years. It started out with what was known as the Water Bridge—a raised aqueduct that rose above the streets and train tracks and wove between the tall buildings and cranes of Zeebrugge. Beneath were rivers of cars and trucks and trains, but up here on the canal, it was more peaceful. The gondolas of the sky tram passed swiftly and silently overhead. After a mile or so, the water bridge descended gradually through suburbs and into the original medieval canal system, eventually delivering the sisters to the heart of the city. Beyond its centuries-old stone walls were larger, newer buildings sprouting up like weeds all around them, staring down in disapproval.

They alighted next to the old belfry, freestanding for over eight hundred years, in a rush of commuters and tourists making their way into the city. The sky tram and road taxis also deposited passengers here, and crowds swarmed around them. A marketplace lined the canal, offering whatever wares anyone could want. It was not dissimilar to Green's Lane, and so Marie held the stolen parasol at the ready in case she needed it.

"Right," Emma said after they were back on solid ground. "Where to now?"

Marie shrugged. "I suppose we go find Mother."

"Brugge is a huge city, and she's dead. Where do you propose we begin?"

"I found you in London, which is almost as large. I can find Mother. And she isn't dead." She held up the new phone that Mr. Davis had provided and gave it a little wave. "Especially without WifeLock holding me back." It felt strange to brandish a phone out in the open like that. Though apparently, it wasn't a problem here. Men and women alike rushed through the city, eyes glued on the devices before them. The openness of it all felt almost obscene.

"Perhaps we could get to our rooming house first, refresh ourselves, drop off our bags?" Emma suggested. "It's not like we're in a rush. We made it out of the country."

"It's hard to believe," Marie breathed. "I keep expecting someone to hassle me for using a phone."

"Freedom is a hard thing to wrap your mind around when you've never had it," Emma said. "It was so daunting at first for me, realizing that I didn't have to wait for someone else's permission to do something. I could just do it."

Marie nodded. "I could do anything. I could even download French literature. Or pornography!"

"Don't download pornography."

"I wasn't going to *watch* it!"

"That's what everyone says."

"I'm just saying, I *could* do it if I wanted." She flushed. "But of course, I won't actually."

"I won't make you go to confession for having threatened it," Emma said in mock solemnity.

"I may make myself go for having even thought it."

"There will be plenty of time for that," Emma said. "After we rest."

"Fine."

Marie looked around expectantly. She knew it was silly, but some part of her had hoped to find their mother there at the docks, waiting for them with open arms. Of course she wasn't. She didn't know they were coming. And it had been foolish to hope for it. It wasn't going to be that easy; no part of this had been, and no part of it likely would be. Instead, they looked up the location of the rooming house that Mr. Davis had booked for them.

"We shouldn't stay there," Marie said. "I don't trust anything that man does."

"I agree," said Emma. "But we have nowhere else to go."

"Can I help you ladies?"

They looked up at a tall, thin man with an English accent.

Marie and Emma looked at him warily.

"I beg your pardon," he said. "I don't mean to frighten you. I just thought you looked a bit lost, and Brugge can be so daunting for two ladies. Are you traveling with your husbands?"

Emma hardened her expression. Marie held up the parasol she'd stolen in Green's Lane and gripped it hard.

"May I see your identification?" the man asked.

Emma tugged at her sister's elbow and led her away without answering him. Marie still held the parasol up threateningly at the man.

"So many ladies leave England when they shouldn't," the man said, picking up his pace to keep up with them. "We have to ensure your safety."

"Don't respond to him," Emma whispered.

"Especially if there is a man on the other side of that channel who is wondering where you went."

They started running, then stopped at the sound of a familiar voice.

"Oh, Mother Mary!"

Their heads both snapped toward the voice. An old lady with curly gray hair and a pushcart was staring at them. They could see the reflection of light on the tears welling in her eyes. They hardly noticed that the man had apparently decided to leave them alone and had moved on to a more attractive or vulnerable target.

"For so long," the old woman said, clasping her hands together in prayer. Those hands which had held and hugged and dressed and fed and bathed them too many times to count. "For so long, I've been waiting here, each day, at this time, waiting for the people arriving in town from the ferry and hoping that one day you would be among them. And finally, you are."

She took a few shuffling steps toward the two shocked sisters, mouths agape until finally Marie was able to form her mouth to say the name on her lips.

"Jane?"

Their former nanny, recipient of their mother's last letter, put her hand to her mouth and then opened her arms wide for Emma and Marie.

Chapter Fifteen

"Dirk!" Jane cried as she threw open the door to her home. The old house was right on the canal. It was subdivided into flats, and hers was on the ground floor. "Dirk, they've finally arrived!"

Marie looked around hesitantly. None of this seemed real. This was not just finding a log to cling to in a flood, this was being pulled from the water altogether. There was no way they were this lucky. No one could be. Nothing was ever this easy.

A young man with short black hair and rectangular glasses emerged from what looked like the kitchen with a dish towel thrown over one shoulder. He appeared to be midway between Marie and Emma's ages. "You're serious?" He spoke English, but with a Dutch accent. "This is them?"

"Our prayers have been answered!" Jane cried as if she were reading Marie's mind. She ushered Marie and Emma into her sitting room and insisted they sit on the sofa, touching each of them on the face with such tenderness in her eyes that Marie thought she might weep again. "The kettle, I've got to put on the kettle. Dirk, get the tea out, we're going to celebrate!" Dirk disappeared back into the kitchen, and they heard the sounds of water running and mugs being set on the counter.

"Oh, you needn't get out tea on our account," Emma started. Marie tried to back Emma up, but Jane was having none of it.

"Nonsense! This is a special occasion. Besides, tea is far less expensive here than in England. Even us common folk can afford it, and afford to drink it! But even if it were priceless, this would be the day I would use it." Her eyes shone again, and tears pricked. "Oh, such a mess I am today!"

Emma looked at Jane as if she couldn't believe she was real.

"I have so many questions," Marie asked.

"Please, ask them!" Jane said. "Ask me anything you like!" She was still bustling around.

"Sit down," Dirk called from the kitchen. "I've got it."

"Thank you!" Jane called back. She took a seat on a chair next to the sofa and gazed at the sisters with flushed cheeks. "Ask, ask!" she prompted Marie.

Marie needed no further prompting. She launched into them without pausing for breath. "What are you doing here? How long have you lived here? How did you know we were coming? Why were you waiting for us? Who is Dirk?"

Jane laughed. "Oh, I've missed your questions, Marie! You always had so many of them." She wiped a tear from her eyes. "And yet you didn't ask the one that I expected."

"Which was?"

"Whether your mother is still alive."

Marie and Emma both gasped.

"The answer, as you may already suspect, is yes. It's why you have come here, isn't it?"

Marie felt dizzy as Emma put her hand to her mouth.

"Girls, you can cry here. You're not in England anymore."

"Oh my God." Emma's voice cracked as the tears came pouring out, which shocked Marie out of her own tears. Emma never cried. Marie put an arm around her, and to her surprise, Emma leaned in to the embrace.

Emma shook with sobs. "I wanted it to be true so badly, I wanted to believe that she was alive, but I couldn't let myself believe it. I didn't want to get hurt again."

Marie pulled her sister in closer. It was true, all of it was true. It was indeed safe to hope, to have dreams, and to chase them.

"Neither did I," Marie said.

Marie had been hiding behind Emma this whole time, counting on Emma to protect her. But who was protecting Emma? Marie had been so used to watching Emma being confident, strong, and independent, she'd never realized that any of it could be a cover for what Emma was really feeling: fear. Emma had been just as scared as Marie, but she'd been so much braver and resourceful in the face of it. Knowing that she had been right about their mother mixed in with Marie's concern for her sister. Their mother was out there, maybe even here in Brugge as Marie had deduced.

It was the anger that she hadn't expected. Marie had expected to feel happiness, relief, hope at the news. Instead, she felt rage swelling up inside of her. She'd had hoped to be right. She hadn't appreciated that she had hoped even more to be wrong. Because if their mother were indeed alive, she had abandoned them and never come back.

But Emma needed her now, so Marie chose to focus on that. She didn't know if she had it in her to take care of Emma the way she needed, especially in light of the fact that the Earth had shifted on its axis, and her feelings were more complex than she had anticipated.

Jane came over, knelt down, and caught both sisters as they fell into her arms. In that moment, Marie had her answer. She and Emma would figure out how to take care of each other, and later on, perhaps they would have their mother again. But in this moment? Jane would take care of them, as she had for so long, and Marie melted into the comfort of that knowledge.

"Why didn't you tell us?" Emma asked Jane, when they'd cried enough tears that there was now enough room for words to come out again.

"I did," Jane said. "In the only way that I could. Your mother's letter communicated the whole plan. And if she was clever enough to write it, then you were clever enough to read it and understand it. But I could hardly tell you myself. You were never alone, either of you. The Earl had surveillance everywhere. Not only among the staff, but in all rooms of Ellthrop. Even in the bathrooms and your bedrooms."

Emma and Marie both blanched at that. In the bathrooms?

"Don't worry, he didn't bother to review the tapes himself," Jane said. "That was beneath him. But you can believe he hired those who did, and who were told to report to him as soon as they saw something. Illicit letters. A boyfriend sneaking in through the window. Things of that nature. And he monitored all staff communications. Remember those smartwatches we all had to wear?"

Marie nodded.

"They were all equipped with listening devices, and they tracked our movements. Mrs. Eastwood—you remember her, the old housekeeper—she would get an alert if we were ever in a part of the house we were not supposed to be in. So you see, there was no opportunity to speak to you alone, no chance to take you away, no way to even give you a letter or sneak you something. We, and you, were always being watched. And your mother knew that, so she planned for it. She knew that you were clever enough to follow after her, and that you'd know where to look to find the hints."

"Marie was smart enough," Emma said. "Not me. And not Alice either."

"It only required one of you to figure it out. But all three of you were clever enough to do it. And where is Alice?"

"With her husband," Marie said. "She doesn't speak to us anymore."

"I'm sad to hear that, but I confess that I am not surprised," Jane said. She looked at Emma. "Emma, darling, I owe you an apology. I tried to find you, but I didn't even know where to look."

Emma shrugged. "No one did, apparently. I didn't hide."

"I should have tried harder to find you," Jane said. "I knew you had gone to London, and it's easy enough to find someone there. I decided you had built a life for yourself and I should stay away. It was wrong. I was wrong. I should have brought you here with me. No, that's not good enough. I should have never let you walk out that door in the first place. I should have brought you here. I needed this job, and I put my position before you. It was wrong. I was wrong."

"Enough apologies," Emma said. They were English, after all, even here in Flanders. No time for regrets or lamentations, and certainly enough feelings had been discussed to last for some time, perhaps even a lifetime.

"Where is our mother now?" Marie asked. "Can we go see her?"

Jane looked to Dirk, who was just coming in with a pot of tea and nice cups on a platter. There was a bowl of sugar and a small pitcher of cream. He and Jane were giving them the absolute best. Dirk looked down steadfastly as he began making the tea.

"I haven't introduced you let. Ladies, this is Dirk. Dirk, this is Marie, Duchess of Suffolk, and Lady Emma Kenfield." Jane gave them a smile. "Don't you worry, Dirk is safe. He won't tell anyone who you are or why you're here."

"Pleased to meet you, Dirk," Marie said, all manners.

"The pleasure is mine," said Dirk, with a small smile.

"How do you two know each other?" Emma asked.

"Dirk is my son," Jane said.

Both sisters' heads swiveled toward Jane.

"You have a son?" cried Emma. "You never told!"

"I didn't even know you were married," Marie said.

"I'm not," Jane said. "I never have been."

The silence grew thick, like a fog that rolled in without warning. So that was why Jane had to keep her job at Ellthrop. She was supporting someone.

"He was born here and raised here," Jane said. "With my sister. I sent home the money from Ellthrop. Here in Brugge, being an unmarried mother is not a problem the way it is back in England, but I had to be careful. And I had to be sure that your father never knew about him. Your mother did. And it's close enough that I could visit when I could. That's why your mother chose to come here. We had a network of people who could help. And once my position at Ellthrop was no longer needed, I came out here to live with my boy the way we always should have done." She beamed at her son with pride. "Isn't he a fine young man?"

"Mum," Dirk said, embarrassed.

"'Mum' nothing," Jane said. "He's taken very good care of me ever since I moved out here to be with him. We've had years now to grow closer. It was better that way, him being raised out here. And he's very trustworthy. He'll help you with your next steps to find your mother."

"Yes," Emma asked again. "Where is she?"

"I wasn't sure where to start to look," Marie said.

Jane nodded sadly. "I'm afraid," she said, "that she isn't in here in Brugge anymore."

Marie nearly dropped the cup. "What do you mean?"

"I mean, that you have to journey farther than you have so far," Jane said. "Your mother had to leave Brugge. And so do you."

John Hart strode into the jewelry store as soon as the buzzer sounded. The bodyguard outside hadn't done anything but give him a single look. Good man. He was smart enough to know better than to do anything more.

He walked past the rows of sparkling necklaces of diamonds, rubies, and emeralds behind glass. Small stones. The sort of stones that were so small that no one at Grayside would bother to bend down to pick them up from the floor. It wasn't worth the strain on the back.

He pushed open the double doors to the small lab where the man he'd come here to see was bent over something or other, his eyes glued to a magnifying glass. John Hart scoffed in greeting. If you had to use a microscope to see it, it wasn't really a gem.

Mr. Harrison looked up at the sound, and his face went three shades paler.

"Mr. Hart," he said, his voice raspy, as if it had gone suddenly dry.

"Mr. Harrison," he said. "I think you know why I'm here."

"I'm afraid I don't."

"Good to be afraid. Smart man." He strode over and plucked the gem from its clamp under the microscope. It was so tiny, only about an eighth of an inch wide. He gave it a disdainful look, then swallowed it whole. He looked at Mr. Harrison to see if he would object. He did not, just as it should be. If John Hart of Grayside wanted to swallow Mr. Harrison's jewels and shit them out, there was nothing the poor man could do.

"An item of jewelry has gone missing from Her Grace's collection," Hart said. "Shortly after the latest Duchess of Suffolk died, we took an inventory of all the belongings in the house. Her Grace is missing the ring that was given to the late Duchess as an engagement gift. It was an heirloom piece, a large sapphire surrounded by diamonds. Bespoke, very valuable. We suspect it may have been on the Duchess's finger when she plunged into the sea, but we haven't been able to find her. Not a trace. Not a scrap of clothing, save for what was on the cliffs. Nothing at all."

"How very curious," Mr. Harrison said.

"It is indeed. The sea floor is rather deep just off the cliffs, the water is choppy, and the jagged rocks along the sides make it a particularly difficult place to search. Most likely, it's at the bottom of the sea and won't be found. But we can't overlook the possibility that the ring was taken by someone, perhaps a member of staff or someone in the late Duchess's employ. We have to at least exhaust that possibility."

He sat next to Mr. Harrison and stared him dead in the eye. John Hart knew that men never wanted to meet his eyes. A person could lose their soul looking into that ice blue. And once they looked, they couldn't look away. He had that effect on people. It worked on everyone. Something about his gaze made them want to tell the truth, out of fear or obedience or sheer terror. It was the closest thing to truth serum that existed in His Majesty's kingdom. And John Hart worked for the

Dowager Duchess. If he worked for His Majesty, England would be a world power. But he didn't, so it wasn't. Just a small island in the North Sea that few people could find on a map.

"So," Hart said, once his eyes had done their work for a few moments. "We both know that if anyone wants to sell jewelry illicitly in England, they have to do business with you. If the ring was stolen, I have no doubt that it came through here." He slid a picture across the workbench toward Mr. Harrison, whose eyes were still fixed on Hart's. "This is a photograph of the ring here. If you saw it, you'll tell me. Have a look at it. And I want your first answer to be the honest one, if you please."

Mr. Harrison gulped, and, now having been given permission to look away, studied Hart's photograph. After a few minutes, he looked back into Hart's eyes, and nodded once.

Chapter Sixteen

Emma hadn't let herself believe that their mother was still alive, or that they were going to see her. But now that she had accepted this, it was as if her mother had died again. The longing and hope Emma had locked away burst forth like a breaking dam, and she wouldn't be able to put it back together. She would have to rebuild the wall around her heart again to protect herself, and she wasn't sure if she had the strength to do it.

Jane sipped from her tea, impossibly calm.

"Your mother came to Brugge because my sister and my son were here," she began. "She had no one left in England to turn to, except me, and no one outside of England to receive her. Things had become desperate. Your father needed an heir, and she kept not producing one. It didn't matter what they say about DNA and genetics and chromosomes. It didn't matter that it was his fault that she kept having girls. It didn't matter that, had he just a little less pride, they could have visited a specialist and had an embryo with a Y-chromosome implanted into her. His inability to put a son in his woman the old-fashioned way offended his pride. Nothing on this earth is more dangerous than a man with wounded pride.

"The more he knew it was true, that it was his fault, the more he punished her for it. He beat her. He got other women pregnant, pregnant with boys, to show that it wasn't him who had failed, it was her. Oh, how she cried, and it breaks my heart every time that I think about it."

Jane set her teacup down, and it made a clanging sound.

"She didn't deserve that. She had been the diamond in the crown of London society the year she met your father, and she knew it. It was not unlike your debutante season, Marie. You reminded me so much of her at your age. She could have had any man she wanted. All of them wanted her for a trophy, and a few would have loved her and taken care of her. So she snagged her own trophy. The Earl was the most eligible man that year. I remember a young baron, heir to a great fortune, who would have treated her like a queen, cherished her every moment. She knew it. But that wasn't what was done then. It's not how it's done now." She looked at Marie. "You were just as trapped as she was, and it broke my heart that so little progress had been made by then.

"After you were born, I was in there helping care for her in the aftermath of childbirth. No one else was there, no one was paying attention. The bad news was being spread. She was despondent that you hadn't been a son, and hated herself for feeling that way, for she loved you so much. She just hated that you needed to be something else. She said I couldn't possibly understand. I told her about my own secret—that I had a son and no husband. And while she'd always trusted me, it reached a new level in that moment.

"We were victims of our uteruses.

"After she had her third daughter in a row, we knew the situation was becoming dire. He had impregnated another of his mistresses. She was able to get a scan—it was a boy. This was different from the others: your mother had had three daughters by now, and her husband was desperate. If your mother was out of the picture, he could marry his mistress in time to legitimize the boy. We had discussed, briefly, publicly passing Dirk off as hers so that we could both be protected, but the Earl would never have gone for it. It mattered to him that it was his son—his flesh and blood. Falsely passing off someone else's son as his own would have been too deep of an insult, and so we never proposed it. I sometimes wonder how things might have been different had we had the courage to do so. She knew her days were numbered. The Earl had beaten her so badly before, he would do it again, and this time she might not survive. She was his property, his to destroy if he wanted. There would have been no justice for her. No consequence to him. There are never consequences to men like him.

"We knew she was going to die. The question was, would it be on her terms, or his?

"We figured out a way for her to disappear, to appear to have taken her own life. If she committed suicide, she would not be allowed to be buried in a church, so no one would look for her. No one would miss her. There would be no funeral mass for her. And she had become such a liability at home that no one in society was acknowledging her anymore. If she were to die, it would be a blessing, something quietly swept under the rug."

Jane gave Marie a piercing stare. "I read of your 'death,' Marie. I suspect that you had reached many of the same conclusions that your mother did."

Marie's face flushed.

"Did you have help like she did?"

Marie shook her head.

Jane clicked her tongue. "Such a shame. Every wife needs a confidante. No woman should have to shoulder the burden of marriage alone.

"So your mother arrived here; the letter you saw had a code inside of it that spelled out a time for us to meet. We had a color for the day of the week and a sense for the time of day. I still remember it: blue for Thursday, and she would reference smell if she would arrive mid-morning. And she referenced the canal, confirming that she would be in Brugge on that day."

Emma remembered the phrase that had been written in her mother's careful hand. It had stood out for its description of the Thames and its appearance and smell: *This time of year, it actually appears blue and smells of sunshine, despite all the boats traversing up and down as if it were a canal.* Emma should have realized it was a code. The Thames was never blue, regardless of the season or time of day. It never smelled of anything but oil and dead eels.

"I planned a visit to my son to coincide with her arrival. She arrived soaking wet from the journey and from all the tears she'd cried. She'd left all of you, and it killed her as surely as your father would have."

The use of the phrase "your father" was jarring to Emma. She had thought of him simply as the Earl for most of her life, especially after he had disowned her. She had no father; he was just the Earl. It had helped to have the distance that the title provided. She suspected it had been the same for Marie as well. Not that they ever spoke about it. Or ever would.

"She was convinced that she'd done the wrong thing," Jane went on. "Abandoning her children was a fate worse than death. I told her that she had been as good as dead anyway, and what use would she have been to you girls if she were truly gone? At least this way, she could spend her time helping you, if only from afar. And so she has done ever since."

Emma scoffed. "She abandoned us, let us believe her dead, and then disappeared from our lives." She had no desire to betray how much all of this hurt her to the core. "She did nothing."

"But she did," Jane countered. "Through me, through your childhoods, she was there for you. I brought her news as often as I could, through whatever means I could. And in turn, she provided things you needed. Marie, she sent books to me, and I put them on the shelves at Ellthrop, knowing you'd find them and be drawn to them. Emma, she saw you, really saw you. And she predicted you wouldn't last in that house, or with the Earl, or in a marriage. So she ensured, through me, that when you left, there was money in Ellthrop for you to make your way to London, that you had a brochure of train timetables that had been carelessly left around the house."

The floor seemed to fall beneath Emma's feet. She remembered her luck at finding a timetable, snatching it from a sideboard in the corridor. She remembered finding the magazine article about the shelter for women like her in London stuffed into her bag, so that when she'd arrived, she'd known where to go to find help instead of wandering about in a large city where the people in the only places she knew would never have recognized her, let alone taken her in. And as for the money—well, when she'd snatched the funds that she'd been squirreling away for months in a hiding spot, she had thought there had been more in there than she'd expected.

Her mother had seen to all of that, just for her?

Tears welled in her eyes again, and she looked away so that no one else would see them.

"Mother Mary," Marie whispered out of Emma's sight.

"She came to London," Jane whispered. The old woman shuffled over and touched Emma's face, turning it toward her, making Emma face the love that she was too scarred-over to accept. "When I informed her you had left Grayside, she chanced it, and returned to England. The war was very bad at that time, as you know, and it was dangerous. She'd never been back before that, and never since. But she went to the shelter, and she walked through, and she saw you from afar, lying on a cot in a group room, fast asleep. In sleep, you looked weary but determined. She told me later that she'd never been filled with more pride than she was in that moment. She slipped a few things into your bag, but left, so that you wouldn't see."

Emma's hand flew to her throat, where the chain with a medal of Saint Christopher, the patron saint of travelers, had rested ever since that night in the shelter. She'd never questioned where it had come from, but it had brought her so much comfort at the time. It had given her the courage to believe that she was not running away from something but rather toward something else.

"She said that was the hardest it had ever been to get on the ferry back to Brugge," Jane said. "She hadn't seen you in so long, and all she wanted to do was drink the sight of you in, to take you into her arms and never let you go. But she couldn't be sure you weren't being watched, and she didn't want to put you at further risk."

Emma clutched the medal, meeting Jane's eye. Marie wrapped her hand around Emma's free hand. There was so much love and support that it was blinding, and Emma had to shut her eyes against it, wanting it to end. She didn't deserve it, the unconditional love she saw. In her mind's eye, she curled up into a ball, hoping it would go away.

Jane kept going. "She waited here, with Dirk, for years, for one of you girls to figure it out. She waited each day by the arriving ferry, to see if you were on it. She would have been there waiting for you today, had it not been for the person who stepped off the ferry six months ago."

Marie squeezed Emma's hand and asked with bated breath, "Who?"

"It was your father."

Marie's hand began shaking, though she continued to cling tightly to Emma's hand.

"But he died six months ago," said Marie.

"Yes," Jane said. "He died in Zeebrugge. He stepped off the ferry, looked into your mother's eyes, surely thought he was seeing a ghost, and collapsed then and there of a heart attack. By the time the paramedics had arrived, he was already dead."

"I never knew he was here when it happened," Marie said. "I had only been told it was a heart attack."

"I didn't even know he was dead," Emma said.

"You knew I was 'dead,'" Marie pointed out.

"I didn't have a news alert set up for him like I did for you."

Marie's hand squeezed hers. "I didn't know that you didn't know."

"I didn't care. I don't care. And I'm not sorry to hear about it." She made a sign of the cross as she spoke, though it was more due to muscle memory than a wish for forgiveness from the divine for such a thought. Her father had turned her out and left her for dead. She would not mourn him now, or ever.

"Even though he never said a word to her, she decided it was too close. So she moved on, but asked me to stay here and wait for you at the dock each day, just as she had done, and when you got here, to tell you where she would be." Jane began to weep again. "And God be praised, you've come."

"Where?"

"She's in Frankfurt Free City," Jane said. "And Dirk will take you to the train station tomorrow to help you book a ticket on the express."

Dirk nodded. Jane's face shone like the sun.

"You can be with her this time tomorrow."

Chapter Seventeen

It was well after midnight, but John Hart was not going to sleep. Not until he'd found what he was looking for. And when John Hart looked for something, he found it. Every time.

His relationship to the Dowager Duchess of Suffolk had many privileges, but one of his favorites was that constables would allow him, as her representative, to review any and all information he saw fit in order to protect her interests and the interests of her estate. The Duke might be a hopeless idiot, and his wife had understandably thrown herself off a cliff, but the Dowager Duchess was still as sharp and clear as an icicle, and she kept everything in that estate running like clockwork.

John Hart was grateful to her for all she'd done for him, and for her sharp eye regarding the jewelry. The disappearance of the Duchess of Suffolk was too convenient, too clean, and with too little evidence left behind. He had learned that piercing gaze and healthy skepticism from the Dowager Duchess, and so when the jewelry was unaccounted for, he went looking.

England couldn't afford a computer system outside of the one airport in London, so if someone wanted to slip out of the country, the ferry to Zeebrugge was the way to do it.

The Duchess's passport hadn't been used, and there was no record of her actually leaving the country. His conversation with Mr. Harrison had proven fruitful, and now he sat before a monitor watching the grainy footage of passengers in Dover boarding the ferry to Zeebrugge.

Cameras didn't always work, and there were a few days that had not been captured at all. Nevertheless, he would review all the footage, and he had been doing so for the last four days. He couldn't trust the immigration records; the workers manning the station were often too drunk to see straight, were amenable to bribes, and frequently forgot to input passport information into the necessary records.

Mr. Harrison had told him that a young woman fitting the Duchess's description had shown him a sapphire ring that bore a strong resemblance to the one that had been used as her engagement ring. That was not hers to take with her, to heaven or to hell, and certainly not to Europe, as Mr. Harrison had posited that she would likely do.

John Hart knew that what he was looking for was impossible, but this he had to see for himself. Besides, if they relied on other methods, they would have to get James involved, and that would be a waste of time for everyone.

So here he sat, watching grainy surveillance footage. And then he saw it.

Saw *her*.

Impossibly alive, and in disguise, but he knew. He'd know that figure anywhere.

He bolted up, shouting that he needed to get on the next ferry to Zeebrugge, and he needed to get on it now.

Marie and Emma should have gone to the train station first thing in the morning. Vanished into the anonymity of Frankfurt Free City, the unofficial demilitarized zone of a Europe that was constantly at its own throat. They should have bought tickets and worried later about how they would cross into the country.

But they didn't.

The sisters lay side by side in Dirk's bed; he had insisted on taking the couch in the front room. Marie lay awake all that night, thinking about what she'd learned. She'd been right, but she didn't feel vindicated. And while she was thrilled that her mother truly was alive, and she had a much better understanding than anyone else of the desperation that had driven Charlotte to leave, she grieved at her mother's loss anew. The anger still simmered, but she tried to tamp it down as much as she could.

Emma had curled herself into a ball as she thought about her mother risking everything to come check on her, but also not taking Emma with her. It reopened the old wound that Emma hadn't been hard to find, yet no one had come for her.

She had stuffed the pain, the feelings, the sorrow, all of it, down inside of her, pressed it down as far and deep as it would go until it had shrunk into nothing, collapsed as completely and thoroughly as a dying star. Her pain had become the singularity around which her entire self orbited, but one that was best hidden from view. She'd long ago made peace with the fact that loneliness was the price of independence.

Neither sister spoke to the other. But they were there together in the shared silence, and that was enough at this point. And in the morning, neither acknowledged that the other had been awake.

They sat with Jane as she watched the morning news on television. Televisions were not the rare commodity here that they were in England, and the sisters marveled at the stories that were covered here. Rather than keeping a singular focus on England, the news was multinational. Stories of the massive travel associated with the annual Rice Harvest in Mino-Aki; the launch of a new multinational space crew; a major speech given in China; the wedding of the heir to the throne of Fanteland. The broadcast was on the pan-European channel, using the shared common language of Latin that most people spoke in an effort to communicate across borders. The sisters had learned Latin as part of their education, but they rarely used it. Most spoke English as a point of pride, using Latin only when strictly necessary. Seeing it on the television was unlike anything they had ever seen.

When they weren't marveling at the television or news of the outside world, they spent time with Jane, the woman who had raised them longer than their own mother had, who had spent years of her life away from her own son in favor of caring for someone else's daughters.

Jane's comforting voice and easy presence brought them each a sense of peace they had been missing since they had lived with her at Ellthrop. Ellthrop had never been a home for anyone, and those who lived there were more akin to museum curators than residents. It belonged to the Earl, and the Earl belonged to the estate. Everyone else was just background noise. It had been a hard place to live. But Jane had made it tolerable in the absence of their mother. And in this time of uncertainty, her presence made this more tolerable as well.

So they stayed an extra day. Then another. And another. They pressed Dirk and Jane about border security. This wasn't England, Jane assured them. They didn't police women here the way they did back there. The passports would be enough.

"I remember my mother talking about you both," Dirk said as he walked them to the station on the morning of the fourth day so they could catch the overnight train to FFC. "She always said she wished she could have tucked you into her luggage and brought you with her."

It was dusk, and the bright lights of the city blotted out the stars above; the noise of the people and music and the buzz of electricity drowned out the sound of any animals or birds or the rushing water. Everything felt so loud here compared to London, especially the volume at which people talked. Even Dirk sounded like he was shouting.

The train station was as tall and long as a cathedral, and just as cold, drafty, and smoky. These were some of the fastest trains in Europe, though they paled in comparison to their counterparts in other countries, such as China or the multinational network that threaded itself across the New World. Dirk took them to the money changer's booth to convert their Sterling into Guilders. He spoke Dutch to the man on the other side of the rickety, foul-smelling booth. Once the money changer saw that Marie had Sterling, he switched to Latin for her benefit. Even with the money changer's hefty cut, they had enough to buy tickets to FFC without selling another piece of jewelry. Marie didn't like carrying around the jewelry, though she was happy not to have to sell it here and attract attention. If they sold it in FFC, no one would ever trace it back to her.

"My Latin has gotten so bad," Marie remarked to Emma as they walked away.

"Really?"

"I'm pretty sure he hasn't been doing this job for 'a year and three thumbs.'"

Emma laughed. "You're right, he hasn't."

"You'd think that after a lifetime of going to Mass I would understand Latin as well as English."

"You hear the same phrases repeated over and over and have been trained to repeat certain phrases back. That's not the same as learning the language. Some thought is required."

"Not much of an opportunity to do that back in England," Marie murmured.

"Of course not. You're either too busy trying not to starve, or too rich to worry. And those who do, well, they get out."

"Like us."

Emma looped her arm through Marie's. The contact made Marie's heart blossom like a poppy. "Like us," she agreed. "And Mother." Marie swallowed. It seemed so impossible that they might see her as early as tomorrow that she feared that saying it out loud might cause it not to happen. So she said no more.

They followed Dirk as he weaved his way through the crowded station. Marie kept her head down, but couldn't help glancing at all the faces and taking in the languages and sights and smells and noises all around her. A sea of anonymous faces. She had never seen so many people in one place before, swarming like bees in a hive. Even Green's Lane was nothing compared to this.

And then she saw it. She shuffled to a stop, causing Emma to stop with her.

"What is it?"

No.

"Marie?"

Marie shook her head, as if coming back into herself after a dissociative event. She looked again. Gone. Maybe never even there in the first place.

"I thought I saw . . ." Her voice trailed off. "Never mind. Must have been my imagination." She began walking and tugged on her sister's arm. "Come on," she said. "Let's get on the train."

"You scared me for a minute," Emma said.

"I scared me too. Being silly. Lot of change, not much time."

Dirk nodded at them and pointed to platform *vier* (Dirk clarified that it meant "four" in Dutch). The idling train was both larger and newer than any in England. It wasn't one of the swift, high-speed trains that crisscrossed other parts of the world, but it would get them where they wanted to go. It ran on hydrogen or electricity powered by a rechargeable battery, but it still smelled of the dust and soot that covered everything and that made the rest of the world sneer and call their area of Eurasia the Dark Corner—the land covered in soot and smog and smoke, the people who had hollowed out the earth, set it on fire, then left the ashes where they fell. The train had no smokestack, its lines were sleek, and there was none of the coal smoke smell that had more or less taken up permanent residence in their noses, which was why everyone in England was always coughing. And unlike in England, there were none of the disabled war veterans or families in rags clustered around the entrances to the trains, begging for a few coins to get them through the night. No buskers or men selling small trinkets, their wares scattered about carefully upon loose tattered blankets. There were no Brothers or Nuns seeking donations for their causes, or for the Church. Nothing that made a train station a train station. It was so sterile. It was truly just a place to board a train.

Dirk led them to the entrance to the train.

"I can't thank you enough for bringing us here," Emma said.

"And for sharing your mother with us for so long," Marie added.

Dirk smiled, but it didn't reach his eyes. "It's my pleasure."

A man blew a whistle, shouted in Dutch. "The train is leaving now, you should get on board."

Emma looked like she was about to say something more, but Marie gasped, grabbed her hand, and pulled her onto the train.

"Marie?" Emma said, forgetting to use the fake name on the documents.

Marie stuck her head out the door. "For God's sake, don't say my name—just get on the train now. It's not safe. Dirk, you too! You can't let him see you!"

"Who?"

"Just get on! Now!" Marie was almost hysterical. Emma followed her onto the train, with Dirk close behind.

"What's happened?" Dirk asked.

"Not here." Marie began rushing down the aisle of the carriage, glancing into compartments before she finally found an empty one and went in, shuffling down low beneath the window, but peeking up just high enough to see out.

"This isn't our compartment," Emma pointed out.

"That doesn't matter now," Marie said. "Get down, now! Before he sees us!"

Dirk and Emma complied. The three huddled together under the window.

"Who are we hiding from?"

Marie shook her head for a moment as a shadow crossed the window above them, then whispered, "John Hart."

"Who?" Emma asked.

"John Hart!"

"Who's John Hart?"

"The Dowager Duchess's enforcer," Marie said. "They must have figured out I'm alive."

"Why would he follow you?" Emma asked. She'd read the articles: Marie was dead. The Duke's family's statement was perfunctory. Her husband's engagement to his next wife was likely already announced. Everything was tied up. Wasn't it? "You don't suppose it's for the jewelry?"

Marie hesitated, then said, "It has to be. I knew they'd eventually figure out it was missing. I just didn't think they'd come looking for me so soon. Or ever."

"You might have mentioned this earlier!" Emma cried.

"Keep your voice down!" Marie hissed.

"He can't hear us outside," Emma hissed back. "And it's too loud anyway. He didn't even see us get on."

"I can't risk it," Marie said. "I won't go back there."

"Just throw the bloody jewels out the window once we get going. It's not like they'll be able to get us once we get to FFC."

"You don't know him," Marie said. "He doesn't operate through official channels. If John Hart wants me back in England, he will bring me back to England, even if he has to throw me in a trunk and drag me back. And even if he gets the jewels, that won't be the end of it. He'll want to make an *example* out of me. So will the Dowager Duchess."

"Marie, I know you were worried about what they were doing to you before, and you did turn out to be right about Mother, but—"

"They'll kill me," Marie said. "Not publicly, that would be an embarrassment to them. But rest assured, they will get back everything of theirs that I have taken. Simply returning it won't be enough."

Emma chanced a look through the window. The aisle was filling with people boarding. Something about this wasn't adding up. Peers definitely cared about their polished stones, but never this much. This had to be a very special piece of jewelry that Marie had foolishly taken, unless . . .

"Are we talking about something other than the jewelry?" she asked, finally.

Marie didn't respond. An elderly couple arrived at their compartment, quickly becoming agitated at them, pointing at their tickets and gesturing at the compartment around them. Dirk tried whispering to them, but that just made the couple angrier and louder.

"Oh, I wish they'd stop," Marie whispered. "They're going to attract attention."

They heard the whistle of the train and the conductor on the platform blew, and they heard the rising din of final goodbyes as people leaned out the windows of neighboring compartments. They felt a jerk as the train began to move.

"Let's go," Marie said. She stood up. And shrieked.

A man with dark hair and a murderous smile was staring through the window straight at her.

"Oh no," she said. She backed up hastily from the window, grabbed Emma's sleeve and Dirk's elbow. "Let's go, now!"

She pushed them into the aisle of the train, past the angry old couple, who were now shouting at them as they exited the compartment they had been demanding a moment earlier. Would nothing satisfy these two? Marie tried to push through the last passengers who were loading their baggage, but none would budge. They shouted and gestured angrily at them, and would not move. Dirk made rapid apologies in Dutch, but it did nothing to move the people out of the way. They were trapped; no getting out now. Emma looked back through the window. The train was moving faster now, but slow enough that he could still jump on if he wanted. John Hart began jogging, then running, to keep up with the train. He banged his hand on the window, looked Marie straight in the eye. With his other hand, he drew something from his pocket.

"Is that a weapon?" Emma cried.

Marie shook her head.

It was a phone. He put it to his ear and began talking as he ran.

"Oh no," Marie said again.

"Who is he calling?"

"I don't know, but he won't call anyone good," Marie said. She looked around frantically. "Have they closed the doors?"

Dirk shouted something to the conductor, who responded and waved his hand. "Yes," Dirk said.

"Good, then we'll get out," Emma said. "Out of FFC before we know it."

"Not if his phone call is to the right person to stop the train," Marie said.

Emma looked at Marie. "He can do that?"

Marie nodded, her expression deadly serious.

The train picked up speed, and John Hart, sprinting and shouting into his phone, was visible in the window one moment, banging on the window some more, then gone. The train accelerated, clearly not stopping. Whoever John Hart had called, they had failed to stop the train. Yet.

Emma blew out the breath she hadn't realized she was holding. They looked around at the angry passengers around them, and gave small waves of apology.

"We'd best find your compartment," Dirk said finally.

"And hide you somehow," Emma said. "No ticket."

"We'll figure something out. I can probably buy one on my phone," Dirk said. "Or even pay the conductor directly, maybe they have a tablet. But let's go sit, and perhaps you can fill us in on what just happened there?"

Marie nodded, and Emma knew in that instance she was right: this was about more than just jewels.

Chapter Eighteen

Marie kept her head down. No interpreter was needed to translate the dirty looks and hushed conversations that followed them up and down the train. Dirk led the way, muttering apologies in Dutch as he led them through two carriages until they were in the cargo hold of the very last carriage on the train. With nothing anchoring the back of the carriage, it jumped up and shook as the train chugged along the track, and they had to grasp shelves and brace themselves against luggage and cartons to avoid falling down.

They caught their breath and rocked with the train for a few minutes before Emma turned her ice-blue eyes at her sister and said, "I know that I asked you this already, but you didn't really answer me. This is about more than the jewelry, isn't it?"

Marie looked away at the blur of trees and towers that passed by the window. The train shook violently as it picked up even more speed.

"Well?"

"I have the largest sapphire in England pinned inside my dress. Of course it's about the jewelry."

Emma shook her head. "I don't believe that. There's something you're not telling us, and we deserve to know."

Marie waited a few long moments before speaking. "It's too dangerous."

"Someone is after us. The danger is already here. And he knows where we're going. So you may as well tell us." She took her sister by the arm. "Marie, what is it?"

"Something bad," she said. "I took from them the most valuable thing in the entire estate, something that they can't survive without." She swallowed. "And you're right, it's not the sapphire. It's more valuable than that. More valuable than any jewel."

"Can you take it back?" Emma said. "They've clearly figured out that you're not dead."

"Might they kill you if they find out you have this thing?" Dirk asked.

"Not right away," Marie said. "After that, I think they will. They were planning to already. And now I'm already dead, so they won't face any consequences when they do."

"So return it," Emma said. "Whatever it is, it's not worth the risk."

"Definitely not," Dirk echoed.

"All right," Marie said. "I'll tell you." Marie looked at Dirk carefully. "You shouldn't listen to this next part," she said. "For your own safety."

"I'm an unticketed passenger on a train bound for a major city, no passport in hand, and am being chased by a madman. I'm in."

"And you shouldn't be," Marie said. "I don't want this hurting you. Or your mother."

"We'll be okay," Dirk said. "Truly. And we've already been involved with this for some time. Helping you, hiding your mother. We're well involved already."

Marie nodded. "All right," she said. "I'll tell you. But only after the next stop. I want you to have a moment to think about it, and I want you to be able to get off the train first. So you aren't carrying the secret if you all decide that this is too much. I want you to think about that choice, and think about it hard, before you decide. Because you have the right to walk away."

"You're being a little dramatic," Emma said.

"I'm being serious. Lives are at stake with this. Emma, if they catch me, you deserve to be able to honestly say you didn't know what I had done. And I don't want you to face criminal penalties for helping me."

"Criminal penalties?"

"Yes."

"But there are no criminal penalties for traveling with someone who's stolen something. Believe me, I should know."

"You're correct."

"There are only penalties for helping . . ."

Emma's voice trailed off, her eyes blew wide, and her face turned pale.

"Marie, what have you done?"

Marie opened her mouth to speak when the door to the luggage compartment banged open and spread blinding light into the dark chamber. Marie gasped as Emma jumped back behind a trunk, pulling Marie behind her. Emma prayed that the noise and motion of the train had concealed their movements. She hadn't had a chance to grab Dirk, who stood tall and innocent in the spotlight of the light from the doorway. Emma peeked through a gap between the trunk and some suitcases so that she could see what was happening.

A young man in a conductor's uniform stood looking at the compartment and at Dirk standing there. The conductor spoke in German, and Dirk shook his head in mock confusion. The conductor tried Dutch, and Dirk feigned ignorance of that language as well. Dirk replied in Latin, and the conductor began interrogating him in the same language. Emma realized that Dirk was doing that for their benefit, so that they would know what was happening, without betraying that anyone spoke English.

"You are not permitted to be in here," the conductor said in Latin.

"I had forgotten something in my luggage," Dirk replied. "I came in here to check."

"It's dangerous. You should have asked a porter for help." Marie found that the more she listened to Latin, the more her memory of it returned and the more she could understand it, like a series of keys clicking into locks.

"I understand, and I apologize for coming in here. I got what I came for, so I'll be leaving now."

He made to exit, but the conductor blocked his way.

"I haven't seen you on the train."

"Oh, of course you did," Dirk lied with easy, confident grace, taking another step forward.

"Where are you going?"

"Strasbourg," Dirk said.

"Please show your ticket," the conductor said.

"I told you, you already checked it."

"I never forget a face. I don't recognize yours. So kindly show the ticket again."

Dirk made a show of patting his trouser and jacket pockets. "I don't seem to have it on me."

"Perhaps on your phone, you have an electronic copy?"

"Perhaps. Maybe I can step outside and join you?"

"We'll stay here until you can produce your ticket."

"I'm searching on my phone now. As it happens, if I'm unable to find it, I can just buy one, correct?"

"Not on this train, no. And FFC issues steep penalties for those who board a train without a ticket."

"Is that so?" Dirk spoke so smoothly. He used a light tone of voice that sounded as if he might be discussing the weather.

The train jolted and a suitcase tipped over, falling on Emma's foot. She stifled a cry and shrank down so as not to be seen.

The conductor didn't respond; instead, he withdrew a flashlight from his belt and started scanning the compartment.

"What are you looking for?" Dirk asked in Latin.

"Are you alone in here?" The conductor asked.

"Of course not. You see all the luggage in here with me? This is the most crowded room I've ever been in." He affected a laugh, but the conductor did not join him.

"There were two girls on the train with a young man. They were causing some sort of trouble. Many other passengers complained. None of them have been seen for a while, but they must still be on the train, as it had already departed by the time they were last seen moving to a different carriage. You wouldn't know anything about that, would you?"

Dirk shook his head. "I don't, but if I wasn't in that carriage, I wouldn't have seen it, would I?" He gave a laugh that sounded more nervous than he probably intended.

"It caused quite a lot of disruption. Some of our regular passengers described a man who looked like you."

Dirk shrugged. "A tall, thin, pale man with dark hair? I'm surely not the only man on the train who fits that description."

"Enough nonsense," said the conductor. "You're getting off at the next stop."

"Which one is that?"

"Genterbrugge."

"This is not the express?"

"Come along."

"I intended to take the express to Strasbourg."

"Come along," the Conductor repeated, this time with an edge to his voice.

"Yes, of course, I am coming now. I have what I came for."

"Haven't you forgotten something?" the conductor asked.

"No, I do not believe so."

"Your luggage, which you came in here to inspect?"

Fourteen agonizing seconds passed.

"Yes, of course, how silly of me." Emma saw him grab for a random bag, but the conductor stopped him.

"What are you really doing in here?" He lifted a flashlight, shone it right at the trunk behind which Emma and Marie were huddled. Then they heard a rush and a commotion. The door to the luggage compartment slammed shut. The conductor shouted, "Hey!" And Emma peeked over the top of the trunk to see Dirk on top of the conductor, wrestling him to the ground. He lifted an arm and motioned for them to get out of the compartment.

Emma nodded and grabbed at Marie, who at first hesitated, then faltered, then followed her sister out of the compartment. Emma pulled them into the toilet across the aisle, and locked the door.

"It stinks in here," Marie said.

"Shh!" hissed Emma.

"Sorry," Marie mouthed, clearly trying to breathe through her mouth. Emma put her ear to the door. It was difficult to hear over the rumble of the train, but she could hear raised voices, one of which sounded like Dirk's. She heard footsteps, and shouting, and then a retreat. Then it was quiet. Absolutely quiet.

"What's happening out there?" Marie asked.

"I don't know," Emma said. "Clearly, Dirk is in trouble."

"Because of us," Marie whispered.

"Yes."

They were silent as the outside of the train. After a few minutes, someone attempted to open the door to the toilet, making them both jump. After waiting a few seconds, perhaps a minute, the person knocked insistently. They ignored it, and the person eventually shouted a curse through the door and gave up.

"We can't stay in here all the way to FFC," Marie said.

"We can't go out there either."

"But if we don't get out soon, won't people become suspicious?"

Marie made a good point. "Okay," Emma said. "Let me listen first, make sure there is no one waiting for us." She pressed her ear to the door. She heard several sets of footsteps and the laughter of what sounded like teenage girls. She nodded, and opened the door. Emma exited the toilet as if she had simply been in there alone then, glancing around, nodded back at Marie. Emma walked forward a few steps, hoping Marie would know to play it cool, and thankfully she did. They walked forward a few rows, until they found an empty compartment. Emma brushed a few crumbs off one of the seats, while Marie ducked down under the window.

"Stop that," Emma said.

"What?"

"You look like you're trying to hide."

"I *am* trying to hide!"

"That is suspicious. We can't act suspicious."

"I'm scared someone will see us."

"Anonymity is our friend. We're just two widows on a train. Nothing more, nothing less."

Marie blew out a breath. "Should I lower the shade?"

Emma considered. "Halfway," she said. "Enough so that people can see it's occupied, but not so they can see our faces."

"What about the conductor? What if he comes for us?"

"I don't think he saw us."

"But he didn't see us earlier or take our tickets."

"We won't have to lie much: we were in the toilet. I was sick. You were taking care of me."

Marie nodded. "Okay, I think I can do that."

They sat in silence for a long time, rocking back and forth with the train.

"Genterbrugge is the next stop," Marie said. "Should we get off there?"

Emma thought. "I'm not sure."

"If John Hart is following us, he may well be waiting for us there. He will have a car or something, to board the train again. I'm sure of it. If anyone could move Heaven and Earth to follow us, it's him."

"I guess we're staying on the train, then," Emma said.

"But if we get off, we are stranded in a strange city."

"That's not a big change from our present circumstances."

"True." Marie paused for a moment. "Is Dirk going to be arrested?"

Emma sighed. "I hope not. I doubt it. He'll probably just be thrown off."

"Maybe he got out."

"Maybe."

Neither one really believed what they were saying, but it was better than the alternative, which was that he was likely in custody with the officials on the train. Emma didn't know what the penalties were for violence on an international train in Flanders, but she suspected they were not soft. But she decided to believe what she'd told her sister, that Dirk wasn't facing any serious trouble.

They sat in silence until they felt the train slow down. It pulled into the station of Genterbrugge, where a cadre of what appeared to be police officers were waiting on the platform. They watched out the window as the conductor ran to the platform and began gesticulating angrily at the carriage. He appeared to be unharmed, though rumpled. The police entered the carriage. Emma and Marie froze, still as deer caught in headlights. They ducked their heads down. Marie folded her hands in her lap, and Emma grabbed a newspaper out of the pocket of one of the seats. The police boarded the train, walking up and down the corridor of the carriage.

The police opened the door, startling the two. An officer said something rapidly in Dutch, and at the sisters' confused faces, switched to Latin.

"Pardon me, ladies. Have you seen a strange man?"

"A strange man?" Marie asked in the same language.

"Tall, thin, pale, dark hair, causing a commotion."

"Oh, perhaps earlier, when we boarded," Emma said.

"Have you seen him since?"

"No," Emma lied. Marie nodded in support.

"You are traveling alone?"

They both nodded in unison.

"No companion?"

"We are widows," Emma said.

The officer thanked them distractedly and made to move down to the next compartment.

That's when Marie saw him. John Hart, on the platform, running toward them. He scanned the train, then made for an open door in the carriage. He boarded just as the officer was beginning to walk away. His eyes darted around, then he caught sight of his prey. His stare bored into Marie's, looking triumphant. In his mind, he'd already succeeded.

No.

She would not go back. He would not make her go back. Not when she had come this close and still had so far to go.

"No." She said it out loud this time. It was a whisper, but at the same time, it was loud. Emma turned to her. "No," Marie repeated, this time even louder.

John Hart came closer.

"No!"

This was not how this ended.

"Officer!" Marie cried. "Him, that man!" She pointed at John Hart, who was now barreling toward her. He snarled. She screamed and pointed even harder.

John Hart was tall, thin, pale. Causing a commotion.

The officer tipped his hat, then directed the rest of the officers toward John Hart. The sisters could hear his protestations that he had not been on the train, but the word of two ladies was apparently enough. Another difference from England; there, the word of any number of women would never outweigh that of a man.

They watched the police question John Hart on the platform; he produced some sort of document, but the officer shook his head. John Hart pointed at it and began yelling, but the officer was unmoved. Whatever authority John Hart might have back in England apparently did not extend here. The more he argued, the more pathetic he looked, and Marie felt her lips curl into a satisfied smirk. Let him get a taste of what it was like to be her: ignored, irrelevant, powerless. The officers brought over the conductor, who was presumably being asked to identify his attacker. A crackled announcement over the loudspeaker system in Dutch stated what was likely the imminent departure of the train, and people dashed both onto and off the platform. The conductor remained there while a different one took his place on the train.

Just at the sound of the bells announcing that the doors were closing, Marie saw Dirk dash off the train and, without looking back, run past the police, John Hart, and the conductor, none of whom paid him any mind. Marie breathed a sigh of relief and pointed him out to Emma, who did the same. The doors closed. The train started moving. And Marie felt her heartbeat slow down so that it was in time with the rhythm of the train.

"He obviously tracked you here," Emma said once they were several minutes out from the station.

"On what, my phone?"

Emma nodded. "What else?"

"But I don't understand. I got it from Mr. Davis. How could he track me?"

Emma nodded, then gestured for Marie's phone, and once she'd handed it over, Emma threw both Marie's phone and her own out the window. Marie cried out as it disappeared from view. She'd grown so used to this small measure of freedom, and already it was taken away from her.

"We can get new ones," Emma said.

Marie nodded. "I guess."

"I had to."

"I know." She looked up at the ceiling. "What do we do now? Do we still go to FFC?"

Emma shrugged. "Do we have any other choice?"

Chapter Nineteen

When they alighted in Frankfurt Free City, veiled novices from a nearby convent greeted them with blankets and bottles of water before immediately ushering them out of the station. They were led through a specific exit over which a passage from the Book of Colossians was carved into the stone. Decades of rain and wind and human suffering had dulled the words to the point that they were barely visible: "Whatever you do, work heartily, as for the Lord and not for men, knowing that from the Lord you will receive the inheritance as your reward."

FFC had a law that impoverished foreigners must work seven years to be permitted any sort of legal status, and another seven before they could have any rights. It was based on the biblical story of Jacob, who had worked seven years to marry Rachel only to be tricked into marrying her sister Leah. He'd then worked another seven to marry Rachel as well. Marie mentioned this to Emma, who snorted derisively. Marie smacked her on the arm. Laughing at a story from Scripture was considered blasphemy in England, and if that was also the case here, they couldn't afford to be thrown out. Not when they'd come this far, and not when they were so much closer to finding their mother.

FFC was the one part of the Holy Roman Empire where they were permitted entry despite being English citizens. The Holy Roman Empire was the single most dominant empire in all of Europe, with both material wealth and the Church behind it. It stretched all the way from the Baltic Sea in the north to the Papal States in the south, where the Pope in Rome ruled over the entire empire. While all Christians were nominally welcome in the Holy Roman Empire, not all were created equal, and certainly not all areas of FFC were open to them.

An official asked them for their passports; they held them out, and without inspecting them, the official sent the sisters to a doorway labeled *Flüchtlinge* in German and *Profugi* in Latin ("refugees"), where they were shepherded away from the more affluent-looking passengers on the train.

The few English lucky enough to leave England typically worked in low-class domestic service, porter, or janitorial jobs abroad, and FFC was no different. It was a function of the poor diet and lack of educational system for which England was infamous; those who were lucky enough to get out were typically unskilled laborers. Or so Marie had read.

The official who scrutinized their passports gave them a skeptical look. Marie's heart leaped into her throat; they had paid so much for these documents, and they had come so far, they couldn't be sent back to England now. She feared that this entry point might have some sort of biometric data check as well. The official leered at them and said he was not sure he'd be able to offer them entry. Too many English trying to crawl into the city like cockroaches, and just as dirty. "But perhaps," he said in Latin, "there may be an arrangement we could make."

"Money?" Marie asked, but the man shook his head. She looked to Emma, who clearly had known what he was asking for. This man had power over whether they entered FFC or not, and whether they could find their mother. And this in a city of men of God.

Marie gulped, and Emma bravely stepped forward. Marie hoped she wasn't about to take him up on his demand. She followed to offer up herself instead, but Emma put up an arm to hold her back.

The man smiled and stroked a long finger along the side of the passports. He opened his mouth, but before he could speak another official entered. Agitated, the first official turned to the new one, and after some rapid-fire and loud German, thrust the passports back at the sisters and jerked his head to the side. "Stay in your zone," he said in Latin. Then added, "You're lucky it's time for my break."

If London had been busy, Zeebrugge was busier, and FFC was overwhelming. The sisters were shepherded onto a bus, which deposited them in their designated zone.

FFC was a walled-off and divided city, built like a labyrinth. There were parts for citizens of the city, parts for citizens and subjects of the Holy Roman Empire outside of FFC, and parts to which foreigners without money, connections, or the right visas, like Marie and Emma, were limited. They were restricted to what they quickly learned was called the "Garden Wall" section. It was less a garden than a narrow strip of buildings, alleyways, and chapels that formed the outermost perimeter. There would be no landmarks for them, no drinks at fancy hotels, no tea or coffee in the Imperial Gardens in the heart of the city. There would be no shopping at the boutiques in the Platz, even if they had the money to spare. Their visa stamp specifically designated their area of the city, and it was crowded, dirty, and anonymous.

But they were not just restricted in terms of areas they were permitted to visit. Women traveling alone, regardless of marital status, were prohibited from entering bars, saloons, and taverns. They were prohibited from entering mixed-group lodgings. So the sisters went to the only place that was open to them: the convent at Saint Hildegard's, where stern nuns in black and white eyed them with great suspicion, after they had been satisfactorily screened for lice. They were treated as wayward women to be saved, and they knew that these accommodations came with a price: attempts at salvation. Women who went into those convents sometimes didn't come back out. They weren't dead, just forcibly ordained. Or so Marie had read.

They needed to buy new phones, though she had no idea where to go to find them. Paying in cash would mean they'd have to pay double, and paying in cash without identification would mean they'd have to pay triple. Paying in cash without identification or a male with them would mean they'd have to pay quadruple. Jane had provided them with a phone number for their mother, but no address, as not even Jane had that. It was for their mother's own protection—should anything happen to Jane or Dirk, her location would be kept safely anonymous, and if questioned, they could honestly say that they had no idea where she was. Men could be particularly ruthless and brutal in retrieving their wives. Even if their husbands were dead, sometimes that wasn't enough to stop their heirs from finishing the job. Wives and mothers were, after all, property. And nobody stole from powerful men and got away with it.

Saint Hildegard's was not connected to the large cathedral in the center of FFC. It was a satellite location meant to save wayward women, drug addicts, and other undesirables of society, chiefly by converting them into the service of the church. So Marie insisted that she and Emma spend as much time outside of the convent as possible, even if it meant forgoing the safety of the sanctuary. "Because the longer we're here, the longer we may have to stay here."

"You're sounding more and more paranoid by the day," Emma said.

"Haven't I been right so far?"

"That doesn't mean you're not paranoid."

"Please."

"Fine. But only if you provide the explanation you promised," Emma said as they sat on the edges of the cots in the small cell they shared.

Marie agreed. "But not here," she whispered. The walls had eyes and ears. Their cell had no door. They overheard two women arguing in the cell next to theirs. The schedule of all the canonical hours and associated masses they were expected to attend was pinned to the wall: Matins, Lauds, Prime, Terce, Sext, None, Vespers, and Compline. They'd be in mass roughly every three hours and have to wake up twice during the night to pray. Marie was tired just looking at the schedule.

A nun sat at the end of the corridor in a rocking chair, staring at them with unblinking eyes through thick-rimmed glasses. Her wrinkled and weathered skin faded into the grooved wood of the chair as if they were one and the same. Perhaps they were; perhaps she had been rooted to this chair for decades or centuries, watching wayward women for all eternity. Her gaze had been so severe when they'd come in that Marie had unconsciously made the sign of the cross.

They met the old nun again as they walked out. They made their way toward the end of the corridor, where the nun glared at them and croaked in Latin, "Curfew is at sundown."

"And what if we miss it?" Emma asked before Marie could clap a hand over her sister's mouth.

"Doors are locked," the nun said. "And fifty rosaries for each of you once you come in the next morning." She narrowed her eyes. "To start."

Marie gulped and nodded. "Yes, sister, we'll be back before sundown."

"I never sleep," said the old nun. "So I'll know."

"We believe it," said Emma, and Marie tugged her out the door before she could mouth off any further. Who knew how many rosaries that would cost them. They had to sign out at the door downstairs, and the nun at the exit, who was much younger but just as scary, repeated the same admonishment.

"Fifty rosaries if you are locked out, unless you commit a sinful act whilst out. Then even more. Perhaps additional work as penance."

Marie nodded demurely, while Emma breezed out the door.

"God be with you," said the nun. "He is always watching. And so are we."

Marie had a feeling that the nuns watched everything far more closely than God did. But that was the life she was used to—being watched at all times, guilty until proven innocent with regard to her behavior and virtue. She made the sign of the cross. "Yes, sister," she said, and vanished out the door, hoping it would be unlocked when they returned.

"Come on," said Emma once Marie had finally exited. "My God, that place is as bad as Ellthrop."

"Using the Lord's name in vain!" They heard a voice cry from within the convent. "Twenty rosaries upon your return!"

Emma took Marie by the elbow and swiftly led her away before they could commit more crimes against God.

"Let's go eat," said Emma. "And then we can talk."

Their options for food were limited. One option was to eat in silence with the nuns, which was simply out of the question. They could go to one of the few restaurants within the walls of their corner of the city, but a look inside of one of these showed that they were likely to be drugged, robbed, or both. The last option was to buy something from a cart and eat it wherever they could find a relatively clean patch of the ground to sit. They found a not-dirty patch of battered pavement in the shadow of the main cathedral on the other side of the Garden Wall. The windows of the bell tower stared down at them like eyes, not protective but rather parochial. They had better behave, even here.

Sitting down with two paper bowls of vaguely vegetable soup, Emma looked Marie square in the eye.

"You'll tell me now."

It wasn't a question but an order. Marie understood that she was out of time. It was only right that Emma understood why John Hart was chasing them.

"I'll tell you now."

She opened her mouth to speak further, and then a shadow crossed over them. A long-missed silhouette.

A long-forgotten voice said, "You're not as clever as you think you are."

Impossible.

They looked up.

The inside of Marie's mouth turned to sawdust.

"Alice?"

Chapter Twenty

Marie looked up at her eldest sister. Alice seemed fully at home in this authoritarian and segregated city that was hostile to English refugees like her two younger sisters. Her face was more lined and severe than it had been the last time either of them had seen her, but not from laughing. Her brow had what appeared to be a permanent crease from frowning in disapproval, which had likely been carved in there over decades of bitterness and her overly developed sense of justice. Her body, never slim, was more filled out now, but she was solid rather than round, like a soldier or a bodyguard. Above her crossed arms rested a large pearl-encrusted gold cross. Sunlight glinted off it, briefly blinding Marie.

They froze, then Emma jumped to her feet, spilling her soup on the ground. It splashed on Marie, who remained motionless with shock, not even wiping it off her face.

"What in God's name are you doing here?" Emma spat.

"Don't take the Lord's name in vain," Alice scolded.

Twenty more rosaries, Marie thought to herself.

"We're a long way past that here," Emma replied.

"Past the commandments of the Lord God himself?"

"I've been through hell over the last decade. God hasn't."

Marie had no clue how many rosaries that statement might cost her.

Alice pursed her lips, as if debating whether to say anything further, when Marie dared to speak.

"How did you find us, Alice?" Marie asked. She was still seated on the ground, afraid to get up. Still didn't dare wipe her face.

Alice gave her youngest and least-loved sister a long stare. "You didn't exactly cover your tracks," she said. "You were spotted by your mother-in-law's employee on the train to this very city. We knew what part of the city it would spit you into. It wasn't difficult to find you."

"But why *you*?" Emma asked, her voice piercing like a dagger. She emphasized the last word so that it was more like an accusation than a question. If words could have shoved Alice out of the city and back to England, these would have done so. "What do you have to do with any of this? You abandoned our family long ago."

"No, that would be you, my dear," Alice said. She made a point of looking Emma up and down, and by the time she was done, she looked like she wanted to wash her hands. "You left, but not without shaming our family on your way out the door. Where is your little bastard, anyway? Did you abandon it too?"

Emma's face turned so red that Marie could feel the heat of her anger radiating off her. Emma took a step forward, as if to attack Alice. She was stopped only by a sharp jerk on her elbow by Marie, who had scrambled to her feet in an instant to stop them from fighting. It was a move she had perfected over many similar altercations, or almost-altercations, in their childhood. Alice had always hidden her jealousy of her sisters under a veneer of contempt, and that had not changed with time.

"Stop it, both of you!" Marie hissed. She gave them each her sternest look, but being the youngest sister, it had limited impact. No matter how old they grew or estranged they became, she was still the baby of the family, and would never move up in rank.

"I notice you never showed any concern for the niece or nephew you thought you might have," Emma pointed out. "Or either of your sisters. Were we all too beneath you?"

"You were a whore that our father properly cast out from the family, so you weren't my sister anymore. And you still aren't."

"The Earl discarded you just as much as he discarded me," Emma shot back. "He just accepted the first offer, something that he always bragged that he was never stupid enough to do when it came to his money. No, he simply got rid of you at the first opportunity. I freed myself." With a poisonous smile, she added, "I hardly think that makes *me* the whore."

Alice's face turned the same shade of crimson as Emma's. Her mouth set in the same grim line as Emma's. And a tendril of hair fell out of place in the exact same place as Emma's. Marie knew better than to dwell on the similarities. The sisters' only real bonding experience had been their shared misery, and they had handled it in such different ways. Alice had embraced mundanity. Emma had untethered herself altogether.

Marie thought one of them might hit the other. But they had been too well brought up for that. None of them were accustomed to intense feelings, especially anger, and no one seemed to know what to do with it. Certainly neither Emma nor Alice was going to apologize. No one was ceding ground in this war.

People in FFC simply walked around, between, or through them. Three women about to fight in the street would draw all sorts of attention in London. Here? Not even worth slowing their pace.

"Well," Alice said, deciding to speak first after eighty-three seconds. "Whatever you say, the shame you two have brought on our father's family has gone on long enough."

"What do you care?" Emma asked. "Like you said, I'm out of the family and have been for a long time."

"And I'm dead!" Marie cried.

"You are most obviously not."

"You know what I mean. Why pursue us? None of it matters to you." *We never mattered to you,* she thought.

"Marie, you stole something that does not belong to you," Alice said. "And you need to give it back. That's why I'm here. I've spoken with your husband. He hadn't known, but his mother finally told him.

He thought it might be best if you agreed to return with me, rather than John Hart finding you first."

A stone dropped in Marie's stomach. "James knows?"

Alice nodded. "He knows."

"He knows . . ." Marie swallowed. "He knows *everything*?"

Alice nodded again.

In an instant, Alice became Marie's only hope.

"Then you have to let me disappear. Forget you ever saw me."

"You know I can't do that."

"Like hell you can't," Emma said. "It doesn't benefit you at all."

"You think the disappearance of my only two sisters benefits me?"

"You certainly have acted like it," Emma shot back.

"Stop!" Marie threw up a hand before they could start arguing again. They might not be drawing attention, but it still had to stop. "Our reappearance does not benefit you any more than our disappearance, so you can just let us go. None of us were due to inherit, and you already have your husband and your son."

"Sons."

"Good for you," Emma sneered. Marie raised her hand higher, wished she hadn't lost the parasol she'd stolen from Green's Lane. She could probably take down Alice with it.

"I had to make up for both of your shortcomings," Alice sniped. "As I always have."

"Listen," Marie said, again trying to make the peace between them. "I have something for you here that might make you reconsider. You remember Mother's pearls?"

Alice did not react. This was all the confirmation that Marie needed.

"I have them," Marie said. "If I were to give them to you, something that I know you always wanted . . ." She hesitated. "If I gave those to you, perhaps you could forget you ever saw us?"

Alice did not respond for a long time, clearly warring with herself. Finally, she said, "You think I could be so easily bribed to do the wrong thing? You think marriage vows are worth less than a handful of hard-ened clam spit?"

"Please," Marie said. She reached into her coat and, after a few seconds of fumbling, pulled out the pearls. She never broke eye contact with Alice. For a moment, she thought Alice might agree.

But then Emma spoke.

"Depends on what you think the wrong thing is," Emma said. "Helping your sister escape to a better life, or being the one to return her back to certain death."

Alice barked a laugh that was harsh and sharp, just like her. She looked away from Marie to Emma. Contempt was easier than sympa-thy. "Certain death? What sorts of ghost stories has she been telling you?"

"Just because your husband is indifferent to you—" Emma began.

"Indifferent? I've had three sons!"

"Just because your husband is indifferent to you doesn't mean that others are so lucky," Emma continued. "Indifference is the best you can hope for from a man. If he pays attention to you, he hurts you."

Marie indicated her agreement by looking down at her feet. She studied the cracks in the pavement below. Mediating this was a lost cause. But at least Alice hadn't left, and she hadn't called anyone.

"If you please your husband, you needn't worry about a thing," Alice said. "And if you can't even find one, that reflects on you."

"Some of us neither need nor want one. We can be more than vessels for their offspring or the punching bags on which they take out their frustrations."

"Of course we can," said Alice. "But you can do it without becom-ing pariahs. There are good husbands out there—good men. You can be more than a vessel for their children. You can be their counsel in business affairs, the bosom on which they rest their head when they have had a difficult day. You can be the first one they speak to in the morning and the last one they talk to before they fall asleep. You can be the one they text message during the day when they see something interesting, or want your opinion on something, or if they take a picture of something they think will make you laugh. You can be the one they discuss the news of the day with. You can be the one they share their deepest worries and greatest dreams with." She stopped, making what appeared to be the first small almost-smile either sister had seen cross her face in a long time, perhaps ever. "Yes, you are correct. Marriage can be all that and so much more."

For a long time, none of them spoke. Neither Emma nor Marie had ever known marriage to be something positive, something enjoyable. It had always been a financial consideration at best and a prison at worst. Their role was as a pawn upgraded to a queen, but still in service of protecting the king, and to be sacrificed without a thought if needed. Even in the novels Marie had read, marriage was no love affair. At best, a husband was kind in his dominion over his wife, but she had never read a book in which spouses were portrayed as confidants or equals.

"That sounds like a lie," Emma said after a moment.

"I don't lie," Alice retorted. "Not like the two of you."

"Please," Marie said. "I'm so happy that you've found happiness in your marriage. It's wonderful news."

"I know," Alice said. "No one thought I deserved anything but a swift marriage and to be swept out of the way. But it was such a blessing. And now here we are."

"Here we are," Marie said. "You've done so well. I don't understand why you want to trouble yourself with bringing me back. I'm trying to obtain the same happiness you have. Is that so wrong?"

"Had you the ability to make the decision yourself, no doubt. But you took something from your husband. And that's unforgivable."

Emma held up her hands. "I need to hear what this is. You've both mentioned her taking something. It's obviously not jewels. So what is it?"

Marie rushed to say that she could explain everything, but Alice interrupted her.

"She's carrying her husband's child."

Chapter Twenty-One

Marie tried to hide her panic behind a scowl.

"You're *what?*" Emma demanded of her sister.

"We're not talking about this here." She grabbed her sister's elbow and glared at Alice as she began marching Emma away. "Please think about what I said, Alice." She thrust out the pearls again, but Alice's face was as immovable and soulless as a porcelain doll's. She wasn't taking them. "We're leaving now."

Alice kept pace with them. "We aren't finished yet."

"Yes, we are," Marie said through gritted teeth, not breaking her stride. Emma stumbled to keep up, which was unusual. Emma was typically the one striding purposely. But Marie needed to escape.

"Is Alice telling the truth?" Emma hissed.

"We need to go," Marie hissed back.

"I said, we weren't finished yet," said Alice. They weaved through groups of people who did not part for them, and Alice kept pace the entire time.

"I won't go with you," Marie said. She gripped Emma's arm so tight that it was sure to leave a bruise. "Not for anything. I'll die first."

"You'd do that to your own child?"

"This conversation is over," Marie said. She made to leave again, but Alice gripped her hard on the shoulder.

"You know that I can't let you leave, now that I've found you," Alice said. "And it wasn't that difficult to for me to do."

"So, what, you get some sort of bounty for finding and returning me? Is that all I'm worth to you now, a few pounds of Sterling?"

"I'm insulted that you think I could be motivated by money or jewels." Alice did seem genuinely offended, and Marie could tell she was becoming angry. "I told you, there is a higher calling at issue here."

"What, God?"

"Yes."

Marie scoffed. "God has no place in this situation." The sun shifted, and the shadow of the cathedral fell over all three of them.

"Given how freely you trample the holy sacrament of marriage, and faked the venal sin of suicide, you have not the slightest idea of God's position in any situation. And it is time you stopped insulting His will."

Emma rolled her eyes. "Oh, will you stop, and just name your price."

"Neither of you are listening to me," Alice said. "I am here as your sister. I am the *only* person who might find you who will not hurt you. I am the only one who will ensure that you will be both safe and cared for. The *only* one. Do you understand me? You've been found out. You can come back to England freely with me, or you can be dragged back in chains. You can give birth in your home, or in prison. But either way: you will have that child in England, and you will go back, willingly or otherwise. You're carrying a child now; it's not about you anymore. You're not allowed to think about yourself; you have to put the child first. It's the law. You have no choice."

No choice. All her life, Marie had been told she had no choice. Her sisters had had no choice. Her mother had had no choice. No choice in vocation, no choice in their futures, no choice in their education or where they lived.

Until their mother had made a choice. And Emma had made a choice. And then Marie had made a choice. Drastic, irreversible, life-altering choices that burned everything in their lives to ashes. And it had been glorious.

She was tired of saying yes when all she wanted to do was say no.

So she said it.

"No!" Marie started walking, but Alice tightened her grip and jerked her back so hard that she nearly fell on her back.

"Don't make me hurt you," Alice said. "Believe me when I say that I will if I have to, but that is not my preference. I am doing all of this for your own good. And the baby's. And in the end, you'll agree with me."

"I am not going back."

"You made a vow! A sacred vow, blessed by God, and you will honor it."

Marie jerked her gaze away from her sister to briefly search the towering heights of the cathedral, challenging God himself to save her. If He would not, she hoped He might have the decency to look her in the eye.

"My husband made the same vow to me, and he was ready to discard me, just like our father discarded our mother."

Alice slapped Marie hard across the face.

"You will never speak of our father like that again," she said. "And how dare you suggest that your rights and obligations in a marriage are equal to those of your husband? You vowed, to him and to God, that you would honor and obey *him*. He did not vow to honor and obey *you*. You broke that sacred law. And as a result, I am quite the least of your worries."

Marie's free hand went up to the stinging mark on her face.

"You had no right to leave," Alice said. "And you have no choice but to return. They asked me to bring you back because it would be the most pleasant way to do so."

Marie looked back at the cathedral, feeling God's judgment of her decisions. She felt her insides turn red with the heat of anger. She felt acid boil in her stomach and creep up the back of her throat, stinging and burning her every inch of the way up. The unfairness of it all. They'd come so far. And now, after all of this, their escape was likely to meet its end.

How dare He do this to her? How dare He let her get this far only to send her back?

The cathedral windows were dark, cold, unfeeling.

If God would not give her answers, she would get them from her sister.

"How did you know where to find me?" Marie asked. If God had led her here, let Him admit it. Let her sister be the mouthpiece for Him, just as she was for all authority. "And don't just say that it was because John Hart saw me on the train. This is a big city, crawling with people. This dirty ring they've confined us to is like an ant colony. I should have been able to disappear. I didn't. Why didn't I?"

"It doesn't matter how I found you; it just matters that I did. And if I found you, John Hart will find you just as easily. At that point, questions become meaningless, because all the answers are the same." Alice gave that faint almost-smile she'd flashed earlier. "You'd be so much happier not questioning things, Marie," she said. "When you simply accept that, you'll find that life is like floating down a stream, comforting and relaxing. And with your head above water." On that last word, she dug her sharp fingernails into Marie's shoulder, drawing blood.

Marie flinched.

Then she heard commotion.

One moment, Alice was there, the glare from her ice blue eyes cutting into her own.

And then the next, she was knocked into the brick wall they had been leaning against, then kicked to the ground. She lay still, unconscious.

People walking by barely glanced at them. One person just stepped over Alice without breaking stride.

Marie looked to Emma, who was panting from the exertion of having attacked their eldest sister. Marie was impressed with her sister's strength; Alice was no small woman, and Emma had no discernible muscles. Emma rummaged through Alice's coat until she found her sister's phone. She stood. Blew a stray hair out of her face.

"I was always so bloody sick of her speeches," Emma said. She took Marie by the hand. "Let's get out of here."

◆　◆　◆

"That was amazing!" Marie cried as they ran through the maze of alleys of their corner of FFC.

"You've seen me do it before." Emma shrugged. She tugged on Marie's hand and led her through the streets.

"Still impressive."

"Not really."

"Take the bloody compliment!"

They said nothing more as they hurried through the streets. Marie traced her hands along the wall that separated them from the rest of the city, as if trying to find some crack through which they could escape.

She skittered to a stop before the doorway of the cathedral, the shadow of which they'd been in earlier. The seat of the Bishop of FFC had a lone door open to the people in the refugee corner of the city. It was small and hard to notice, but it was there.

Perhaps God was offering her a way out. Good. He owed her one.

"Sanctuary," Marie whispered. "Here, they'll grant it. And they have to provide it."

"Are you sure?"

Marie nodded. "The cathedral is the one place in the whole city where anyone can go. And they honor sanctuary. I saw it in a book." She tried the door, but it was locked. Fitting that a door would be placed there but limit who could enter. She should have expected it.

Marie pounded on the door, starting slow then faster and faster until it was a constant rat-a-tat-tat on the old wood. "Sanctuary!" Her voice grew louder as she went on, repeatedly shouting and pounding on the door. It was worn smooth by centuries of desperate people seeking entry. "Sanctuary!" Marie shouted. She heard scattered laughter behind her, and wondered if they were laughing at them. At the very least, they were not offering to help.

Finally, she felt the door give a bit as it was unlocked on the other side. An old nun covered head to toe in black opened the door and gave them a look—just as piercing but slightly less menacing than the ones from the Sisters at the convent where they were staying. This nun's face was lined with nearly a century of prayer, sorrow, and judgment. She stepped back slightly and left a small gap in the doorway.

Without waiting for an answer, they charged in. The ancient door slammed shut behind them, and the latch clicked into place. The cathedral might recognize sanctuary, but you first had to get through the locked door. Marie couldn't help but notice that the nun hadn't acted very quickly to close it until they were safely inside. Leave it to a woman to shoulder all the important work, God's and everyone else's.

They stood looking down the nave toward the altar, which felt a million miles away. The silent nun, shuffling at a faster gait than might be expected for a woman of her advanced age, indicated for the sisters to follow her. She led them from the stone foyer away from the nave and around a corner. They followed her down an ancient corridor lit only by low candlelight. They made their way down a winding spiral staircase. The stairs were old, the edges smoothed from a millennium of people walking up and down, and Marie began to feel trapped. Would they never end? Eventually, they alighted at what Marie assumed was the crypt, which felt hundreds of feet below the church. Marie wondered where they were being taken. To where bodies were buried? Some ancient relic? Instead, the nun unlocked a door to reveal a small chapel blanketed in darkness. She gestured for them to enter, and they did. The old nun shuffled around, lighting candles here and there.

The nun shut and locked the door behind them. The sound of the rusty, iron latch slipping into place echoed throughout the small room. Slowly, the room begin to reveal itself in the dim candlelight, as if waking up after a long hibernation, and they realized that it was less a room than a cave.

The air was dusty and old, as if the space had been kept empty for a long time. The walls were thick with secrets whispered over the course of a millennium. They were so far below the cathedral and buried so deeply into the crypt that the chapel was carved into the limestone of the earth itself. Stalactites and stalagmites were the pillars and arches, forming a bridge from this world into the next. It was the sort of room in which you felt not only the age of the cathedral, but the age of the earth itself. If you didn't believe in God before you walked in, you certainly did after. Like incense, the Holy Spirit wafted around them. It felt like a hug, like comfort. Marie's anger at God began to dissipate. She should never have doubted as she had. As she forgave Him, she silently asked Him to forgive her.

Secrets were safe here, but lies were not.

"Do you think we've been imprisoned?" Marie asked.

"Maybe," Emma said. "But it's more secure than it was outside."

"I don't suppose we'll be found here by accident."

"I'm sure we'll be found, and not likely by accident. But we'll have to worry about that later," Emma commanded. Their eyes were beginning to adjust to the dimly lit room, and they could see more with each passing moment. "Come, let's sit."

They found their way to the front row of pews facing the altar, genuflected, then sat down. A single flame burned in a red glass candle holder before them, making their faces appear more flushed than they really were. A crucifix hung from some unknown place in the ceiling, making it seem like it was floating in the air. Maybe it was. The chapel had an otherworldliness about it that made the impossible seem not only possible, but likely.

Behind the altar were two paintings that, while faded with age, time, and dampness, appeared to deliberately contrast each other. On the left was the appearance of the Angel Gabriel to the Blessed Virgin, telling her that she was to give birth to the Messiah. On the right was the Blessed Virgin crowned with the sun, moon, and stars, fighting the war for heaven as depicted in the Book of Revelation. Fighting for her son.

The same woman, the same mother, in two roles. One as devout. One as warrior. And in both situations, brimming with courage.

"No more stalling," Emma said. "Is what Alice said true?"

Marie took a deep breath, shut her eyes, and nodded.

Chapter Twenty-Two

"I never lied to you," Marie said. "Not once. I was a barren wife whose dowry had kept the estate afloat for a few years, nothing more. By then, the money I brought in had run out. I had become a liability in every way. And there were so, so many willing women looking to do what I could not. They were certainly auditioning for the role. Just like the parade of women with our father."

Emma sat, listening, not judging, which made Marie relax. She was so used to being talked over that speaking uninterrupted was still a novelty. Marie had won some trust by now, despite her very conspicuous omission.

"I had resigned myself to my future. I had served my purpose, and was soon to be discarded like any other single-use object. As Alice said, you are happiest when you do not ask questions, and I had stopped asking any. I convinced myself that I was happy to do as my husband commanded, even if that command was to die. I knew of our mother, and I was not going to pursue it. I had lost her, just as I had lost you. I was nearly at the point of doing myself in."

Emma put her hand on Marie's. Only now did Marie realize she was trembling. Emma squeezed her hand. Marie squeezed back.

"And then I did not bleed when I should have. Not for a day. A week. Two weeks.

"I bribed a servant to procure me a test. It was a servant I thought I could trust, though that was foolish of me. I had already dismissed the only one I could trust. I took the test. I was pregnant. I was thrilled—this was my ticket to a new relevance, a justification of my position. And I was also terrified—what sort of life was I condemning this child to? What cycle would I be taking part in perpetuating? Our mother had either died or faked her death to escape this life. Would my life really be any better now that I was a mother myself? Or was it simply prolonging a situation that had no hope of improving, only now with someone else to share in the misery?"

There was safety here in darkness, in low light, with no one to listen but God and her sister, and the words came pouring out like warm oil. It was like Confession, but with the safety of your secrets staying within the walls. Priests were known to report back to husbands and fathers the sins of the women in their lives.

"My husband owns this child, just as he owns me. And yet I could not let them do it. I could not let this system claim another life. I knew it was wrong; it was wrong against God, it was wrong against James, and against the child—I made my own choice, for once. I could well be carrying the next Duke of Suffolk and have deprived him of his birthright. And I knew I was as good as dead for even thinking it. It was a great sin. But I don't regret it. I would do it again in a heartbeat, even if I knew they would follow me this far, and even if I knew I was putting not only myself at risk, but you and Jane as well." She met her sister's eyes, and a candle flickered. "I won't apologize for it."

"I couldn't ask you to," Emma said.

"Thank you," said Marie, feeling absolved.

"How long did you wait?" Emma asked. "Before you left?"

"That same night," she whispered.

"But you had everything ready to go, everything planned."

Marie nodded. "You're right," she said. "I was hoping to go after Mother. To find you. I hid away the money. I read the books. I made the plans. But Emma, I was too afraid to actually do it. It all seemed too impossible. That wasn't me—I didn't take risks. Reading books without my husband's permission was risk enough. I was going to go along, ride the river, despite my dangerous thoughts. So I put them away. I was going to trash the whole plan. I resigned myself. Only foolish heroines in books do what I do, not sensible women like us. Not in the real world, where freedom is so rare as to be its own source of magic."

"Well," Emma said. "As you know, it's a crime."

"I know."

"A pregnant woman who leaves the country without her husband's permission is guilty of kidnapping his child."

"I know."

"And Alice, your husband, and his mother know."

Marie nodded. And if she were to terminate the pregnancy, it would be murder. Church Law allowed for easy extradition between countries, and there was a well-established bounty system to return such wayward women. Those passports that showed they were widows were literal lifesavers now. If they were believed. If no one dug any deeper into them or bothered to investigate. If they weren't forced to go through biometric scanning.

"If they find you," Emma said, "you will give birth in that prison cell Alice was talking about." She swallowed. "And then they will hang you right after."

Marie shook her head. "I won't go back."

"You may not have a choice. Alice is just outside these walls."

"I understand that," Marie said. "But we've made it this far. We've escaped from John Hart. We've escaped from Alice."

"Lord knows who they will send next."

Marie looked at her sister. In the dim candlelight, she looked older. The weight of the years living on her own combined with the stress of the last few days was clearly weighing on her. Emma acted like she could run through fire without getting burned, but she was just as breakable as any other human. She wasn't untouchable; neither of them were. No one was. They were English refugees; their lives were cheap. Marie had planned everything like it was one of the adventures in her books, but this was real life. Real life had consequences.

Emma had given up everything and followed her blindly. And for what?

"I was telling you the truth," Marie said. "You can walk away now."

"I've come too far," Emma said. "And so in for a penny, in for a pound, as they say."

"Sunk cost fallacy," Marie said, parroting a term from a book she had read. She hadn't understood much in it, but had remembered that term. "You could leave now. And should. After what I've done. After what I've taken from you."

"You silly girl," Emma said. She squeezed her sister's hand again. "I'm not leaving you to these people. And you've taken nothing from me. I'm here because I love you. You being back in my life . . . you've given me so much."

Marie's throat constricted so tightly with emotion that she thought she might choke on it. How she'd longed to hear this from her sister her whole life. So many walls were falling down. They'd been scraped bloody, and now they were raw and exposed to each other.

"We're in it now, together. So let's carry on. It's what we English women do best. We carry on. And we survive. And we do it best when we do it together."

"Together," Marie agreed.

Marie's thoughts drifted back to the darkest days of her childhood. After Alice had married and Emma had gone, Marie had had nothing to do and no one to talk to. No late-night chats with Emma in her room. No more walks around the grounds or posing along with the portraits in the picture gallery. No giggling during parties thrown by their father and stepmother. No one to commiserate with her over how impossible it was to be around their brother.

Just after Emma had been cast out of the family, her bedroom had been emptied. By the next morning, it had been as if Emma had never been there. Not a scrap of paper, not one hair elastic, not even her scratchy drawings on the walls—the walls had been repainted a deep red, Emma's least favorite color. The first time Marie had walked in there and found that every trace of her sister had been removed, she'd collapsed on the ground of the empty room and sobbed. All she'd had left of Emma then were her memories, and who knew how long any of those would last?

Earl Kenfield and his wife had begun a swift campaign to pretend that Emma had never existed outside of the household as well as inside. She had never been out in society, nor presented to the King and Queen as a debutante, so there was no damage control to be done. If asked, they told people that Emma had drowned while swimming. It was kinder that way, to everyone. First Marie's mother dead, and now her sister; Marie would be sure to garner sympathy from a few suitors, at least. That may open some doors that would otherwise have been closed.

Marie had seen what had become of her sisters. Emma, gone. Alice, married off to the first man who showed interest. Beneath her rank and station, shorter than her, not attractive. But Alice had insisted. Desperation, according to Emma. And Emma . . . Marie had shuddered at the thought of what must have become of her. She'd desperately wanted to contact Emma, but had no way of doing so. She had not been allowed a phone, and Emma had left no other means of reaching her. And Marie certainly couldn't ask their father for help.

So Marie had done everything her father and stepmother had told her. If they'd told her to wear blue because it accentuated her eyes, then she'd worn blue. If she were told to stand still and smile at an event, nothing could crack that grin on her face. If she were told to attend a dinner, she went. If she were told to actually eat at a dinner, she nibbled. If she were given a glass, she held it, but never sipped, for a girl could never be seen imbibing alcohol. If she was introduced to someone, she gave a slight bow and mastered the art of pretending to be fascinated by everything he said, which was always about himself, his son, or both.

As she'd grown older and her body developed, Marie had spent hours in her room, getting her hair styled or her already small waist further tightened by a girdle or corset or shapewear. Her body had been manipulated into perfection by surgeries or exercise, starvation, or binging. Whatever she'd been told to do, she'd done it. Her father had always seemed so pleased to parade her about, and the glow of his approval had been enough to warm her once she was back home and dismissed from his sight, not to be seen again by him until the next time. She had always counted the seconds whenever they were together, desperate to hold on to each one.

"Always leave them wanting," Marie's stepmother had told her. "Make them crave it. But never let them sample it. And never go with a man where you cannot be seen." So Marie hadn't. She'd planted her feet in the polished marble floors.

Then she'd turned eighteen, and her life had been over.

After she'd been presented to Her Majesty the Queen and given the seal of approval, the offers had poured in. Men had met with her father, sent their sons to her home, filled up her dance card at social events before she'd even crossed the threshold. Once one man would make an offer, her father would go to the others and explain the current state of the bidding: the second son of one Earl could offer a large estate, so another Earl would offer up his heir while also promising a lavish townhome in Belgravia and a yacht docked at Bournemouth. Then her father could parlay that into the sons of the Dukes—he'd categorically confirm his daughter's virginity and assure them that she would be as soft to the touch as the English rose that she was. Earl Kenfield could promise shooting parties with His Majesty the King—they were old chums, as everyone certainly knew—and that his daughter would produce the heirs they needed.

All the while, Marie had sat there smiling. Still. Not speaking. She'd been the object of bidding, expected not to say a word. If she'd spoken, that would have ruined everything. It was the mystery, her stepmother had told her, that she had to keep alive. Make them wonder what was under those gowns; never give a hint. Smile shyly from behind a fan, make them work to figure out what amused her.

"But shouldn't I get to know any of them?" Marie had dared to ask her stepmother once she'd learned that her father was in final negotiations to marry her to the first son of a Duke.

"Love is for the poor," her stepmother had scoffed. "This is what you have worked your entire life to do."

"But what if we can't stand each other?"

"You'll have enough space at Grayside to never see each other again. Few women are lucky enough to have that kind of peace, which only money can buy."

Chapter Twenty-Three

Their pact sealed, Emma and Marie turned their attention to the more immediate problem: How had Alice been able to find their exact location in the middle of FFC, just after their arrival?

Alice had claimed they had been seen boarding the train. While it was possible that John Hart, having lost them, had called reinforcements, it didn't make sense to Marie. The Dowager Duchess would never have sent John Hart as a first attempt with Alice as the second. John Hart was her first and only, and when he came, he meant business. There would be no second after him. He was it.

That meant that Alice had been conscripted into this by someone else, and possibly even earlier than John Hart. Perhaps she'd been following them the entire time. There was no chance that Alice was more clever than John Hart, but there was an excellent chance that Alice had simply gone about her task more quietly. Perhaps both had been dispatched, and while John Hart had found them first, Alice, like the story of the tortoise and the hare, had simply been slow and steady.

But then how had they both known where to go? And how had Alice found them so quickly, the same day they arrived, and walked right up to them?

Emma had had the presence of mind not only to take Alice's phone but also to power it off immediately. It almost certainly had a tracking device on it, with Alice being a married woman and all; but now they had to chance looking at it. Alice's phone was not locked, of course. A wife with a locked phone was liable to stray, or so they said, so most phones couldn't be locked.

They powered it on. There was hardly any reception, all the way down here. But they were able to find the apps that Alice had most recently used, listed in the order she'd accessed them. Right there on the top was one called WifeSpot. A tracking app for women. Up popped a map of FFC, with the segmented areas of the city neatly delineated by thick black lines. Landmarks appeared with symbols on them. There were two blinking red dots on it.

"That dot has to be Alice's phone," Marie said, pointing at one that was still in the center of the cathedral. "Us."

"But if that's Alice's phone," Emma said slowly, "then who is the other one that's moving around?" She pointed to the second dot, which showed frantic and erratic movement outside the cathedral—where they had left Alice.

Marie opened and closed her mouth a few times, but words would not form.

With a sound of disgust, Emma shut the phone off. Not that it would change anything. Whoever else was following them would likely have the same app and information, and for all they knew others had followed them to the city, surrounding the cathedral.

"Did you bring anything with you that could be used to track you?" Emma asked.

Marie shook her head furiously. "No. I left everything behind when I left Grayside. And it can't be tracking a phone; it's tracking Alice. And this is her phone."

"There must be something," Emma said. "Maybe they put something on you, somehow, after you left? In the clothes you wore?"

"How would they have put it on me?"

"Maybe in the jewels?"

"Your friend Mr. Harrison would have spotted something," Marie pointed out. Emma shrugged in agreement. "Besides, if I'd had a tracker on me the entire time, wouldn't they have found me immediately?"

"Or at least used it to find your body."

They sat for a long time, because the same realization had dawned upon both of them, and it was too terrible to utter aloud.

She had to have some sort of a tracking device on her, whatever or wherever it was, and had the entire time. Alice's phone had proven it. As she'd suspected, they hadn't looked for her body after she disappeared. She was dead and gone, and that was all they needed to know. It was convenient, just as she had anticipated. She was already ignored and largely forgotten outside of Grayside, so little explanation was needed for others. As a suicide victim, she never could have been interred in a Catholic cemetery, so there would have been no burial or funeral. And even if she could have been, they still hadn't searched for her. They hadn't cared. They hadn't bothered.

She'd expected it, counted on it, even. But that didn't change how much it hurt to have it confirmed.

"Then why didn't they stop us before we left England?" Emma said.

Had they waited that long? They must have. More than a week before they tried to find her. That hurt even more. And if what Alice said was true, that they knew she was pregnant, then they were probably watching her tracker right now, scrambling for a way in.

"So what now?" Marie asked, her voice flat, as she pushed down the heartache.

"We have to get out of here somehow," Emma said, stating the obvious. "But at the same time, we can't leave. Sanctuary will protect us, right?"

Marie hesitated. "I mean, it should. But if a man shows up demanding the return of his wife? I suspect the Church would be all too happy to hand us over. To comply with God's law."

Emma clicked her tongue, partially in agreement, partially in disgust that Marie was most likely right. This chapel was sanctuary, but could also function as a prison. After all, the old nun had locked them in and bolted the door.

"So we either walk out that door, where we will be arrested and returned to England to death or something worse, or we stay in this chapel forever," Emma summarized.

"Those do appear to be our options."

Marie clawed at her clothes. They felt filthy. "I can't even change my clothes." Had something been dropped or sewn into her? She patted herself down, felt each layer of fabric in the low light. She removed her outer layers and tossed them to Emma, who searched them while Marie retreated to a corner to search her undergarments.

Nothing. Marie returned to her sister and retrieved her clothes from Emma. She dressed in silence, now wondering what to do.

There was definitely nothing on her. But she was still being tracked. *How?*

They stared at the altar at the old, faded painting of the Blessed Virgin in front of them. Her eyes were not faded; they were a deep and piercing blue that likely did not represent what she had actually looked like in life. Her golden hair fell around her shoulders, peeking out from under the veil that covered her head. She was pregnant, and the Angel Gabriel was standing before her. Faded gold writing shaped in an arch around the painting read, "Benedicta tu in mulierbus, et benedictus fructose ventures tui." *Blessed art thou among women, and blessed be the fruit of thy womb.* Even the chapel mocked them. The wall seemed to disappear into darkness, and the jagged walls of the cave contained a number of hidden crevices where the candlelight could not reach.

The longer they sat in the room, the less quiet it seemed. The acoustics were tremendous, and every scrape of their shoes, clearing of a throat, or tap of a fingernail on the wooden pew echoed all around them. If they whispered, it sounded like a chorus. They could see how people went mad when they got lost inside of caves. They didn't dare walk around, for the footsteps would have sounded like an approaching army.

And yet, at the same time, that was precisely what they thought they heard.

The sisters flew to their feet at the unmistakable sounds of someone approaching. It wasn't the near-silent shuffle of a Sister. This was someone else, striding with purpose. This was it. They were found. Sanctuary was canceled. They'd come all this way only to fail. And since they were in a Church, they couldn't, and wouldn't, dare to fight back.

The steps grew louder, and the sisters' breath quickened. It echoed off the cave and chapel walls. They drew closer together, clasping hands, desperately looking for a place to hide. Would one of the crevices fit both of them together? One of them at all?

Marie shut her eyes and prayed. She prayed the Paternoster. The Ave Maria. She began making a dent in those twenty rosaries she'd been assigned. Her lips moved quickly over the words that had been repeated thousands of times over the course of her life. They never stumbled, not once. She needed God to listen to her today, here in this holy chapel that was either to be their salvation or their doom.

The steps grew louder—and then Marie realized that they were coming not from behind the heavily barred door but from a crevice in the back of the chapel that, in the low light, had been completely hidden. From that direction now came a middle-aged woman with brown hair cut short, like a man's, glasses, and what almost looked like a white laboratory coat.

"Sister Maria Josephus said you were here," said the woman. She spoke English with a German accent. So she was local, and somehow knew their language. She gestured for them to follow her back through the crevice from which she had come. "Come along. We haven't any time to lose."

◆ ◆ ◆

They didn't dare make a sound. It wasn't clear whether this woman could be trusted. But they knew what awaited them on the other side of the door. They knew what probably awaited them if they stayed. So they went with the devil they didn't know. They followed her through the hidden crevice.

The crevice was actually a triangular-shaped doorway. It was dark, but the woman led them through with the light from her phone. The path they walked was natural, not manmade, or at least was well disguised as a natural path, as if God Himself had carved an escape route. It was a good disguise—no one would have found it had they not been looking for it. It was also narrow—once they made their way through the doorway, the sisters had to contort themselves and shift their weight from side to side to avoid scraping the cave walls. The woman's phone lit the way only a few feet at a time and gave no indication of where they were going or how far it would be; nor did the woman herself offer any guidance. It was a true test of faith, in the midst of a cathedral. Marie could feel a downward grade as they walked—they were going deeper into the earth. The air got colder, damper; and the texture changed. Like the Earth was inhaling them deep into its lungs.

After a long time—several minutes—they arrived in a large space, with a ceiling as high as any cathedral. There were no electric lights inside, but they were illuminated by torches and what appeared to be large spheres filled with bioluminescent algae, which gave a soft, neon-blue glow that reflected on the multifaceted surface of the cave. The torches would have to be replenished, but the algae could illuminate the cave for an indefinite period.

And it was bustling with people.

The room was part makeshift hospital, part refugee clearing center, and was as chaotic as a train terminal. Nuns shuffled about, comforting children and talking to parents. Women, and a few men, in white coats tended to the ill and injured. Young people scampered and weaved throughout the crowd, faces pensive with purpose, carrying stacks of papers. Babies cried or napped in makeshift cots. One old man played a violin that echoed throughout the room. The lives and fears and hopes and dreams were a symphony of humanity, all buried here deep in the Earth, hiding from the constraints placed upon them in the world above.

The woman led them to an area in the hospital section of the room and gestured for them to take a seat next to a bed. She pulled out a backless stool on wheels that had a peeling cushion and produced a tablet from what seemed to be nowhere.

"Right," she said. "My name is Ingrid, and I work with the Underground Refugee Network. What I have ascertained so far is that you are English and are seeking sanctuary. Might you explain to me what your issue is?"

Emma and Marie looked at each other, then back at Ingrid.

"Perhaps I could give you some more background. The URN is a network of doctors, nuns, and other sympathetic individuals dedicated to helping people escape dire situations in their home countries. We specialize in helping those from the most impoverished nations that are dangerous for women, like England and France, along with the occasional person from Iberia, seek new and better lives elsewhere. As I'm sure you can appreciate, we cannot assist every refugee in their quest for a new life, which is why we perform this intake. Everything begins here, in what we call the Bridge Room. This is the first step where you leave your old life behind and journey toward your new one—a bridge from one place to another. Perhaps you can tell me what it is that you are running from, or running toward?"

Where could they even begin? And how could they be certain that they would be protected if they divulged anything?

"What happens to those you cannot help?" Emma asked.

"We work with people in the Church. Many women join a convent, while others sometimes find their way to another city where they might have better luck."

Many women join a convent. They didn't have the options here that they thought they might. Plus, they were still being tracked.

"Are you from a convent?" Emma asked.

"I took holy orders," Ingrid said.

"You're a Sister?"

"It's less important for you to know about me than it is for me to know about you."

"If you work with the Church, then you presumably follow Church Law?" Marie asked.

Ingrid hesitated. "We work with them when necessary, but I must stress to you that this is an underground network. We work with people in the Church, not the Church itself."

"Is there a difference?"

"Very much so. There are many of us who find the priorities of the Church misguided. Too much of a focus on sexual issues, not enough on caring for the poor, the needy, the infirm. Christ would be appalled. And so we help those who need such assistance that is not available through the official channels, but which we believe are fully supported by Scripture."

"So . . ." Marie took another leap of faith. "So if a woman were to, say, escape her husband by coming here . . ."

"We are often, though not always, able to help."

"And if she's carrying his child?"

"Our mission is the same."

Marie relaxed ever so slightly. This was good news. And there were so many people here, surely she could trust that what she was being told was true. It seemed so surprising that so many, perhaps hundreds, people could be here, undetected.

Undetected.

"I think I'm putting everyone at risk," Marie said. Ingrid looked at her placidly while Marie's stomach dropped through the stone floor. She tried to jump off the bed but Ingrid put her hand on her shoulder to stop her.

"Somehow, I don't know how, I am being tracked," Marie continued. "I can't figure out where it is or how to turn it off. And I know I'm being tracked by very bad people. But you should probably get me out of here right now."

Ingrid nodded. "Ah, you must have a WifeChip. Very common in England. Most women aren't even aware they have one. The good news is that we're so far underground that you are unlikely to transmit a signal they can reach. But no sense in playing with fate. We will help you by having it removed."

"What's WifeChip?"

"You had to get some shots when you were married, did you not?"

Marie nodded. "Vaccinations, plus blood tests."

"And the needles were very large?"

"Yes. And painful."

"Often, a small microchip is injected or otherwise inserted into you, so that you can be tracked by your husband."

Marie felt the Earth tip on its axis and take her with it. "What?"

Ingrid was all business, as if she hadn't ripped a hole in Marie's understanding of her life. "Yes. It's pretty standard for all married women in England." Ingrid looked at Marie, and her face softened with compassion. "Ah, they never told you."

Marie shook her head, no. How long had her husband tracked her on his phone? Had the Dowager Duchess done the same? Was that how John Hart had found her?

Why hadn't any of them simply picked up a phone to find her at the bottom of the sea, if they had believed she was there?

"And they never asked you, correct?"

Of course they had not asked her. Women did not have the capacity to make their own medical decisions—their fathers, husbands, or brothers had that power. If a woman had no immediate male family, they had to find the nearest male relative, who was often a stranger and might approve everything or deny everything. Many a woman had died as a result of the inaction of a male relative who either could not be reached or could not be bothered to respond.

She thought of Emma, alone in the world for thirteen years. How had she gotten medical care, disowned as she was by the family? She was too ashamed to ask.

"When can you take it out?"

Ingrid patted the hospital bed next to her. "Right this moment. I'll draw a curtain around us so that you can have some sort of privacy. It doesn't take long."

"What do you do with the chip once you remove it?"

Ingrid gave one last smile.

"We smash it with a hammer, of course."

Chapter Twenty-Four

"You've seen chips like this before?" Emma asked as Marie lay down on the bed.

"All the time," Ingrid said. "This has become somewhat of a safe house for women escaping abusive husbands in England."

"I see."

"Church Law is hostile to women and their autonomy. The Holy Roman Empire is no different; the laws of the Church apply here the same as they do everywhere else in Europe. But FFC? Very progressive when it comes to women's rights. It's an oasis in the desert. You can own property here, and make your own medical decisions, and even earn half as much money as a man! Did you come here from Brugge?"

Marie sat up sharply. "How did you know?"

"Well, you certainly didn't come via France, did you?"

Marie shook her head. Ingrid began prepping her tools.

"This is an underground network for women escaping England; if you're caught fleeing a husband here, you'll be sent home. FFC and most other nations have no issue with sending you straight back. A man only has to say you are his wife for you to have violated Church Law." She lifted Marie's skirt, lowered the waistband of her underwear, and sanitized her hip with rubbing alcohol. "There's a more or less well-defined way to escape England. First, from England to Brugge. It's among the most progressive cities—you know, a port city; anything goes there—but also the riskiest because it's so easy to be sent back to England. You were lucky to get out." She pinched a bit of Marie's flesh. "Local anesthetic. This will sting for just a moment, then you'll go numb."

"Will it hurt the baby?"

"Baby?"

"Yes."

Ingrid's voice softened, but her grip did not. "No. Not at all."

Marie signed with relief and nodded. She winced at the pain, but appreciated how quickly she became numb.

"Give that a few minutes to work. Anyway, once you're here with URN, we can get you out."

"We don't want to get out," Marie said. "We need to find someone here in FFC. We need to contact someone back in Brugge, and they will connect us with her. But we can't get reception here, so maybe there's a better way?"

"You can't stay here," Ingrid said. She put on a surgical mask. "FFC is so segregated, unless the person you're looking for is in your sector of the city, you'll never connect. They lock down the sections pretty tightly. The doorway to the cathedral is the only way out of the Garden Wall, and most people don't notice it. It gets closed off a lot; you were lucky it was open when you knocked. FFC may be progressive, but since that's so well known, there's a network of bounty hunters here. Is that who was after you? Sister Maria Josephus said you were being chased by someone."

Emma, who'd been listening this whole time, said, "In a way, yes. But it's someone who's personally connected to us."

"Then there's even a greater need to get out."

"But if my chip is removed, they can't track me anymore, right?" Marie asked.

"It doesn't matter," Ingrid said. She pressed a finger on Marie's hip. "Your mobility in FFC is so restricted, they are likely to find you anyway. It's crowded, but it's contained. And where one bounty hunter has appeared, others will shortly follow. You are probably staying in a convent, correct? One of those nuns will probably turn you in at some point. They have to sell out the women who come there; the nuns starve otherwise. Can you feel me pressing down on your hip?"

"Yes."

"Needs another minute or two, then. We may have to give you some more. Anyway, you can't leave this sanctuary and go back to FFC. First of all, we have to keep this network a secret, and if you go back out, you risk letting the authorities in FFC know we are here. We remain secret because the Sisters of the cathedral actively hide us, and because once you come in, you do not go back to FFC to let others know."

"Does that mean you won't let us come back out to FFC, even if we wanted?" Emma asked.

"We can't risk you talking," Ingrid said. "I'm sure you'll insist that you would never talk, you'd keep it secret, and so on. And I believe that you believe that. But when people are desperate, in dire straits, are facing significant punishment back in England? They look to trade information. We can't afford to be that trade."

"We could escape," Emma countered.

Ingrid actually laughed. "Of course you can't escape," she said. Even in freedom, they were still not free. "This is a one-way trip. Once that iron key in the chapel turns, you're committed. Sister Maria Josephus has been our eyes and ears in there, and the only reason we've been able to successfully smuggle out as many women as we have is that people are not seen coming and going from that chapel. Do you think the Bishop knows what's going on here? He trusts Sister Maria Josephus because he believes she's harmless. She took a vow of silence that she breaks every time she helps us by writing down what happened, and we burn it immediately. She has a true talent for getting women in and out of that chapel deep in the cathedral's crypt. It stays locked until she puts someone else in there. And even if there were a way out once you got there, would you be able to navigate the system of caves that brought you here?"

"System?"

"You didn't think there was just one pathway direct from the chapel to here, did you? It's dark and a series of twists and turns and false turns and branches you could take. Some have tried. They've all gotten lost in there.

"Besides, with the chip still in you? They've likely figured out that you're in the cathedral somewhere. So we have no time to lose. While they wait for the Bishop to allow them to search for you, they believe you're safely ensconced inside. Once they find you are not, they will check, but you will be long gone, on your way to the next stop."

"But what about our person here in FFC?" Emma asked.

"You'll have to contact them after you leave," Ingrid said. "If you have any phone, no matter where it's from or how recently you purchased it, you'll have to surrender it here. We'll destroy it along with the chip. And we'll provide you with a new one in your new location. We have a good track record of getting phones that work both there and here." She pressed on Marie's hip again. "Can you feel that?"

"Feel what?"

"Excellent, we're ready to begin. Most likely, it's in your hip bone. I'll use some tools to locate and remove it; I'll probably have to scrape it out. Once done, you'll have some pain in your hip, and it'll be a while before you're able to run. We'll have you rest for a day, and then we will take you."

"Take us where?"

"Strasbourg."

"But that's in France."

"Yes."

"We're English. That's the most dangerous place in the world for us to go."

"No, that would be England upon your return in handcuffs," Ingrid said. "And France is the one place where the English authorities will never be allowed to come look for you."

"But . . . but isn't it illegal for us to be in France?"

"Hold still," Ingrid told her. "I need to start an incision. And no more questions until we're done. But in answer to your last query: it's illegal to be *you* everywhere. You might as well be illegal in the one place where no one from England can come after you."

They said nothing more for a long time. Ingrid sent Emma to sit some distance away so as not to contaminate the area. She worked silently on Marie's hip before saying ruefully, "I can't get it out, not with these tools. Whoever inserted it either really knew what they were doing, or were so clueless as to bury it in the hip bone. Either way, it's not coming out of there without a full surgery, and we'd have to put you under completely. You need a specialist for this, with better equipment than we have here."

"Can I have that full surgery if I'm pregnant?"

Ingrid waited a few moments before responding, "Do you intend to keep the pregnancy?"

"Of course!" Such a question was practically obscene to a woman raised her entire life in the Catholic Church.

"Then we will take precautions to keep the child safe. But know that there are risks."

Risks. Every step she took was risky. Each risk begat more risk. All she wanted to do was sleep. Marie tried to prop herself up on her elbow but couldn't, so she collapsed back down. "Can you at least destroy it so that it stops transmitting my location?"

Ingrid made a face. "I can try to destroy it, but I don't think it's going to work, and I don't want to risk your safety. You'll already walk with a limp for a few days as it is."

Marie sighed, nodded, and waited for Ingrid to close the incision. Once she had done so and left so that Marie could rest before moving to their sleeping quarters, Emma pulled her chair over and lay her head on the bed so that she and her sister were facing each other.

"Everything has to be so complicated, doesn't it?"

Marie laughed. "To think that I thought I had it all planned out— we'd get to Brugge, then be done."

"I've lived among the underground for some time," Emma mused, "but never experienced it so literally before."

"I didn't even know there were caves in FFC," Marie said.

"That wasn't in a book?"

"I'm starting to learn that the most real things aren't in books. Every moment I'm learning something new."

"Well," Emma said. "We've got this far."

"And I was broadcasting our location the entire time." Marie felt a sting of pain and briefly winced before continuing. "You need to get out of here, Emma. They can't track you the way they track me."

"For all we know, I have one of those too. I wouldn't put it past the Earl to have us all tracked."

"Was that even a thing when we were children? How recent is this technology?"

"No idea."

Marie considered for a moment. "I wonder if Mother had one."

"If she did, no one ever looked for it."

"Our father would have told us," Marie said. "He would have wanted us to know exactly how firmly we were under his thumb, exactly how much freedom we did not have. He never kept things secret like that. He'd have wanted us to know so that we wouldn't have tried anything."

"I suppose," Emma agreed.

"And I wonder if James insisted upon it."

They lay there together for a long time before Emma said, "Was it ever a good marriage for you?"

Marie sighed. "In the beginning, sure. At least, I thought so at the time. I don't know what really makes a happy marriage. But I was happy enough. I had a new home to explore. I had new things to occupy my mind, new people to meet. I was a married woman, and a Duchess at that. I didn't have to do a lot of the 'wife' stuff that I thought I would, which I had some mixed feelings about. His mother certainly ran the household, which I didn't have the first idea how to do anyway.

I thought perhaps she would take me under her wing, train me. That never happened. I was clearly there for one reason, and one reason only: to produce an heir. And I never managed to do it, until it was too late."

"Your timing was always impeccable."

"But I do remember this one time," Marie went on, so lost in memory that she didn't acknowledge what Emma had said. "We were at this ball held by the King at his Christmas residence in Norfolk. James and I had been invited, and it was our first Christmas as Duke and Duchess of Suffolk. So we took extra care in how we dressed: our finest clothes, the best jewels, you name it. I remember I wore red, and what a daring color it was, but it paired so well with the diamonds and the sapphire ring on my finger. I remember James had never looked at me so intently as he did that night. I thought it might be the dress but hoped it was me. I remember he led me out to the dance floor and swept me up in his arms; it was the longest we had ever been physically entwined before. I'd never really realized how good he smelled to me until that night. I must have pleased him, too, because I remember him taking long breaths into my hair, like he was trying to learn my scent as well. I remember the feeling of his hands on my hips. We'd been married for some months by then, and this was the first time he'd put a hand on my body and just rested it there for a long time. I remember the heat from his body—I never knew another body could be so warm. I'd never been so close to one for so long. We stayed like that all night, and after the dance, we made love—really made love—for the first time. It wasn't just him visiting my bed to put his seed in me and leaving. He kissed me everywhere, cared about my pleasure, and stayed with me all night. And the way we moved together . . . my Lord God in heaven, it was like magic. It was like God himself was guiding us one move at a time. And I remember so vividly thinking, This is what I was made to do. I was made to be his other half."

She sobered. "It never happened again. After that night. It was like a spell had been cast over us that evening, and it popped like a soap bubble. Incandescent for just a moment, then gone, no trace of it ever having been there. That's what was so heartbreaking about the whole marriage—I know what it could have been, because I experienced it. It was real. And we never managed it again."

Emma reached over and took Marie's hand. She squeezed it, and her sister squeezed back. Then she took a deep breath.

"I never told you the real reason why I left home," she said.

Marie lifted her head slightly in surprise. "You didn't?"

"No. I mean, I didn't lie to you. I couldn't live the life that I was meant to, not the life that the Earl would have planned out for us. And I couldn't have just borne it out. It would have suffocated me to death."

"What do you mean?"

Emma looked more conflicted than Marie had ever seen her, like the words themselves were strangling her.

"Emma?"

Chapter Twenty-Five

Emma took a few breaths. This was harder than she had expected. She could never speak these words anywhere above ground. But down here, in the labyrinth of caves that was to lead them to freedom? This was the place to share secrets.

"I've known that I was . . . different . . . my whole life," Emma said. "That I could never truly love a man the way he was meant to be loved. I could never *be* with a man, the way that you were with James. I knew that I could never change; it was in my bone marrow, my DNA, every cell in my body. I was drawn to girls, especially the ones at our boarding school. Some of them were drawn to me.

"It didn't feel wrong, no matter what the Church teaches. It felt *right*. And no matter what I did, what I read, what I thought about it, I couldn't change that feeling. I had heard of what happens to girls who dare speak this feeling, and I had no interest in being put through any of that. I couldn't be married off like I was supposed to. So I thought I would do what I had to: I left. I used a lie that I knew would ruin my reputation, but it was far less bad than the truth. The truth could put me in prison.

"I knew that if I told the Earl privately, he'd call the doctor to come in and take care of it that night, that no one would ever need to know. I couldn't do that. They wouldn't find anything in there. They would find that I was not only lying about being pregnant, that I was still a virgin. So that's why I announced it when and where I did: so there would be an audience, and he would have no choice but to send me away then and there, and that no one would risk looking for me."

Emma exhaled, a weight lifted from her shoulders, one she had not realized she had been carrying until she noticed its absence. She looked at Marie, who was staring at her wide-eyed. But not with anger or shame.

"I'm so sorry," Marie said.

"Don't be. I was born this way."

"No, no, not that. Goodness, no, not that." Marie pulled Emma's hand to her lips and kissed it. "I'm so sorry that you were so alone. And that I never went after you."

"None of that matters anymore."

"I hope . . . I just wish I had been as brave as you," Marie said. "I wasn't born the same way, but our home was just as you described it: suffocation. Slowly. Maybe that's what it's like to freeze to death—a gradual loss of feeling until you simply become numb."

"I wonder if Mother was like me," Emma whispered. "I never thought about it before, but after you described your theory, and after Jane confirmed it was correct, then I wondered. Is that what Mother had fled? Maybe we both had this affliction." Maybe she wasn't so alone.

"It's not an affliction," Marie said. "It's natural."

"That's hardly the word people use."

"That's the ignorant talking. People who claim to preach the Bible but don't actually know what it says."

"Oh?"

"Matthew 18:20. 'For where two or three are gathered together in my name, there am I in the midst of them.' And there is Galatians 3:28, 'There is no male or female, for you are all one in Christ.' And maybe even the First Epistle of John—chapter 4, verse 16, if I'm not mistaken: 'God is Love.' So it's really quite obvious: any gathering of two or more in love is blessed by God. Love never had any place in my marriage. But I cannot imagine that the Lord Jesus Christ would shun any relationship between two good people who are gathered together in love."

Emma's eyes welled with tears, but they did not spill over. "I never heard it interpreted that way before. But I find it hard to argue with you."

"I'm sure that's why women cannot be lawyers. We'd win every argument."

Emma gave a choked laugh. "I'm sure you're right."

"If we had equal rights, we'd be unstoppable."

"They say there are countries where that's possible."

"And maybe someday we'll find our way there," Marie said. "As for whether our mother was like you, I don't know. But you and I are going to find out together. And soon."

Emma wasn't sure whose hand was squeezing whose now, but it grounded her. She'd shared her deepest secret, and had been rewarded.

"Can I ask you a question?" Marie asked. Emma nodded. "Have you ever found love? Or at least someone enjoyable who you could spend some time with?"

Emma laughed. "I've not been alone. But I've also not been in love. It's different when you have to keep it under wraps. It's difficult to find each other. It's difficult to conduct a proper relationship. I can hardly marry the person I might fall in love with. And while having a flatmate should not trigger as many questions, it might in a flat like mine with only one bed. So I have to be careful. Perhaps I've been too careful. But there are places I can go to find others who are like me, and for now, that has been enough."

"I hope you don't settle for that life," Marie said.

"There is joy to be found in purely carnal encounters," Emma pointed out. "The sins of the flesh are among the most decadent."

"I suppose," Marie said. "I won't pin my hopes on you. I just hope you find happiness, whatever form that takes for you."

Now it was Emma's turn to kiss her sister's hand.

Chapter Twenty-Six

Getting into FFC involved stepping off a train and entering through the correct doorway. Getting out of FFC involved a long maze of dark caves that neither Emma nor Marie could have hoped to navigate without help. After what felt like hours, they climbed an endless number of rusted stairs, then exited via an unmarked black door in a nondescript building in a cow pasture just outside of the city. Ingrid walked out briskly, as if she were leaving her own home for an appointment, and Marie and Emma followed her out, similarly acting as if they belonged there and had someplace to go. The cows paid them no mind as they made their way to a waiting truck. They climbed in the back, nestled between boxes of other unmarked and undeclared cargo. Without a word, Ingrid vanished, and the truck rumbled to life. Marie and Emma had no idea if she was going with them or if they'd ever see her again. It would have been nice to have the chance to thank her, or at least say goodbye.

"Do you think it's safe to talk?" Marie whispered just loud enough to be heard over the roar of the engine.

"Probably not," Emma said.

"We've come this far," Marie said.

Emma turned to look at her. "What's on your mind?"

"I guess . . . we're just so *unwanted*. We grew up thinking England was the envy of Europe. I never truly understood it until I got outside of it."

Emma didn't say a word, just silently urged Marie to continue.

"Just, on top of not being wanted by my own husband, my own father, or my mother-in-law, it's hard. Are we just condemned to not be wanted anywhere?"

Emma shrugged. "I've been living a very different life from you. I've been unwanted the entire time. There's a lot that money can shield you from, but once you're away from it, you realize just how much it distorts the reality of everything around you. I mean, where we come from, women are treated as rare and valuable objects to acquire. When you get outside of that world, you see that we're just someone to take advantage of. Either way, we're meant to be something used by men—as a work of art, or as garbage."

The truck rumbled over a hole in the road and knocked everything about. A box fell on Marie, and the sisters struggled to replace it in its spot.

"I guess I could at least think to myself, 'I'm English.'" Marie said. "Like, no matter what people thought of me, I could feel superior. But now I see that more people don't bother to learn English because it's exclusive or too hard to learn. It's because it's not worth it."

"Probably for the best," Emma said.

"What do you mean?"

"If we could, don't you think Englishmen would swarm the Earth like locusts? Devouring everything they could get their hands on?"

"No."

"We would," Emma said, assured. "If I've learned nothing else, it's that we're never satisfied with what we have. Everyone wants more land, more wealth, more power. We've been fighting the same war for generations so that we might hold on to a little more land. We've exhausted our own. Why else would power be given to the wealthiest landowners? Because then we can squeeze every last drop out of every last acre. We always want more. We'd take and take and take. The whole world would never be enough for us. So it's probably for the better that most of us are penned in to our small island."

Hours later, following bumpy roads and heart-stopping customs and border checks, they came to a shuddering stop and someone, presumably the driver, threw open the back of the truck. He jerked his head back, indicating the sisters should get out. They did, and scurried like mice around to the front of the truck. There they saw Ingrid, who must have been in the cab with the driver. Her presence put them at ease as she led them forward.

"Forward" was, of course, a relative term. Unlike the regimented and segregated FFC, Strasbourg was built as if someone had laid out a city nicely on a picnic blanket, then grabbed the blanket by the ends and tossed it into the air, leaving everything where it fell. There was no order, no streets arranged in nice, straight lines. Just chaos—houses might be built next to mechanics' shops, and stables wedged between dance clubs and clinics. People sat in the middle of ancient cobbled streets in the shadow of medieval buildings, drinking wine straight from the bottle, while indifferent drivers in cars and motorcycles lazily swerved around them. The air was filled with a tossed salad of languages. Posters crudely tacked to signposts advertised missing property and people. A woman leaning against a wall was approached by a man, who whispered in her ear, presumably inquiring about prices. She kneed him in the groin. Two men walked up to a third, who was speaking on a mobile phone; they smashed his phone on the ground and dragged him away despite his loud protestations and cries for help. No one slowed their pace or even looked at him.

It seemed like the kind of place where faces were easily forgotten, commerce was conducted underground, and life was easily discarded.

Perfect.

A person could disappear in a place like this, for better or worse, and that was just what the sisters needed. They were one illicit surgery away from freedom.

"This way," Ingrid whispered once they moved away from the bustling interior of the city. She took them to a barn at the dead end of a road that was only half paved and gave a distinctive knock at the door.

It opened, and she led them inside. They were met by three men in surgical masks, one of whom barred the door behind them. The barn had some hay on the floor, and a couple of docile cows lowed in the back. There were some windows high up in the rafters that let in a little light and fresh air, but it definitely smelled of livestock. The smell of poverty. An odor that a well-bred lady like Marie could easily go her whole life without smelling, and had certainly tried to avoid.

"What happens here?" Marie asked.

"The surgery," Ingrid replied.

"In a barn?"

"My sister is not having surgery in a barn," Emma said, stepping in front of Marie.

"It's secure here," Ingrid said simply. "Who would presume that a medical procedure would be completed in such a place?"

"But—" Emma began.

"But, what, exactly? Do you want to go to a hospital, where soldiers and bounty hunters and police officers will demand your identification before treating you? Do you think you will last long without your English citizenship being discovered? Do you think you can have surgery to remove a chip in any known hospital?"

Both sisters wanted to say "yes" but knew the answer had to be "no."

"WifeChips are recognized by Church Law," Ingrid said. "The Church prohibits their removal. You are the property of your husband, and it would violate the Tenth Commandment to remove anything that would permit your husband to retain the control he has over you. Your marriage is a covenant relationship; do you understand? Even if you leave your husband, you are still his wife in the eyes of God, both in this life and the next, and his will and ownership and control remain over you, no matter what you might argue or try for otherwise."

"Is it . . ." Marie's voice trailed off. She wasn't sure what she had meant to ask. *Is it sanitary? Sterile? Safe? Secure from intrusion?*

Is this really my life now?

She didn't finish the question, and was not offered an answer. Of course this was her life now. She'd chosen it, the first choice she'd ever made for herself, and for her child. It had to be a good one. She had no alternative.

The men in surgical masks said nothing, but gestured for Marie to follow them to the back of the barn, past the cows, to a stall where all the straw had been cleared out and plastic sheeting hung from the ceiling in what Marie guessed was an attempt at sterilization. One question answered, at least.

Before she could take off her clothing, Ingrid put her hand on her arm. "You must pay them first," she said.

"Pay them?" This had never been mentioned.

"Yes, you think they do this work for free?"

"Are they doctors?"

"They can perform the surgery," Ingrid said. "They will take good care of you. But for the risk of what they are doing, they must of course be compensated."

"I guess that's only fair," Marie said. "How much?"

Ingrid named the price, which made Marie blanch. How did people who hadn't smuggled out a duke's jewels afford this? She didn't voice the question aloud, for she really didn't want to know the answer.

"Excuse us then, please," Emma said. She took Marie by the elbow and led her away from everyone.

"What are you doing? I need this surgery."

"I agree," Emma said. "But we have no choice."

"So why are we leaving?"

"We aren't. But we're also not taking out our jewels in front of them. That's how women get robbed and trafficked."

"Ingrid is a nun!"

"And how many priests have children with women whom they've taken against their will?"

"They do that?"

"Hasn't there been a book written about it?"

"You know there wouldn't be."

Marie retrieved the jewels and laid them out. They were down to the sapphire that Mr. Harrison had declared he could not sell, the necklace, and the pearls. "Which do you think?"

Emma considered. "For what they're demanding from us? I suppose the pearls."

"The ones Alice refused?"

"You're right. That makes it even better."

They hid the remaining jewels, and then Marie turned to Emma, feeling like the baby sister more than she ever had in her life. When she spoke, her voice was small and frightened.

"Will you stay with me? While I'm unconscious?"

Emma threw her arms around her. "I won't let you out of my sight."

In returning the hug, Marie knew that Emma was promising more than just this surgery.

Marie's eyes fluttered open, but her eyelids felt so heavy that she had to immediately close them again. It was just too much effort. She felt as if only a few minutes had passed but at the same time sensed that it had been hours. She had never been under sedation before, and hoped to never repeat the experience again. She was groggy from the drugs, and even though they had given her painkillers, she could feel a dull ache in her side where she knew there was a new incision. She groped around until she felt a thick bandage on her hip. She hoped no one had helped themselves to her organs.

A hand stilled her.

"Leave it," a voice said. "You don't want to hurt yourself."

That voice.

It was impossible.

She had believed she would never hear it again.

There was no way she was this lucky. God would never bless her like this.

The hand covered hers.

Heart in her throat, she forced her eyes open again and looked straight into the bright-blue eyes of her beautiful mother.

"Hello, darling."

Chapter Twenty-Seven

What Marie had always remembered most vividly about her mother was the shape of her fingernails. Not too long, not too short. White at the tips, pink otherwise, with perfect crescent-shaped cuticles. Whatever new humiliation Charlotte's husband had cooked up for her, her fingernails had always been pristine. They were the mark of a woman who did not have to work, whose hands were not needed for any sort of labor and could serve a primarily decorative function. They were works of art that befit the woman of Ellthrop and the pedestal on which she had been placed.

Marie remembered the feel of them on one particular day, as Charlotte had gently stroked the hair out of Marie's face. Marie had been seven, and she and Charlotte had been lounging together on a couch, Alice and Emma on either side of them, watching the television that was limited to programming approved by their father. They'd been watching Evensong service from Northampton Cathedral, and the haunting choir, echoes of the pipe organ music, and chanting of the monks had spread out of the television and into the air of Ellthrop over one hundred miles away. Marie could practically smell the incense, as if it too were wafting out of the cathedral and into the room.

She'd also felt the sadness radiating from her mother. She'd know by then that her mother had been pregnant four times in the last seven years, each one ending after only a few short weeks or months. With each failed pregnancy, Marie had felt the disappointment that her parents held for her—her very existence reeked of failure.

Yet in that moment on the couch, she had felt content and safe. She and her sisters had been bickering earlier, tossing barbs back and forth about their respective appearances and behavior until Charlotte had silenced them. Marie had not taken part in the insults; instead, she'd treasured her opportunity to sit with her mother, casually like this. Such things happened far too rarely.

Charlotte had absently twisted a lock of Marie's hair. Marie would always remember the slight tug that she'd felt—not pain, just a bit of pressure as the hair had looped around her mother's finger, capped with one of those perfect, crescent-moon fingernails. They were soft fingers that had never touched a tool, had never written much beyond the obligatory social letter, and spent much of their time demurely folded in their owner's lap, often in gloves for protection. Marie's soft, downy, ash-blond hair had slipped like silk through her mother's fingers. Around and around, then gone. Around and around, then gone.

They should have been participating in the Mass, sitting and kneeling and praying and standing and sitting and kneeling and praying and standing and sitting and kneeling and praying and standing and sitting and kneeling and praying. And on any other night, they would have done so, particularly if their father had been there. But he hadn't been that day, and Marie had not known where he was, and their mother would not allow herself to think of where he was. So they'd lounged, and they'd absorbed, and would tell no one of their apostasy.

Charlotte had broken another taboo by asking her daughters, in the midst of the service, "What is your favorite thing about Ellthrop?"

Marie had piped up first. "The pond!"

Though she could not see her mother, she'd felt her smile as she looped another strand of hair through her fingers. Around and around, then gone. "Why do you like the pond the best?" her mother had asked.

"The calmness," Marie had said. "I can be quiet there, but not like quiet in the house. Instead of sitting still, I can lie down, or run around, or walk. Instead of paying attention, I can look at everything. I can listen to a bird, or look for a rabbit, or look for fish and frogs. I can lie down next to it and close my eyes and imagine anything I want."

"The word I think you're looking for, Marie, is freedom," her mother had replied.

"Freedom," Marie had agreed. "That's what I like best about the pond."

"There's a big tree at the edge of the grounds," Emma had said. "It's full of branches that reach up to the sky and touch the other trees. You can climb up them and probably even climb into another tree from it. But I never do. What I like about the tree is that there's also a little hole in it. It's big enough that animals, like maybe badgers, have lived in there. But now it's empty. And it's the perfect size to go in and hide."

Charlotte had looped another strand of Marie's hair, around and around, then gone, before she'd asked, "Why do you like to hide?"

Emma hadn't responded. Marie had felt her mother's body shift a little to look at Emma. "Are you hiding from something?" her mother had added.

It had been several long moments before Emma had answered, "No."

"You can tell me, you know, if you are."

"I'm not!" Emma had raised her voice. "I just like the idea of a small space that's just for me. And I'm not going to show any of you where this tree is because I don't want to share it."

"I know what tree you're talking about!" Marie had cried excitedly. "I can see it from the pond."

"Mummy, don't let her use my tree! It's mine!"

"I don't want to use your stupid tree. You stay away from my pond."

"Girls," Charlotte had admonished. Marie and Emma had been well behaved enough that only the one word from their mother had been enough to nip any quarrel in the bud.

"It seems to me," Charlotte had continued, "that Emma wants security."

"I want privacy," Emma had said.

"Those are often one and the same."

Emma hadn't responded.

They'd listened to the choral service for a few more minutes, and Charlotte had continued to twirl Marie's hair throughout.

"What about you, Alice?" she'd finally asked. "What do you like best about Ellthrop?"

"Everything," Alice had said.

"Everything?"

"Yes," Alice replied. "I love the house. I love my room. I love my bed. I love the pond and the trees. I love the chapel. I love the parties that you and Papa host. I love the dinners we have as a family. I love when Papa joins us for them. I love the sunsets and the picture gallery and the stables. I love that we're all sitting here together now. I love everything about it. And I never want anything to change."

Charlotte's fingers had paused at the end of Alice's answer. The hair had simply fallen away from between those perfect fingers and into Marie's face.

"Nothing at all?"

"No," Alice had declared, with great conviction in her voice.

Charlotte had sat in silence, and the choral evensong had filled the room. Evensong was the mass held at twilight, just as the last whispers of daylight faded away and the black expanse of night descended. A time of transition, when the line between life and death felt just a little bit blurred, and when you believed just a little bit more that there was a life after this one. It was the time when the voices of the hundreds of millions who had lived and died before your life was even a possibility could just barely be heard at its edges.

"So," Alice had said, "what is it you think I really want?"

Charlotte had picked up Marie's hair and begun to loop it again.

The words she'd spoken would be the last she would ever say to her daughters. By morning, she would be gone.

"The impossible," she said.

Chapter Twenty-Eight

Marie shook her head. Her mouth felt like it was stuffed with cotton. Surely she was looking at Emma and was delusional with the painkillers she had been given.

But Emma was on her other side, taking hold of her other hand. Emma's eyes shone with tears, emotional in a way that Marie had never seen before. Probably in a way that Emma had never let herself be before.

"You were right, Marie," Emma whispered. "You were so, so right."

The hand from the other woman, impossibly her mother, cupped Marie's cheek. Marie dared to let herself believe that she had done it. That she had been right. She sighed, and let herself gaze.

Their mother somehow looked like she hadn't aged a day from the last time they'd seen her. Had she had surgery to remove the years from her face? Or had she just looked older than her age when Marie was a child? Marie remembered the fights, the humiliations, the repeated pregnancies that had ended in one sort of failure or another. The stress of managing a large household staff, the constant pressure to look beautiful; how so many of her father's accomplishments had been made possible only by her mother's hard work, though she'd never taken an ounce of credit for it. Marie closed her eyes briefly, exhausted just thinking about it. She'd experienced but a fraction of the horrors her mother had, and she knew the pain they caused. Yes. That was enough to take years off anyone's life. In "death," her mother had regained her life.

Marie briefly wondered how close her mother had actually come to ending her life, rather than just faking it. And what had driven her to survive.

She opened her mouth to speak, but all she could croak out was, "How?"

How did you find us? How did you survive? How did you convince everyone you were gone?

A breath. And the deeper questions came.

How could you bring yourself to walk away from us? How did you sleep at night knowing we were left behind? How long would you have waited if we had never come to find you? How could you have resisted contacting us for so many years?

And finally, how much did any of that matter anymore? They were all here, all together, at long last. It was greater than Marie had ever dared to hope.

Charlotte brushed her hand through Marie's long-unwashed hair. The fingernails were no longer perfect crescent moons. The skin was no longer soft; these fingers had known daily labor for many years. They felt unfamiliar. Marie flinched, but Charlotte did not.

"You're fine," Charlotte said, answering the one question Marie had not meant to ask. "And your baby's fine."

Marie blew out a breath in relief.

"And the chip is out," Emma said.

Charlotte smiled. "You're free. We're free."

Marie nodded. All of them. Free.

Free.

What a concept.

No more men watching her from afar. No more being tracked by people who treated her as a wayward piece of property. No more being branded like a piece of livestock, no longer carrying within her what was effectively the receipt for her purchase. No longer being nothing more than the property of a man who wanted to dispose of her. She could leave if she wished, without looking over her shoulder. To be sure, she was far from safe. An unmarried woman from England was not truly free—no woman in a country governed by Church Law was. And France was quite possibly the most dangerous place they could be.

And yet Marie felt as if a too-tight belt wrapped around her midsection had finally been loosened, and she inhaled shakily with what felt like the first deep breath of her life. Full of oxygen, she felt each cell within her perk up just a little bit more. And though she knew it was too soon, she would have sworn on anything that the baby within her did a little flip in celebration.

She wondered if it was a son or a daughter.

She knew which one, in her old life, would have conferred value upon her, and which one would have condemned her to ridicule. But here, in this new life, this new world, she knew which one she preferred.

Marie looked to her mother and her sister.

"You're so beautiful," Charlotte said. She brushed her hand through Marie's hair again with her ragged fingernails and looked at Emma. "You both are."

Emma nodded, but looked away.

Charlotte cleared her throat. "I owe you an explanation, and an apology. I'm not sure which one I should give you first."

Emma shook her head, saying what Marie wished she could. "Jane told us," she said. "And Marie figured out the rest."

"Jane doesn't know the full story," Charlotte said. "She protected me, helped me land on my feet. She urged me to truly disappear, to go deeper into the continent, but I needed to stay as close to England as possible to be near you two, and near Alice."

Marie saw Emma stiffen at the sound of their eldest sister's name. "We saw her," Emma said.

Charlotte nodded, her jaw tense.

"She doesn't believe you're alive."

"Good. It's safer if she doesn't. Safer for all of you." Charlotte sounded like she was trying to convince someone, and it wasn't her other two daughters.

"You're the least of our worries," Emma said. "We have more to fear. Marie's mother-in-law. Her lackeys."

"They teach you to fear the men," Charlotte said. "What they don't warn you about is the women who do their bidding."

"I think he's doing hers," said Emma.

"That may be true, but a woman without a man is a being without value. Her greatest power, creating life inside of her, is her greatest weakness if she has no man with her to legitimize that life. Most women internalize this. I did. I'm sure you did. I was raised not just to be a wife and a mother, but to conceive that I could *only* be a wife and a mother. And I raised you to believe the same."

"And then you walked away from it," Emma said. "You walked away from us."

Charlotte nodded, obviously conceding that she could not argue the point. "I did."

"Do you regret it?"

The question hung in the air, making it thick with tension. Charlotte's silence was answer enough, but they waited for her to speak anyway.

"I'm not sure how to answer that."

Emma's response was the stab of an icicle, cold and sharp.

"Try."

"I don't think you'll like it."

"I'm sure I won't."

"And this is not the time or place for it."

"Don't make us wait any longer than you already have."

"You have to understand, it wasn't about you."

"Jane already told us that."

"And I did what I could to protect you all these years."

"She told us that as well."

"Then I don't know what more I can say."

"You didn't answer my question."

"No." Charlotte's voice was a shard of glass.

"No, you won't answer it?" Emma asked.

"No is my answer."

Silence.

"So," Emma said. "You don't regret it. You don't regret leaving us."

"I don't regret saving you."

"Saved us?"

"Yes."

"No one saved us. No one saved *me*. I had to run away. Be disowned by my father. Leave behind my sisters." Marie heard the years of fear that Emma had suppressed start to rise to the surface. Now that Marie's immediate safety was assured, now that there was no way for anyone to continue to track them, Emma had the luxury of dealing with these fears. "To be a fallen woman on the streets of London; do you have any idea what I had to do to survive?"

Charlotte nodded her head. "I came to you," she whispered. "Didn't Jane tell you? Risked it all, just to see you breathing."

"You didn't wake me up," Emma said. Marie swore she could see the light reflect off a tear in Emma's eye that danced on the edge of her eye, peeking out to her eyelashes, but not daring to step out over the precipice.

"I wanted nothing more than to wake you up," Charlotte said. "To gather you into my arms and carry you out of there, carry you with me across the channel and never look back."

"Why? Why didn't you? Why did you leave me?"

The tear finally dared to spill over.

Emma looked angry at the prospect.

Marie felt herself shake, opened her mouth to speak, but the words choked in her still-dry throat. She lifted her hand to try to grab their attention, but she was weak, and clumsy, and Emma and Charlotte were laser-focused on each other.

And the dam broke for their mother.

"Because I couldn't do anything for you."

"What are you talking about?" Emma whispered.

"I truly had believed that by leaving, I was doing right by you girls. You and Alice. Oh Lord God in Heaven, Alice. She was the only daughter your father was truly happy to have—she was the first, surely a son would follow. And then when the son never came, he grew colder and colder toward her, more and more disappointed, as if blaming her for beginning a trend.

"Without a son, there was no future for Ellthrop, not one that would have included you girls. It would have gone to your father's younger brother, and all of you would have been thrown out on the street. Your survival depended on your having a brother. *My* survival depended upon it.

"I couldn't give him to you. The one child we all needed to secure the future evaded us over and over. Oh, but that didn't mean that I didn't love you. I did. I do. I loved you more and more each day. But I was also saddened for you. If your father could have an heir, and if the future of Ellthrop were secure, the pressure would be off the three of you to make up for the lack of it with loveless marriages. You would have a chance to marry the person you chose—or to not marry at all. So I made sure he, and you, could have that security, even if it meant that I could not be part of your lives any longer. I thought I was giving you that choice. But it was clear soon enough that I thought wrong.

"I was sickened, knowing what I had failed to do. I know that science says women are not responsible for the sex of the baby, but that didn't change what I knew in my heart: that I had failed to provide you with protection and security.

"I'm sure Jane told you about the insecurity in which I found myself. I don't believe your father would have actually killed me, and certainly he wouldn't have wanted to. But I think he could have grown desperate enough to do it. Particularly when his favorite mistress became pregnant, and the scan revealed it was a son. So much was riding on that child, for your father and for you. I couldn't deny you that future.

"So I did what all good mothers do: I sacrificed myself for the sake of my children. A legitimate son for your father would have meant security for the three of you: good marriages, a home to stay in, and a good name.

"Faking my death wasn't so difficult. I knew they would not look hard for me. There was another woman waiting to become the next Lady Kenfield, and my sinful death meant there would be no Christian burial or funeral. Tidy. Everyone could move on. Even me."

Emma had crossed her arms and was looking away from Charlotte, processing all of this. Marie reached out her hand to her mother's, who took it and squeezed. Marie understood what that pressure was like, how impossible it was to live under the inability to perform the one task the world demanded. How it suffocated you to live under the weight of your own useless body. How easy and hard it was to pretend to die, knowing that no one would look closely enough to unravel your death.

Marie was happy to have had a model to follow.

"I thought I was saving you," her mother went on, "and even though it destroyed me to walk away, I truly believed that what I was doing was right for all three of you. It was the only world I had known, and I thought what I was doing was right."

She sighed. "And then I arrived in Brugge. The world opened up to me—it was like I was cracking the spine of a new book. I realized the possibilities that we had all been denied. I thought about what lives you could have if you left England. If you lived in Brugge, you could have a life even if you didn't have a husband. I fantasized about getting all three of you out. But I knew I couldn't actually do it; you wouldn't be able to leave the country without your father's permission, and he would never give it. I watched from afar as you grew up, hearing it all secondhand from Jane, and I ached inside. I thought I had protected you, but I saw that the toxic environment of our home had only metastasized from there. I learned how you suffered."

Charlotte reached out her other hand to Emma, who slowly uncrossed her arms and took it. Marie could feel the surge of emotion through Charlotte's other hand as it squeezed hers even tighter.

"And . . ." Charlotte choked back tears. "And I was powerless to help you get out. I could only hope that through the clues Jane left for you, one of you would figure it out and come find me."

The tears fell.

"But I never dared to dream that *two* of you would do it."

Whatever defenses Emma had left fell as she too began to sob. She and Charlotte grasped hands over Marie, who raised hers to join as well. With strength that was returning to her, she pulled them both in close to her, and the three held each other for a long time.

"You're awake," Ingrid said as she entered the room. She made no comment about the three crying women. "Give the patient some space, please, and let her move about."

Marie found her voice, which scraped her throat as she spoke. "Is it true, you got it?"

Ingrid nodded. "Yes, all of it." She held up a jar with a tiny microchip inside. "You're free."

"Wonderful," Marie said, wiping her eyes. "But why did you keep the chip?"

Ingrid smiled. "Because some women like to finish it off themselves." She withdrew a small hammer from the pocket of her coat. "Would you like to do the honors?"

Marie nodded, and, with great help from her mother and sister, got out of bed. She shuffled over to a table and held out her hand. The pain from the procedure was still there; she knew she probably wasn't actually feeling her bones, but she could swear she could feel where the chip had been dug out from her. Ingrid gave her both the jar and the hammer.

Marie unscrewed the jar and tipped the chip onto the table. She raised the hammer. With one movement, she'd be free forever.

Then she paused, hammer hovering in midair. Her hand trembled slightly, but she did not move.

"If I destroy it," she said, "they will know this was where I last was."

"That's right," Charlotte said. "They'll never know where you went from here. You will have the same freedom I did. Chips like this didn't exist back then."

"But they'll know where to start looking," Marie said. "Maybe they're already here."

Emma put her hand over Marie's so they held the hammer jointly. "Do you need my help?"

Marie thought for a moment, then nodded.

She removed Emma's hand from the hammer. And then she set it down on the table.

Chapter Twenty-Nine

"How did you find us?" Marie asked, as Emma helped her into a new set of clothes provided by URN. The clothes were well used but of high quality. It felt both familiar and wrong to wear them. Their quality suggested that the sisters were far from the first women from their social situation who had made this journey and left their clothing behind for others who followed behind them. Slipping into them was a disguise, but also felt to Marie like she was returning to something more familiar.

Charlotte smiled. "Jane."

"Jane?"

"When her son was thrown off the train, he notified Jane, who notified me. They used their connections to get you into the right hands. Jane and Dirk have worked with URN for years. She said that Dirk even gave you a hint of where you could be safe, and Jane told me to come here, that you'd be here after you were brought across the border."

"You know," Emma said, pulling a sleeve down Marie's arm (Marie winced in pain as she did). "Remember what Dirk said when he was in the cargo compartment of the train, when they were asking for his ticket? He asked if he was on the express to Strasbourg. He was giving us a hint of where we would end up."

"But we couldn't do anything with it," Marie said. "Why would we have put any significance in that? We ran to that cathedral by random chance, with Alice pursuing us, which no one saw coming." She stood up and shuffled around the room a bit. The pain in her hip was receding but still there, a dull ache. "He never could have foreseen that."

Emma gently took her elbow to offer support, but Marie waved her off. She needed to be able to stand on her own two feet now, literally and figuratively. Who knew how much more running was ahead of her? "He was thinking ahead all that time?"

"If you hadn't ducked into that cathedral on your own, someone else would have brought you there," Charlotte explained. She stood up and walked along Marie's other side. "I don't know who, maybe someone at your lodging—you probably stayed in a convent in FFC, right?" Marie nodded. "URN has people placed in most of them, and eventually you would have been brought to the cathedral. After I fled Brugge, I was supposed to wait for you in FFC, but once John Hart began chasing you, a change of plans was necessary. We had to get out of his reach."

Marie nodded, with a wince of pain as she took a turn. "You know John Hart?"

"The Dowager Duchess knew your father," Charlotte said. "She used to come to Ellthrop with her husband, and John Hart would always be there with them, attending to her every need. He was so young, just a teenager. He went everywhere with her."

"Still does," Marie said.

"If her wine looked less than half-full, he ensured it was topped up. If she looked bored or flushed or pale, he would see to it that she was swiftly moved to a comfortable seating position. He had what was almost a sixth sense with her, always knowing what she might need or want. And he did it unobtrusively. You saw John Hart, but not until he was actively attending the Duchess. He had this ability to evaporate into the shadows, where he'd observe but never speak. It was as if you could only see him when he wanted you to see him."

"What do you think inspired that level of devotion?" Emma asked.

"Love," Marie said. "Look at Jane, and how devoted she's been to us. The level of devotion is no different."

"Jane disappeared from our lives, though. She moved to another country."

"Only after she was dismissed by our father," Marie pointed out.

"She could have followed me, or followed you, or even followed Alice, instead of moving on. She went to where her son was, not to where we were. It's not the same."

"You're right," said Charlotte. "It wasn't. But you're on the right track."

Emma gave the smug smile of the big sister who'd gotten the better of the baby of the family. It was as if the decades had fallen away. "How do you mean?"

"There were rumors," Charlotte said, "that he was her son."

Her daughters' heads whipped toward hers. Marie stumbled. "What?"

John Hart, her husband's brother? The secret son of the Dowager Duchess? It seemed impossible; but at the same time, something fell into place in Marie's mind. Something about it fit perfectly. The way the Dowager Duchess trusted him, and the way he would do anything for her. The way he'd scrutinized Marie's every move from the moment she'd arrived at Grayside, as if he were a discerning part of the family rather than a servant with, now that she thought about it, a never-defined and nebulous role in the household. Servants and private secretaries were known to be loyal to the families they served, but though some estates claimed that those who lived below stairs were just as beloved as those who lived upstairs, there was always a clear demarcation between the two.

With John Hart, that had never been the case. Ever.

"The rumors weren't loudly spoken; but yes. Someone as powerful as the Duchess of Suffolk is bound to have gossip spread about her. I never knew her very well, but knew of her. The thought was that before she'd met the Duke, she'd had born a son out of wedlock. It was hushed up and taken care of, as these things often are. The Duchess was from a very powerful family; they could have hidden something like this away quietly and not impugned her reputation. Then years later, a teenaged

John Hart joined her household. Supposedly he was the son of a woman who lived on the grounds that her family owned. He bore enough of a resemblance to her that there was talk almost immediately, and it never quieted down."

"It did quiet down, because I never heard about it," Marie said. Even with all the ways it made sense, it still did not make any sense. "And I didn't see any resemblance between them." Not that she'd looked closely. Both of them had scared her, and she hadn't wanted to make eye contact.

"I've seen pictures of the Duchess in recent years. She's had enough cosmetic surgery done to dissolve the resemblance. She started soon after the rumors did. And if she kept you locked up at Grayside, you wouldn't have come into contact with anyone stupid enough to repeat the rumor around you."

"Wow." Marie's footing became uneven as her vision began to go black around the edges. This time, she accepted the support of her mother and sister. "I'm all right," she said, but they led her back to bed anyway. As soon as she lay down, her vision began to clear, and she felt better. "Did you ever find out if it was true?"

"No," said Charlotte. "To be honest, there was a large purge of people from their inner circle when it was first circulated. But it didn't matter, really, because by the time the whispers began, she was such a formidable woman that no one dared dig too far." She huffed a laugh. "After all that trouble to keep the scandal quiet, and she blew it up by employing him in her household as soon as he came of age."

"Stupid," Emma said.

"No," Charlotte corrected. "She was flexing her power like few others could. The scandal of her youth couldn't touch her anymore, because she had the money and the power to keep it away. She'd been married for years and produced two more sons. The succession was secure. And she'd brought a lot of money to the estate through her dowry. Few women have that kind of freedom."

"I'll say," Emma said. "Pretending to be pregnant out of wedlock was my one-way ticket out of that world. It didn't have to be true—it was enough that I said it."

"But you were a young woman of marriageable age," Charlotte said. "That's not what happened in her case. Once the rumor about the Duchess came out, she was already a Duchess, with her husband's power behind her. She'd produced the heir and spare, so any disparagement of any of them would have sent the entire Dukedom into chaos. To disparage her would be to disparage her husband and, more crucially, her sons. That couldn't be allowed."

"They gave her that value," said Emma. "And without them, you have none."

"Exactly," said Charlotte. "And that was what I was faced with, and what your sister was faced with. If you lose your value to your husband, you lose your value altogether. In our cases, we hadn't produced sons for them. So we became disposable."

"But not anymore," Marie said. She chanced sitting up. The world didn't spin, so she sat up more. "So now what?"

Charlotte smiled. "Now everything."

"But first," Marie said, "Emma, remember when I asked you to help me?"

Emma knew that she was being tracked. In fact, she was counting on it.

She walked to the Strasbourg train station, which was as bustling and busy as any other station in Europe. She kept her head down as she wove through people and cargo, catching snippets of conversations in French and English and Latin and German. She glanced up at the departures list and waited for the language to switch to one she could read. One train was due to leave in three minutes, from a nearby track. Perfect.

Emma approached the train. Windows and doors were opened as passengers boarded and others alighted. In the chaos, Emma wrapped her fingers around the vial containing the chip, deep inside her pocket. She boarded the train. With a practiced hand that had stolen many valuable items from her employers' homes over the years, she pulled out the vial and tucked it firmly into the back pocket of one of the few empty seats. She heard a conductor give what sounded like the last call for boarding, and she quickly stepped off the train just as it began to pull out of the station.

She hadn't even bothered to look at where the train was going; she had only looked at the departure time. So now that she had the luxury of doing so, she checked it out. Paris. The beating heart of enemy France, a place where John Hart could not follow. For all he knew, Marie was headed there, beyond his reach forever. He'd have to go back to the Dowager Duchess as the failure he was.

Smiling, Emma turned on her heel.

Chapter Thirty

Strasbourg edged up against the shores of the Rhine river. On the other side of the river were the walls of the Holy Roman Empire. It was France's only peaceful border. France had been engaged in a war with England along its northern border for a millennium and against an ever-encroaching Islamic Empire to the west for hundreds of years. Therefore, it had every interest in keeping the Holy Roman Empire happy. To do so, it had agreed to house any refugees, migrants, transients, or other undesirables within its borders. This meant accepting such people who crossed the Rhine into France from the Holy Roman Empire even as it prevented them from crossing in the other direction.

Marie looked at the wall from the other side of the river, in Strasbourg, where she sat on a blanket with her mother and sister. Emma had just returned from her errand to the station and had reported that her mission had been successful. They ate a simple meal of apples, cheese, and bread. They lounged under a tree, shoes off, sunglasses on. Strasbourg could be dangerous, as could most cities full of desperate people fleeing something, but here, on this riverbank, on a sunny day, full of people, relaxing seemed to be the easiest and most obvious thing in the world.

They had wandered over here after Ingrid had finally released Marie. With Marie's chip gone, they were no longer traceable. So they had walked, with no destination in mind. Walking instead of running, because they could.

"Be careful," Ingrid had said. "And you must never, ever mention our organization to anyone, to protect those who follow in your footsteps. God be with you."

"And with you," Marie had replied, punctuating the gratitude with a most un-English hug. Ingrid had been equally uncomfortable with it, and instead had shooed her off.

It was only after they'd left the sanctuary of the stables and taken up their place on the riverbank that Marie realized, half an hour into their idyllic afternoon in the sun, that her jewelry was missing. The discovery broke their reverie.

"She stole it!" Emma shouted.

"Don't be ridiculous," Marie said. "She saved us, saved me. She wouldn't have stolen it."

"You had the jewels when you went into that stable, and now that you've come out, you don't have them. In between, you were unconscious and at their mercy." Emma made a noise of frustration. "We should have checked before we left."

Marie's blood ran cold in her veins, but she beat back the tendrils of doubt that she felt creeping in. Emma had to be right. Emma had warned her that anyone would take it from her at the first opportunity. And she'd failed to be skeptical of the person offering to help her.

And yet. "I won't believe it."

"What you believe won't change the facts," Emma shot back. "We were so distracted with each other that she took advantage of us. It's my fault; I should have thought of it. I should have seen it coming. She saved you, but do you really think she did it out of the goodness of her heart? For no payment at all? Of course she didn't ask for any, she just took what she needed. I bet they do this all the time. Imagine all the underground activities your jewelry will fund."

Marie chewed on the inside of her cheek. She tasted blood.

"Then I hope she did take it, because then it's going to a worthy cause."

"Better that than her own pocket, which I fear may have been the result."

"I'll never know," Marie said. "And I'd rather not know. I'm free, truly free, for the first time in my life. I'd like to enjoy it."

"Free and penniless."

"Then I am truly starting anew. And without any jewelry on my person or the money to show for it, I can't be accused of having taken them, now, can I?"

"If you think you have to have the jewelry on you to be credibly accused of theft, I have bad news for you."

"Girls," Charlotte said with a warning. They might have been small children again quarreling over a toy. "Enough. The jewelry is gone, and how it happened won't change where we are now. It doesn't matter, in the end. What matters is that we're here."

Marie felt heartened by Charlotte's platitudes. Her mother was back in her life and was going to make everything okay. "Where do we go now?" Marie asked.

"Back to Brugge," Charlotte said. "You'll stay with Jane until you're back on your feet. Especially since John Hart now believes you're in Paris."

"What about you?" Marie asked. "You don't live there anymore."

"Where do you live, anyway?" Emma asked.

"I was in Brugge, but now I move around from place to place," said Charlotte. "I was in FFC most recently. Now I'm not. It isn't safe for me to stay in one place, which means it isn't safe for you to stay with me."

"But we've only just found you," Marie said. She took her mother's hand and squeezed it tight, as if physically preventing her mother from leaving again. "You have to take us with you. I'm dead, and we have new identities. We're free and can follow you anywhere."

"And I don't understand why you have to move around," Emma said. "You've been 'dead' for so long that no one would be following you. No one knows."

Charlotte looked pensive for a moment but shook her head. "It's not safe," she repeated. "I'll help you get back to Brugge and stay with you until you're set up with Jane. It's only a couple of hundred miles, but it's difficult to get there from both France and the HRE when you don't have any legal status. It's a wonderful city."

"Why did you leave it?" Emma asked. "Jane said you were there for a long time, and then you vanished."

Charlotte said nothing, just watched the river. Armed soldiers patrolled the wall, sneering at anyone on their side of the river who made eye contact.

"It doesn't matter anymore," Charlotte said.

"I think we should just stay here," Emma said. "We can disappear here too. With all the comings and goings, it might even be easier than in Brugge. Plus, we're in France. It's hard for anyone in England to follow us here."

"There were so many shops and businesses," Marie said. "I wonder if we could get work here."

"What did your books say?" Emma asked.

Marie shrugged. "I never thought I would come to Strasbourg, so I never paid much attention to it. But from what I remember, there was a lot of the same nonsense you usually read about France: that it's immoral, full of baby-eaters and blood-drinkers. That border towns like Strasbourg are full of human traffickers, though there's probably some truth to that. I don't know; it's probably as difficult a place as any for us to set up a home."

"It would have been easier with the jewelry," said Emma.

"Don't be so sure about that," Charlotte said. "Lots of people come through here with jewelry. The market could be depressed."

Emma shook her head. "If it were worthless, Ingrid would not have stolen it."

They all sat in silence after that, watching the river and the occasional swan riding along the current. Back in England, the swans were all property of the Crown. Did they belong to anyone here? Could someone kill a swan and not be arrested for poaching? What were the laws in France? Were they the same if you were English as opposed to French? Marie wondered if she could get by here using Latin. She knew using English was a lost cause. Where would they live? Even if there was work available, what was she even qualified to do? She was an English woman of noble birth; she was raised for the sole purpose of birthing the sons and heirs of noblemen. And now she was pregnant—would she be able to work here? Would they let her once her belly began to swell? And once the child was born, what sorts of help was available? Would she end up in a workhouse, like the kind that still existed, albeit unofficially, for destitute unwed mothers in England?

Marie couldn't breathe. She felt wetness on her face. She realized she was having a panic attack. She also realized that she had been voicing her concerns out loud, her voice becoming more shrill and hysterical the longer it went on.

"Marie." Charlotte rubbed her back as she spoke in a soothing voice. It reminded Marie of how Charlotte had cared for her whenever she was sick as a child. Unlike most Countesses, when her daughters were sick, Charlotte had nursed them back to health herself. Marie was so full of love at the memory that she felt her heart begin to crack. "Marie, relax."

"What have I done?" she asked, through the shaky sharp breaths she was forcing herself to take.

"You've done what I always hoped you would do," Charlotte said. "You've saved yourself. And you aren't going to end up in a workhouse. Not by a long shot."

"I can't raise a child on my own," Marie said. "I wasn't thinking straight, and now it's too late. Was it the hormones that made me do it?"

"You're not raising this child on your own," Emma said firmly. "I'm going to stay with you and help you."

"I wish you could help," Marie said to Charlotte. She wasn't in England anymore; she could share her feelings. "I don't know if it's pregnancy or seeing you again, but I don't want to let you go. I don't want to do any of this without you."

Charlotte sat there for a long time, not responding to either of her daughters. She seemed to be at war with herself, then having reached some sort of decision, she nodded.

"Okay."

The sisters looked at her. "Okay, what?"

"Okay. I'll stay with you. I'll do this with you."

"You mean it?" Emma's voice was so full of hope that Marie felt her heart crack once again.

"Is it safe for you to do so?" Marie asked.

Charlotte gave her daughter a smile that did not reach her eyes. "It's safe for you if I do so, yes."

Marie laughed and wiped at her nose in a way that would have had half the society of England clutching their pearls in disgust. "So back to Brugge?"

"No," Charlotte said quickly. "No, not Brugge. We can't go back there. We'll stay here in Strasbourg, at least for now. Emma and I have started over before, and we'll do it again here with you. And the baby. As a family. Together."

The thought warmed Marie like treacle. She felt the damp grass beneath her. Was this patch of earth where they were to live? She remembered the danger and disorder of the city when they'd first arrived. It was a distinctly refugee community. It wasn't unpleasant, but it wasn't familiar either. Maybe that's what she needed. The less familiar, the better.

"I like the idea of staying here," said Emma, "but it's too close to where we were last seen, even with the chip gone. Besides, staying in France feels . . . wrong."

"Then where?" asked Marie.

Emma considered for a moment before blurting out, "Rome."

Marie's heart sank. "Rome?"

"Yes."

"No."

"Yes. Rome. That's the best option," Emma said.

"I can't be an unwed mother in Rome."

"You wouldn't be. Remember, officially, you're a widow. It's far. Latin is spoken widely, so you can communicate. It's perfect. At least for now." Emma nodded as if it were a done deal.

Charlotte had been watching her daughters as they volleyed, like watching a badminton game. Back and forth.

"There's no . . . with no money . . . how do we even get all the way to Rome?" Marie asked.

"Well, Rome is the destination, but that doesn't mean we get there today. We'll work a bit, earn some money, go a little ways. Then work some more, earn some money, go a bit farther, you get the idea."

Marie considered. She looked to her mother for guidance.

Charlotte looked pensive. Then said, "Okay, let's do it."

When her mother said nothing further, Marie pressed her sister. "Why Rome?"

Emma shrugged. "When no place is truly safe, you can't go back home, and you have to move forward, the appropriate question really becomes, 'Why not Rome?'"

Chapter Thirty-One

It was risky to ask around for free lodging in a city full of desperate people fleeing desperate circumstances, so they didn't even try. Charlotte had enough money with her to get them a room at an inn that night. Since they couldn't risk using electronic payments, as would be required by any reputable place, she found them the nicest place she could that accepted cash and didn't ask questions.

At least it had a door that locked.

The room was dingy; even in the still-light evening, it was shrouded in darkness with only a tiny window, about a foot square with some sort of residue on it that kept out most of the sunlight. Directly under the window was a lumpy bed that would struggle to comfortably fit one person, let alone three. Not much room on either side of it, and no rug on the discolored wooden floor to allow someone to sleep there comfortably either. To the right, a door left ajar revealed a tiny toilet and washbasin.

Marie shut her eyes. This entire room was smaller than her closet at Grayside. She had walked away from that life of luxury and comfort, of status and titles, in hopes of finding something, anything, better. And now she found herself here, in this room, her hip still harboring a dull pain from the surgery. Was it better?

She opened her eyes and saw her mother and her sister. And yes, God yes, it was better. So much better.

Charlotte put on a smile and said that they should try to get settled. Marie limped about. Coming out of anesthesia was exhausting by itself, and too much had happened today. A weight she hadn't known she'd been carrying, a tightness in her stomach that she hadn't known was hurting her, suddenly dissipated, and despite her pain and exhaustion, she felt as light as air.

None of them had clothes but what they were wearing, though they stripped down to their last layers. There was talk of who should use the washbasin first, but in the end, no one did. That could wait until morning. Everything could wait until morning. Charlotte declared herself exhausted, and laid down on the bed in the middle. There was just over a foot of space on each side of her slender frame. She stretched her arms out wide. Marie recognized the invitation and in her shuffling gait she hobbled over and laid her head on her mother's right shoulder. She closed her eyes, sighed, and breathed in her mother's very distinct scent that she had never forgotten. It was real. This had happened. They had made it.

For once, Marie didn't count the seconds. She lay there for a few long moments, maybe even several long minutes, before she heard more shuffling and then a dip in the mattress as Emma nestled in on their mother's other side. Marie's eyes were still closed but she could feel tension leaving her mother's shoulders, like she'd been carrying her disappearance all those years and now, daughters in her arms, they were finally here, as they should be, all together.

Alice's absence was felt. There would have been no room for her, not in the bed, not on her mother's shoulder, not anywhere. And in a way, that was fitting. But Marie grieved for her anyway—for Alice's decision to work against them rather than with them, for her refusal to listen to them, for her damned superiority complex that she used as a shield against her fear that she never quite fit in with the others, for her decision to dive head-first into the life that had been laid out for her and cling to that certainty like a life raft. No matter what Alice said, she couldn't be happily married. Marie didn't know a single person who was.

But Marie forced all those thoughts out of her head. She had read somewhere in the library at Grayside about mindfulness, the concept of not thinking about the past (which could not be changed) or the future (which was still unwritten) in favor of living in and savoring the present. So she decided to do just that. The steady breath of her mother, the warmth of her body, the comforting and familiar feel of her arm around her. The quiet of the room. The watery light coming in through the dingy window. The ache in her hip from the surgery, the bandage wrapped around it, the pain in her feet from walking around. The child growing in her belly, whom she could neither feel nor see yet but knew was there, growing bigger every day. The absence of a chip in her bones to monitor where she was and who she was with—the freedom of being anonymous and lost.

It didn't matter that she was a grown woman. It didn't matter that she'd been married and pregnant and ran away from her marriage and her home and faked her own death. She was a girl who had not fully appreciated how much she had missed her mother until she had her back, and that part of her was ageless. She sank deeper into her mother's side, and Charlotte's arm wrapped around her tighter. Marie could just feel the dampness of a tear that ran down her mother's cheek and into her hair.

She unhinged her jaw and allowed herself to feel relaxed from head to toe, unclenching muscles that she hadn't realized she had tightened, as if in perpetual fight-or-flight mode.

Tomorrow, who knew where they would be? If Marie had her choice, she would stay like this forever, in this sour-smelling room, crammed together in a too-small bed with a too-thin mattress, all three of them snug and comforted and ready to face the world.

Marie had never questioned her decision, and this moment, this time here, sealed it for her. It had all been worth it.

She drew in a deep breath, and was asleep before she exhaled.

For as long as she could remember, Emma had been running away: from her true self, from her family, from Ellthrop, from the shelter, from convents, from men who wished her harm, from women who wished her harm, from her own fears, from her own insecurities. She had been on the run for so long that she had forgotten what it was like to simply lie still and breathe. She wondered if she was even capable of doing it, if her body had any of the necessary muscle memory to simply stop.

She had debated before allowing herself the physical and emotional closeness of lying down with her mother and sister in bed. Two people who had been out of her life for what she had assumed would be forever were suddenly the only two people she had left in the world. Even after Jane had confirmed that their mother was still alive, Emma had refused to let herself believe. She had come to associate family with pain for so long that she couldn't open herself up to the possibility—it was no different than handing someone a knife and then presenting your wrists to be cut.

And now here it was, impossibly real. She couldn't hide behind a shell of doubt anymore. She had to face down what she was truly scared of: love.

In the years since she had run away, Emma had avoided getting close to anyone. She hadn't developed any friendships. All her work had been underground; even her house-cleaning job that she'd taken for the veneer of plausibility to wash the money she got from her illegal work had paid her under the table. Romantic relationships had been out of the question in a country where it was outlawed under both criminal and Church Law. There was nothing but pain in relationships and associations, so she'd never tried.

Lying here, next to her mother and near her sister, she was stiff as a plank and coiled tight as a spring. Here in the dark, with the two people who had loved her the most and whom she had loved the most, she had to admit that the thing she had really been running from all her life was herself.

Her mother's arm wrapped around her and pulled her in a little closer. She pillowed her head on her shoulder and heard her mother's heartbeat. That soft, steady sound was all it took for Emma to shatter.

One tear fell. Then two. She didn't move, didn't start crying, didn't say a word or make a sound. But the tears spilled. Her mother made no reaction except to pull her in a little bit closer. Marie was asleep, her breathing slow and steady. The room was dark, even if it was still daylight. There was safety in this darkness. No one would see. No one would hear. Except her mother. And with that thought, Emma decided to finally, finally, stop running.

Charlotte had lain here for hours, with her daughters curled up sleeping next to her as if they were little girls again. She was exhausted, needed to sleep, but she did not and would not. She had lost so much time; she was not going to miss a single solitary second of her time with them.

So many years had passed. They were women now—grown, old enough to marry, old enough to be pregnant. And yet here, in her arms, they were what they always had been and always would be to her: her babies.

One baby was missing. Alice. *Oh, Alice.* Her arms craved that third baby right now, but she swallowed that pain. She would enjoy what she had. She would not mourn what she did not.

As the years not spent with her children unrolled through her mind like an endless scroll, she asked herself the question that she had never permitted herself to answer or even entertain: Had she made the right choice?

She had always told herself the same story she had told her children: that she'd had no choice; that it had been either leave or be killed; that she couldn't have taken them with her; and that her absence had set them up for the lives they were supposed to have: stable, comfortable, and married to important men. That there would have been no way for her to be there for them, and it was best for her to just step aside. She'd repeated it to herself over and over and over. She'd said the words aloud that very day.

She knew, deep down, every time, that it had been a lie.

She'd regretted walking away almost as soon as she'd done it. She had forced herself to take each step forward, away from her old life and toward the unknown, telling herself that it was the right decision. She had lied to herself every minute of every day ever since.

She'd spent most of her time in Brugge, waiting for them, until she had to flee. She had intended to return to Brugge as soon as she could, waiting each day, hoping that she'd see her daughters again. Of course it had finally happened after she'd left. She should have come back sooner. It probably would have been safe by then.

She finally let herself listen to the words that had been in the background of her life, that she'd become expert at tuning out: *should have, should have, should have, should have, should have.*

Should never have left in the first place.

Should have tried to take her girls with her.

Should have made contact.

Should have taken Emma with her from the shelter.

Should have taken the ferry to Suffolk when she saw the notice of Marie's marriage.

Should have sent Alice a present when she had her first child.

Should have told them the truth herself.

Should have done everything differently.

Charlotte let the mantra play out as she counted the cracks in the ceiling and felt the dried tears on her face and the dampness of where Emma had silently wept into her side.

She let the words and regret wash over her, let them drown her, and then let them recede. When they'd finally dried out, she was resolved.

No more.

Her daughters, clever and resourceful as always she knew they would be, had figured out what she had done. And Charlotte had tracked them down. Too many years wasted, no more time to spend on regrets. Once they left Strasbourg together and were on their way, they would talk, and she would tell them everything.

Chapter Thirty-Two

There was no handbook on how to create an itinerary to get to Rome when you were a refugee traveling under a fake identity while pregnant with a child whose father was still alive and married to you. But Marie was determined to put one together anyway.

Strasbourg had a library in the center of town, near an open-air market that had been set up in the summer sun. The library was across the street from the cathedral and next door to a brothel. It was a former house, built in the medieval half-timbered style, that had been converted from living space into room after room packed floor to ceiling with books. What might once have been a bedroom was now the repository for European, Chinese, and Islamic history. The corridor that led to what had likely been a water closet was a wall of tomes covering the long history of the Church. The former kitchen was now full of scattered tables where a handful of people pored over books, laptop computers, and notebooks. What had been a roasting hearth in a prior century was now packed tightly with bookshelves. There was no easy way to find anything in the library—it wasn't curated in any way, there was no guidance, and it didn't even appear to be alphabetized. But at least many of the books were written in Latin, and after spending enough time perusing all the shelves, Marie found a few titles that would help them make a plan. On the third day, she took up a spot on one of the tables in the no-longer-a-kitchen and dug into a book.

Emma had wanted to leave immediately, to put as much distance between them and their pursuers as possible. But Marie had been tired of running first and planning later. It was too chaotic and stressful, and now they didn't have to actually run anymore. No one was chasing them. Plus, after all this time on the run and after the surgery, she was exhausted. She still walked with a limp. She needed a rest. Emma had found work as a barmaid at a tavern, where she could listen to people discuss their own plans to flee to places of safety now that they'd made it as far as Strasbourg: what routes were relatively easy to get to; which cities would welcome them with open arms versus which would turn them away; countries where you could get by with Latin versus those where you needed to learn the local language; which countries required identification to work and which did not. Useful things, things they would need to know in planning their evacuation. Emma and Marie had blundered into Strasbourg based on nothing more than Marie's research and their own wit. They were going to do this the smart way going forward. Marie accumulated her research material and found a spot to spend her afternoon.

Was there nothing better than getting lost in a book? Rome spread itself out before her as she reviewed. Things weren't as terrible as she had thought they would be there. According to the book she was reading now, Rome had a thriving district for pilgrims around the world. It opened its arms to those who were tired, who were poor, who were helpless and hopeless. It invited them in. It was one of the few places in Europe where Latin was spoken everywhere, not as the second language as it was in most other nations. There were even organizations that would sponsor their trip, on the belief that every good Christian should visit Saint Peter's Basilica and pay their respects to the bones of Saint Peter himself, the first Pope and the rock upon which Jesus Christ Our Lord had built his church. Two millennia on, the Church was still there, indivisible and strong.

Emma had been right. Rome had great potential.

The road to get there, though, was another story.

A boat down the Rhine was not an option to anyone who was not a citizen of France or the Holy Roman Empire. Other foreigners had been banned after a long history of refugees jumping off their boats and onto HRE territory. Based on what Emma reported, their best hope was to somehow get to the South of France and then on a boat to Rome via the island of Corsica and the Kingdom of Sicily. Marie supposed they could get to Switzerland and, having crossed the Alps, get into Genoa and from there to the Papal States. But that overland route was decidedly the riskiest. Marie doubted she could handle much mountain climbing, given her condition. She mentally crossed that option off the list.

So getting into the South of France was to be it, then. It wasn't the safest route, but more so than the others. The least bad option. But if they kept their heads low and acted demurely, they might be able to make the three hundred miles it would take to get to the Mediterranean port. If they did it before the baby came, they could probably avoid detection.

Marie mentally kicked herself again for the loss of the jewelry, which could have funded a plane ticket to Rome directly. She had told Emma that she did not regret it, but now, penniless, she had to admit that Emma had been right to be upset. Things would be difficult, and even if Marie had agreed to leave immediately, they had no funds to do so anyway.

She was poring over the texts for the fifth day in a row when someone sat down across from her at the table. She kept her head down so as not to attract the wrong sort of attention. The person coughed, revealing himself to be a man, and she whispered "God bless you" without looking up.

The man coughed again. She chanced a small look, then snapped her head up.

"Dirk!"

Jane's son smiled and nodded. He looked more tired than he had when she had last seen him on the train. That had only been just over a week ago, and he looked like he'd aged several years in that short amount of time. "I'm glad to see you made it safely here," he said.

"Not as glad as I am to see you. We were so worried, and even in the midst of that chaos, you managed to give us a clue!"

"Without context, I'm sure it wasn't the least bit helpful."

Marie shrugged. "We made it."

"My mother will be pleased to hear it."

Another patron looked over and glared at them. They were being noisy, and Marie suddenly felt bad. She began gathering up her notes. "Let's get out of here, yeah? Find a place we can talk."

Dirk nodded and held out his hands to carry her books and papers. Marie gratefully handed them over. She hadn't realized until that moment how much she had been doing for herself, versus what her life had been before. Before she'd left Grayside, she'd never carried any of her own bags, trays, or other belongings, and truth be told, it was still unfamiliar to have her hands occupied all the time. Her entire life, she'd lived in homes with enough wealth to pay someone to do such menial tasks. Her husband, James, had even hired someone whose sole job was to go to his closet and bring out a selection of clothes for him to wear each day. Marie wondered if he'd ever been inside the closet himself. She remembered asking James once why he called for the valet every time he wanted a pair of socks and didn't just get them on his own. He'd snapped at her, "Because that's what he's paid to do." And that had been the end of her asking James any questions.

Dirk and Marie stepped out onto the street.

"What happened to you after the train?" she asked him.

He shook his head. "Let's not talk about it while we walk, yeah? You know? You never know who might be listening here."

Marie nodded. He'd probably done this before with the others he and his mother had helped.

"Where should we go?" she asked.

She watched him consider for a few moments before he asked her, "Where are you staying?"

It was the most inappropriate request, even if she knew there was no inappropriate reasoning behind it. A gentleman simply didn't ask himself into a woman's private home.

"Sorry," he said with a blush. "In Flanders, that isn't a strange question. People go to each other's homes all the time. But I forgot it's different in England."

Marie felt embarrassed to reply for some reason.

Dirk looked around for a few more moments before gesturing toward a bench that faced the river. It was a nice day, full of people taking advantage of the sun to sit and soak it in. The bench was secluded enough that they could speak yet also out in the open. Dirk looked around a bit nervously, which prompted Marie to do the same. They sat on the bench, spaced an appropriate number of inches apart. Dirk set her stack of books and notes in between them, and that boundary made Marie feel more safe.

"Is everything all right?" she asked.

Dirk looked around once more and shook his head, no. She could see a bead of sweat on his forehead.

She dropped her voice to a whisper. "What's wrong?"

A crow cawed as it flew overhead. A group of teenagers huddled together on the grass laughed uproariously at something that someone in their group had just said. A man walking behind them began cursing in French at the person he was speaking to on the phone.

Dirk swallowed, then responded. "That man who was after you on the train."

"John Hart?"

"Yes. He found us. After I got back to Brugge."

Marie's hands flew to her mouth.

"He came to our home. He found my mother."

Tears formed in her eyes and threatened to spill over. "Did he hurt her?"

Dirk swallowed. "She got away, thankfully. She's in hiding in Brugge. She had to destroy her phone. She'll be fine; Brugge is an easy city to get lost in when you want to. But she was—she *is*—concerned for your safety. She asked me to come here to make sure that you'd gotten to Strasbourg via the underground that I'd hinted at. And . . ." Here he paused for breath. He was shaking. Marie could only imagine what he'd been through, how difficult it had been to get here, given the number of borders he'd have to cross. "And she wants to be sure that you connected with your mother."

Marie instinctively reached for Dirk's hand but drew it back. Touching would cross a line. "After all of that, she's still concerned for us?"

Dirk nodded.

"That's . . . that's so kind of her. And you. It must have been difficult to get here, and to find us."

"I've been looking for a few days," he admitted. "There was no real way to reach you anymore."

"I'm glad you kept looking," Marie said. "We might have already been gone, but I convinced them to stay for a few days so we could properly plan before we went on. Maybe with you here we can finish the plan."

"You said 'them,'" he pointed out. He looked hopeful.

Marie nodded. Her face broke into a grin, and the tears finally spilled over. "We found her, Dirk. It worked. You did it. We can never repay you for what you've given us."

He shook his head. "That was you. You figured it out. We just provided a small bit of assistance once you arrived, is all."

"No, it was so much more."

"No," Dirk insisted. "You figured out that your mother was still alive. You obtained the identification necessary to leave the country. You came to us without warning, and you got on the train and continued to your destination. And you got to Strasbourg on your own. That is all . . . it's such an accomplishment. I wish my mother were here with me to see it."

"Why didn't she come with you?" Marie asked. "Wouldn't she be safer here?"

"She wanted to," Dirk said. His voice was strained, like he was trying to impress upon her how much he meant what he was saying. "But it was hard enough for me to get here, and with that man following her . . . best if both of us weren't trying to cross a border. So she sent me."

Marie put her hand to her heart.

He gave her an intense look and dropped his voice. "I know I caught you off guard by asking if we could go to the place where you're staying, and I apologize for my rudeness. It was abrupt and inappropriate."

Marie nodded. "I'm sorry that I reacted the way I did. You have to understand, people don't just say things like that where we're from. So you caught me completely by surprise. I think . . . I think it would be fine. And I know my mother would love to see you, and love to even talk to Jane. Perhaps they could do a phone call or video call while you're there?"

Dirk nodded. "We'll see what we can manage, and what's safe at the time." He paused. "So . . . it would be okay if I went there?"

Marie flashed a smile. "Yes, I think it would be more than okay." She stood up. "We could go now if you want. Everyone should be back now."

Dirk stood and picked her books and notes up again. "Please lead the way."

Chapter Thirty-Three

From where she stood in the hallway, there was no noise behind the closed door, but Marie knew that her mother and sister would be in there. Marie knocked twice in rapid succession, then twice slowly, then quickly three more times. It was the secret knock they had come up with to let the others know it was safe to open the door to their shared room. Perhaps a bit silly, but Marie had insisted.

Emma opened the door a crack to confirm that it was Marie, then opened it wider. Her eyes opened widest of all when she saw that Marie was not alone. "Dirk!" she cried. She stepped aside to let him in. "What are you doing here?" She turned around. "Mother, did you see?"

Charlotte had been combing some hair out of her face in the wash-basin. "Dirk!" She crossed the room and took his hands in hers. Her eyes shone. "It's good to see you."

"You as well." Dirk squeezed her hands back and appeared to swallow down his own emotion. "I was so pleased to find Marie, and to learn that you had all arrived safely. It was a close call, back there on the train. I had no time to give you what little warning I could. And knowing you would be in FFC, where they're downright hostile to English people, and you didn't know where to go or who to ask for help . . . well, as I said, I'm so pleased that it worked out."

"What brings you here?" Charlotte asked.

Dirk filled her in on his mother's situation. Emma narrowed her eyes, while Charlotte put her hand to her heart.

"Why didn't she just call our mother?" Emma asked.

"I told you," said Dirk. "She had to abandon her phone. She's in hiding. That man, John Hart, came after her. She lost her contacts. But she still fears for your safety."

"She is a good friend," said Charlotte. "She has always held our family's well-being high in her esteem. Few people walk through this earth with a friend so dear as her."

"But you came all the way here?" Emma asked. She crossed her arms. "All the way from Brugge?"

"Yes," he said. "It was worth it, to see you."

"Isn't it amazing?" Marie asked. "He found us all the way here, and wanted to ensure we were all right."

Dirk blushed and fiddled with his phone, looking like he was trying to take a photo.

"What are you doing?" Emma asked. "You keep playing with your phone."

"I—I'm sorry. I'm trying to take a photo of the three of you to send to my mother. I just want to put her mind at ease."

"We can just pose for one," Marie said. She gestured for her mother and sister to join her. "Though we certainly don't look our best."

"Why don't we do a video call?" Emma asked. "I'd love to see her."

"I agree," said Charlotte. "It would be lovely to see her, hear her voice. Maybe you could give me her new number?"

Dirk nodded. "I know that she would love nothing more. But let me text her first, to make certain that it is safe."

"But—"

"Imagine if you'd had a call to answer in that train compartment. Wouldn't that have made things worse?"

Emma nodded with a sigh, conceding the point. "Yes, of course," she said.

Dirk lifted his phone. "Let me do that now."

"But could you take our photo?" Marie asked. "Just . . . we haven't had one since we were children."

"Of course."

"I'll go get my phone," said Charlotte.

"I'm happy to take it with mine," said Dirk.

Charlotte looked to Marie, who looked to Emma, who paused a second or two before nodding. Then both Marie and Charlotte nodded.

Dirk indicated with his hands that the three should stand together. Charlotte stood in the middle, a daughter on either side, just as they had fallen asleep that first night in here. Dirk snapped the photo.

"Thank you," he said. "It looks good."

"Can I see it?" Marie asked, gesturing to the phone. Dirk nodded and showed her the photo. Marie felt a swell of emotion she could not name. There it was, proof that this was real. It was their first picture together in decades. And it was the only photo they had ever taken in which they were all smiling. They all smiled so rarely, she realized. Marie couldn't believe how much it transformed their faces.

She gulped. "Would you send us a copy?"

Dirk nodded. "Of course."

Before she could stop herself, Marie reached out and clutched Dirk's hand. It was something she would never have done in England. "Thank you," she said.

"It is the very least I can do." He tapped at the phone a few times. "There, I've messaged her. Now we wait to see if she can talk."

Charlotte motioned for him to sit on a corner of the bed, but he shook his head. "Tell us about your journey," Charlotte said. "Or would you prefer to sleep? You must be tired."

Dirk nodded. "Yes, it's been a harrowing few days." He held the phone in a vise grip. "But no, I don't need to sleep."

"Well!" Charlotte clapped her hands together. "If you won't sleep, then you must let us at least feed you. There's a tavern around the corner where Emma has been working, and they offer discounted meals. It's not fancy but it's at least edible. Let us take you. No argument." She pointed to the door. "Let's go."

Once they were seated with their meal of watery stew at a dank table in the grimy tavern, Marie looked at Dirk apologetically. "I'm sorry it's not more."

Dirk took a hearty spoonful. "It's exactly what I need," he said. "You're too kind."

"It's the very least we could do," Marie said. "After all you've done for us. And all that you and your mother sacrificed for us."

"I'm glad Jane was able to get out," said Charlotte. "She was always so resourceful."

Dirk nodded. "That she is."

"I don't know what I would have done without her," Charlotte continued. "The way she helped me all those years, helping me escape, disappear. It's no wonder she was able to do the same."

"She did put a lot on the line for you," Dirk agreed. "Prioritized you over everything else."

"It was very selfless of her." Charlotte gave a small smile. "I don't know what I did to deserve a friend like her. At Ellthrop she was my only friend, and stood in my place to raise my girls when I no longer could. Then later, after she moved to Brugge herself, we were equals. It was a time for which I will always be grateful. I needed a friend, and someone who could teach me to live independently. I had no idea how. Those years with her were among the best of my life, and I hope we'll be able to return at some point, when things have died down."

Dirk smiled. "If it's one day possible, I would welcome it. And I know she would too."

"No sense in dwelling on things that are impossible," Emma said. She picked at her stew with a wooden spoon, ladling it up and then dropping it back into her bowl.

"What's the matter?" Marie asked Emma.

"Nothing."

Before Marie could push further, Dirk jumped. His phone was buzzing. He swiftly accepted the call, and the flushed face of Jane filled his screen. "Mama!" He rushed out the doors. Marie, Charlotte, and

Emma followed. They found him around the side of the building, speaking to Jane in rapid Dutch.

Jane smiled at her son through the pixels. "Heb je het gedaan?" She sounded like she had been crying.

Dirk nodded, tears in his eyes. "Ja."

"Hoe kon je? Ik had je gezegd, om dat niet te doen!"

"Hoe kon ik niet? Je hebt ze al alles gegeven. Ik liet ze je leven niet nemen."

Next to her, Charlotte furrowed her brow.

Jane sighed and then with a shuddering breath said, "Laat me ze zien."

Dirk nodded and angled the phone toward everyone. They crowded together to drink in Jane's face. She looked upset, but otherwise safe.

"Are you all right?" Marie asked.

"What happened?" Asked Emma.

Charlotte said more evenly, "Jane, what's the matter?"

Jane huffed a breath. "I'm so relieved to see all of you."

"Not as relieved as we are to see you," said Marie. "Dirk told us what happened. He had us so worried about you. Can you tell us where you are?"

"Of course she can't," Emma hissed. "She's in hiding. It might not even be safe for her to talk now."

"It's good to see you, Mama," Dirk said. "We shouldn't talk here, in public. We'll call you later."

Before she could respond, Dirk ended the call. "Let's go back," he said. "I'm worried about someone here seeing her. You never know, right? Let's go back to your room, we can call her from there."

"Very well," Charlotte stood. "Let's go." Without another word, she led them out of the tavern. They stood outside the door to their room a few minutes later. Charlotte was expressionless. No worry about Jane, no particular concern about anything.

It wasn't until Charlotte put the key in the lock that Marie realized that after years of living in Brugge, her mother probably understood Dutch.

"I just want you to know," Charlotte said to Dirk, "that I forgive you."

She turned the key.

"Girls, *run!*"

Emma grabbed Marie's hand and tried to take off, but Dirk grabbed them by the arms and pulled them back. Charlotte scrabbled over to try to free them, but Dirk shoved her away.

"I'm sorry," he said. "I had no choice."

The door flew open from the inside.

John Hart stood in the doorframe with a gun pointed at them.

Chapter Thirty-Four

Marie reeled back and tried to run, but Dirk's hand on her arm was firm. He yanked her and Emma toward the doorway. John Hart stepped back to let them in. Charlotte stood there, motionless, eyes locked with John Hart.

"The late Countess Kenfield," John Hart said. "It's been a long time."

"Indeed," Charlotte said. "You look more like your mother every day."

"All these years you've been running," he said. "It was only a matter of time before you were caught."

"No one was chasing me," said Charlotte.

"An oversight," said John Hart. "And you know why." He turned to Marie. "And the late Duchess of Suffolk, following in your mother's disgraceful footsteps. You took something that doesn't belong to you." And then to Emma. "And your sister, with her unnatural proclivities."

Emma tried to pull away from Dirk, but he held firm.

"What are you doing?" Emma asked.

"I didn't lie to you," Dirk said. "He did take my mother. He threatened us, held my mother hostage until I led him to you. He knew that we knew you and were helping you."

"How?" Marie asked.

Dirk didn't answer.

Marie's stomach sank. "The chip. They saw us staying with you in Brugge." They had been so fixated on being currently tracked in FFC, they had not stopped to consider that they had been tracked the entire time in Brugge.

"He was very keen to assist," said John Hart.

"My mother gave her entire life for you and your family," said Dirk. "We were both abandoned by our mothers. But your mother abandoning you meant that my mother had to pick up the pieces. She left me to take care of you."

"Dirk . . . ," Charlotte said.

"You never thought about how selfish your decisions were," said Dirk. "You only thought of yourself, always. My mother will never say it, but I know she feels that way. How could she not? She gave up her child in favor of yours."

"I don't have time for this," John Hart said. "Bring her over to me," he commanded, pointing at Marie with the gun. Dirk led her over, and John Hart's vise grip replaced Dirk's.

"Don't hurt my daughters," said Charlotte.

"Don't worry about us," said Emma.

"You don't have to force me," said Marie. "I'll go back. Willingly."

"No!" cried Charlotte. "You can't go back."

"It's fine. Please, leave them alone," said Marie. "I'm the one you want. I'm the one who ran away, and you're right, I took my husband's property with me. I left without his permission. Take me back. But don't hurt my mother and my sister. They're innocent in this."

John Hart smiled like a snake. "You seem so sure about that."

"Just, please. I'll go with you. I'll go back to Grayside. But don't hurt my family."

"I won't," said John Hart. "But they aren't your family anymore."

He pointed the gun at Charlotte's stomach and fired.

Chapter Thirty-Five

According to Gilbert Wainwright's *A History of China*, citing the recently translated Chinese book *Classified Essentials of the Mysterious Tao of the True Origin of Things* and Roger Bacon's *De nullitate magiæ*, gunpowder was invented in China in the ninth century AD as a means of seeking immortality. It was first used in warfare within a century, and it was called flying fire. Like a virus, it spread along great trade routes: from China to the Mongolian Empire to the Islamic Empire and, though the details of when and where and how were never recorded, it made its way to Europe and, eventually, England. Each time, this attempted elixir of eternal life was made only for causing death.

August Howard's *Weaponry through the Ages* discussed how gunpowder transformed murder so that guns could permit someone to kill their target from far away, without risking a sword or knife returning the favor. Howard said that bullets travel at over eighteen hundred miles per hour and can travel up to fifty yards. You could kill a person without having to look them in the eye. Suddenly, taking a person's life required no greater effort than swatting a fly.

Some of the most famous deaths in English history were from the piercing of a bullet. King Phillip III's youngest son, Prince Raleigh, in a duel. The singer Rose Randolph in a robbery. The Viscountess Tillman Mullaney, along with her lover, Joseph Sherwood, by her husband.

An average of thirteen Londoners were killed by guns each year, according to the *Times*. Of those, ten were typically killed by a family member, while the remainder were someone who was known to the victim. On average.

An old edition of *Green's Anatomy* stated that a person shot in the abdomen could die within a few minutes or a few days. Or not at all. The sooner medical attention was provided, the better. But in a refugee area like Strasbourg, legitimate medical services were hard to find. And they had no money left.

Books could teach you so much. But they could never prepare you for the reality of watching your mother bleed to death in front of you.

◆　◆　◆

Emma tore herself from Dirk's grip and ran to her mother. She threw herself over her, whispering apologies, while Charlotte struggled to shush her. Marie tried to do the same, but John Hart wrapped his arm around her waist to keep her from running.

Emma ran bloody hands through Charlotte's hair. Her face cracked open and she began to sob.

Marie screamed and tried to make her way to her mother and sister, but John Hart's grip was unyielding. Emma could hear her sister struggling but did not dare take her eyes off their mother.

Dirk looked at John Hart with wild eyes. "You swore you wouldn't hurt them!"

"You got what you wanted. Your mother is safe," said John Hart to Dirk. "Our bargain is complete."

◆　◆　◆

Marie struggled, but John Hart's grip tightened even more. She tried to bite him, and he hit her on the side of the head with the barrel of his gun. Her vision went black and full of stars, but she remained on the right side of consciousness. She remained aware but powerless to go to her mother. Powerless to apologize: for not searching for her sooner, for not being the son that could have changed everything, for not leaving Strasbourg days ago. For going to Jane, which had triggered all of this. Marie went limp as a rag doll, and the grief and regret weighed her down. She opened her mouth to try to vocalize all of this, but it just came out as a guttural wail.

"Don't make me hurt you," said John Hart.

Dirk ran to Charlotte's other side. Charlotte's breath gurgled, and her body went rigid then limp as she went into shock. Emma was sobbing and making her own apologies for things that didn't matter anymore.

"But I have my other orders."

John Hart pointed the gun at Emma and fired. She fell to the ground with a cry.

"Emma!" cried Marie. She tried again to go to her family, but John Hart stopped her again. Dirk made to attack John Hart, but he pointed the gun at Dirk.

"It makes no difference to me whether you live or die," said John Hart to Dirk, "so don't give me a reason to pull the trigger. It costs me nothing more than a bullet."

Dirk stopped, looked conflicted for a moment, and then went back to Emma. Emma was sobbing but conscious. For now. Charlotte had stopped moving.

"Remember," John Hart said to Dirk. "You didn't see anything or hear anything. Ever. If you forget that, you know that I know where to find you."

Dirk shuddered, then nodded shakily. He took Emma's hand, and she pulled it away just before she went limp herself.

"Let's go," said John Hart to Marie, sounding bored. "I think you've caused quite enough of a fuss."

Chapter Thirty-Six

Emma felt the life leaching out of her, one heartbeat at a time. It was like a countdown timer, only she didn't know how many moments she had left. Was it minutes, or only seconds? She didn't know. And at the moment, she didn't care. What was there to live for now, with her mother dead and her sister taken back to the prison that she'd finally escaped?

There was no clock in the room, but she could hear the seconds ticking away nevertheless. In her childhood, their father had always been so meticulous and made it clear that spending time with his children was a burden. So there was always a time limit. Every moment spent in the presence of her father was measured and counted. Tick, tick, tick. Every one of those seconds was spent in fear: fear of disappointing him, fear he would not love her, fear he would hurt her. She'd become accustomed to counting them—first as a means of trying to stretch out the time, and then as a means to assure herself that this, too, would be over. She had counted the seconds ever since. And now, here she was, in the final countdown.

Damn Marie. Damn her for making her have a family again. If she'd died without reconnecting, it would have been clean. Neat. Easy. It was why she'd kept herself out of reach from everyone starting from the moment she ran away from home. The less you were attached to, the less there was to mourn when the end finally came. You were a feather on the wind and could be carried away, wherever made the most sense.

Mere survival had few perks, but there was something to be said for just muddling through rather than trying to do something. Mere survival meant that you never failed until the end.

This could have been her sole failure. Instead, it was just the most recent.

She had now lost her mother twice. She had far preferred the first: her mother was there one day, then gone the next. Out of sight and eventually out of mind. But watching it happen? That was far worse. Especially since it wasn't clear to Emma why her mother had to die. John Hart had already taken Marie. What did the rest of them matter?

Her own injuries? An afterthought. The only two people she loved were now gone, truly gone, with no chance for further reconciliation. Best to get on with dying now. If she could have laughed at herself, she would have. Emma Kenfield, English until the very end.

Emma felt the blood emptying her not just of life but of regret. As much as she'd cut herself off from everyone and everything for her own self-preservation, she regretted that she had done it, and that it had been necessary in the first place. She hadn't wanted to admit it to her mother, her sister, or even herself, but she'd never felt more alive than when she'd reconnected with them. For just a few short, beautiful days that had led to her losing everything, including, her life.

Had it been worth it?

She took a shaking breath, which she thought was probably her last. She exhaled.

Absolutely. She would have done it again in a heartbeat.

She felt weightless. It wasn't like drowning. It was letting go.

It wasn't so bad.

She heard voices from the past echo all around her. The din of voices, as if she were walking through a crowded room full of everyone from her life. No distinct words could be heard, though the occasional laugh or exclamation could be identified. Her mother, her sisters. Jane. The Earl. Her stepmother. Her brother. Voices of people she'd had various dealings with, both aboveboard and under the table. Even Dirk's voice was there, which she batted away in her head. This was all his fault. He couldn't come with her. He didn't belong here.

She was sinking deeper and deeper while simultaneously floating farther and farther away. It felt like hands were cradling her and taking her wherever she was going next. It felt safe. It felt warm. It felt like home.

She let herself be carried away.

Chapter Thirty-Seven

Marie didn't remember John Hart carrying her through the streets of Strasbourg, where a man carrying a struggling woman through the street would hardly merit a glance. She didn't remember him throwing her into the back seat of a waiting car. She didn't remember John Hart loading her onto the private plane that the Dowager Duchess had arranged for them, which had been sitting in Brugge until Dirk had texted his mother the photo of the three of them, along with their location. She didn't remember the short flight back to England. She didn't remember being taken from the small airfield and into another car that took her back to Grayside, which looked and felt like a graveside more than ever.

But there were things that she did remember. She remembered the feeling as if she herself had been split open the moment the bullet from John Hart's gun had pierced her mother's body. She remembered the look in Emma's eyes, and how the bullet had shattered the wall she'd built around herself. She remembered falling forward and down, starting from the moment they had all realized that Dirk had betrayed them, all the way until now. She still felt like she was falling. And there was no one to catch her.

She fell through her reentry into Grayside, not by way of the grand double doors of mahogany that were as old as the family title itself, but rather via the back entrance through which coal had been shoveled for centuries. The Duchess of Suffolk was tossed through here like the rest of the material that was meant to be discarded after use. Burned until there was nothing left of her but smoke and ash.

She followed in a daze. There was no point in fighting. She'd left to save herself, save her child. Now, she'd lost her mother and her sister. She'd lost her hope. All that she had left was her baby, and she knew that she would certainly lose it too. There was no way she'd be allowed to raise it. They would see to that.

Marie blinked and found herself in a room in Grayside that she didn't recognize. It was small, the walls yellowed with age; a bed with a thin woolen blanket, a washbasin, and no windows. Marie had been so blinded with grief that she wasn't even sure where in the house she might be. She thought it might be part of the downstairs portion, where the servants lived and worked and never pestered those who lived above-stairs unless they were providing some sort of service. When they did their jobs well, they were like ghosts. A fire lit, food prepared, drapes opened, clothes laundered and laid out, baths drawn? Someone did all those things. Now here she was, living among the ghosts.

She ran her hand over the blanket, as if stroking the fur of a pet. It was the only solid thing in her life.

Absently, she rubbed her stomach. It was still far too early for her to show, but she knew that the baby would begin to make itself known, proudly announcing itself to the world at large. Marie would be just the vessel for its growth. She'd never get to be its mother.

She heard someone clear their throat. She looked up. When she saw who it was, she instinctively sat up straighter.

There she was.

The Dowager Duchess.

Marie studied the Dowager Duchess's face in a way she never had before. The resemblance wasn't there, superficially. The years had carved their way into the Dowager Duchess's face so deeply that even the cosmetic surgery she'd had done couldn't fully erase them. Her hair was coiffed and styled so that not a single strand dared stray. It was like a general's helmet. Her bearing was regal; she was the type of person who always seemed so much taller than they really were. She wore clothes that, even from a distance, obviously cost a lot of money and were made from fabrics that most people were not fit to even touch.

John Hart, by comparison, had a servant's bearing—always standing at attention, as if awaiting his commanding officer's order and eager to pass inspection.

But the predators' eyes that washed over Marie to find her weakness? The way they reduced one to a quivering mass with a single disdainful look? Yes, Marie saw it now. And she wondered how she'd never seen it before. She'd been taken in by the superficial differences and hadn't probed beneath the surface.

"So," said the Dowager Duchess coolly. "You're back."

Marie's arm instinctively wrapped around her belly.

"Yes," said the Dowager Duchess. "We know all about that." She took a step closer and stared down her nose at her daughter-in-law. One Duchess of Suffolk to another, and the ranking wasn't even close.

Yet something rose inside Marie. She was beaten, but she needed answers. She needed to understand. The Dowager Duchess could give her at least that much.

"Why did you bring me back?" asked Marie.

"Do you really not understand?"

"I really don't," said Marie, finding her courage blooming within her like a red tide. "James can have another child. Lord knows that he has no shortage of women waiting to replace me. I'm conveniently dead. There was no reason to bring me back."

The Dowager Duchess had never laughed as long as Marie had ever known her. Marie had long thought that she no longer knew how to laugh. Perhaps she had once, and the muscles had atrophied. When something surprised the Dowager Duchess, she raised her eyebrows a fraction of an inch. When something amused her, she minutely lifted the corner of her collagen-filled lips. And when she hosted a dignitary, she softened her jaw and widened her eyes. The Dowager Duchess did not laugh, not in front of anyone.

But here, now, in this unknown room, the Dowager Duchess laughed. It was the bark of a seal and the caw of a rook, the screech of nails on a blackboard, all in one. It was the bray of the souls in hell. It was a slap across the face by a hand with sharp nails that sliced your skin and left a sting. It was the stained glass wall of a cathedral shattering into a thousand pieces—something timeless and beautiful and holy being destroyed. Marie reared back from the sound, pressed her hand tighter to her stomach. It was a sound she never wanted to hear again.

"Oh," said the Dowager Duchess. "You believe this is about your spawn?"

The Dowager Duchess walked over to the bed and sat down next to Marie. The bed sank next to her. The temperature plummeted. Marie held her breath, certain that if she dared to exhale, her breath would be visible.

"My dear," said the Dowager Duchess, "none of this has been about you."

Chapter Thirty-Eight

"You have just spent some time with your mother, so there is no doubt that she has shared a suspicion that John Hart is more than a garden-variety servant." The Dowager Duchess gave Marie a side-eye look, and Marie was too afraid to even think about denying it.

"John Hart was born in a convent under circumstances that no longer matter. There was great interest in ensuring he had a loving home to grow up in, and his mother urgently and desperately wanted him to be raised far enough away that no one would know their relationship, but also to be raised in a manner that befit his status as the son of a high-born young lady. Such a thing happens, but it is difficult. Secrecy and trust is paramount.

"John Hart's young mother was fortunate to have a friend who was devoted to her. Not in an unnatural sense, but like a sister. And when John Hart's mother found herself in her predicament, she took to a nunnery, as was the custom, for her confinement. While there, a novice from a good family, the youngest daughter of a life-peer baronet, befriended her, helped her through the darkest moments of her life. John Hart's mother knew that she could never keep him or raise him, and it was essential that she give birth under wraps and return to her life so that she might debut with other young women before the Queen that season. That novice was there every step of the way. When she became consumed with her fears and emotions, the novice had the good sense to hold her hand and slap her across the face so that she could focus on the important next steps she must take.

"The child was born, and his mother was faced with giving him up. She had spent her confinement steeling herself for what must come, but when faced with having to do it, she had a moment of weakness.

"The novice understood. And as she always had, she knew what to do. She left the convent and took the child back to her home to be raised by her family. The family gave the child their own surname and fabricated a relationship that would fool anyone who looked at him. There was no visible trace of his true parentage.

"The novice and the young mother remained in discreet correspondence for years. The novice kept the young mother apprised of her son's progress, in such a way that no one who read the letters would know what they were reading. There was no connection between the novice and the mother, and no way to trace them back together.

"The novice ended up leaving the convent before taking her final vows. She'd never wanted to be there, and the boy gave her a sense of purpose. She wanted a family and life of her own, but while she was from a good family, she was not from a titled or landed family, so her options for a husband were limited to her own class. But the now former novice had grander ambitions for herself, and once the boy was grown, the novice named her price for her discretion and her work ensuring that he had been raised right. She knew that his mother, now married to a man at the highest level, would do anything to keep her secret buried, and her price was high. Her price was that she wanted to marry a titled gentleman. But not just any titled gentleman. She wanted an Earl, the shooting friend of her father's who already had a wife."

Marie's stomach sank, but she didn't dare interrupt or move a muscle.

"She began as his mistress. It was all very indiscreet at first: against a tree during a shooting party, or in a closet during a dance. She described their intimate encounters as wicked. She said that he loved the idea of defiling something sacred. Of all his mistresses, she swiftly became his favorite. It was all so sinful, she said she could just taste it. They both found it an irresistible aphrodisiac.

"And then she became pregnant.

"This was not cause for concern. This Earl had sired a number of illegitimate children over the years. But time was ticking away. He had no heir, and he needed one soon.

"The former novice said she would have the child and would make its paternity known. And the Earl, well, he embraced the idea. His wife had given him only daughters, no sons. This young woman could give him the son he'd needed. He could not let his brother inherit the Earldom. So he knew he had to somehow get out of his marriage. He had never hidden his dalliances with others from his wife; indeed, he'd been rather open about it. He amplified the affair, drove his wife to insanity until she did the honorable thing and ended her life. And thus Louise Goodman became the next Countess Kenfield. And just a few short months after the wedding, she gave the Earl what he'd always needed and wanted: a son and heir."

The Dowager Duchess gripped the blanket with her clawed hand.

"For twenty years this arrangement worked. Until the day, six months ago, when the Earl and Countess Kenfield went to Zeebrugge. They had never been. They stepped off the ferry, and immediately saw something impossible. The Earl's late wife, the former Countess Kenfield, very much alive and well. Standing on the deck. Staring at them both. Like she was a ghost, reminding them of their sin.

"The sight of her scared your father to death. He suffered his heart attack as soon as his eyes found the eyes of your mother. They stared at each other until his heart gave out. In the commotion, she vanished."

Marie suppressed a smile at her mother's final revenge. She couldn't decide whether it was her father's cowardice or her mother's courage that had killed him. She decided it didn't matter.

Oh, if only Emma were here to listen to this.

"Countess Kenfield returned home, buried her husband, and watched her son inherit the Earldom. He made for an excellent master of Ellthrop, just as she'd always hoped he would.

"The problem was, with your mother still alive, he was a bastard, just like the other children that her husband had sired with women to whom he was not legally married.

"In an instant, it was clear what would happen if anyone else knew your mother was still alive. The Countess's entire life would fall apart.

"We were all very content to let *you* go. But there was the matter of your brother demanding the Kenfield jewelry back. We searched and realized it was all missing. The sapphire engagement ring, a highly distinctive piece, might have appeared on the black market. And then we learned about the child you carried. Your husband's child. So I sent the person I trusted most to investigate. And he found you in Brugge, and saw who you had been in touch with. He understood the implications. He alerted me."

The Dowager Duchess released her grip.

"We were content to let the child go. We were content to let the jewels go. But knowing that your mother was alive, and that you knew and were going to find her . . . that was too great a risk. Your mother had to be eliminated, officially and completely, so that your brother's succession to the Earldom cannot be questioned. Louise could not allow that, and after what she did for John Hart and his mother, I cannot allow that to happen to her. Questions are problematic. Questions lead to trouble. So questions must not be asked. All loose ends must be tied up."

She stood up and made for the door.

"That's what this was all about? Not the jewels or your grandchild. It was to stop them from spilling your dirty secret?"

The Dowager Duchess glared. "I didn't kill anyone."

"You know what I mean."

"I think it is your dirty secret that could not be allowed to be shared, and that dirty secret is the fact that your useless mother lived. That loose end needed to be tied up. And it was. Neatly."

"What about Dirk? And Jane? They know too."

The Dowager Duchess shrugged. "With what proof? John Hart saw to that. He is . . ." The Dowager Duchess appeared to swell with the closest thing to motherly pride that Marie had ever seen in her. "He is impeccable."

"Is that what I am too? A loose end?" Marie asked.

The Dowager Duchess turned around. She moved that corner of her perfect mouth ever so slightly.

"You're here so that you cannot share what you know with anyone. And as long as we have you, we might as well wait until we know whether you're carrying my son's heir. If you are, that son can easily become my son's child with his new wife. For, of course, he's already found a new Duchess, though they haven't been to the Church yet. Insurance, you know, just in case the new Duchess proves as useless as you at the one thing you were born to do."

"He'll never agree to that," Marie said.

The Dowager Duchess barked that horrible laugh again.

"My dear, he will do as he is told, just as you will. You know that he will."

"And then, what, I just give my son up?"

The Dowager Duchess raised her eyebrows a fraction of an inch. "Can you not figure it out? You're the loose end, after all."

Marie gulped. "And if I'm carrying a daughter?"

The Dowager Duchess barked her horrible laugh again, turning the blood in Marie's veins to ice.

"Use your imagination."

She left, slammed the door behind her. The sound of the key turning in the lock was deafening and final.

Chapter Thirty-Nine

Marie couldn't tell if days or weeks or months passed while she was in that room, with no windows and a door she couldn't open. No way of knowing whether it was morning or night. She could only measure time by counting her heartbeats and by the swell of her belly, which grew firmer and larger each day. It was still small enough to not be obtrusive, and could be hidden under her clothes. But she knew that wouldn't last for long.

Her baby was growing, and she was alone. She wanted her mother more than ever.

Food was delivered by anonymous servants who kept their heads down. They retrieved the empty plates. They never responded to Marie, no matter how often she tried to speak to them, to tell them who she was, to ask who they were, to ask what day it was, to ask if she could see her husband, see her mother-in-law, see a doctor, see *anyone*. They slipped away, silent. Her requests were never granted, even if they were passed on.

She would lie back and rub her belly, contemplating this child whom she was destined never to know. She would think about her mother, and in the privacy of the room, she would cry. She no longer had access to books, so she escaped into fantasy. Charlotte would have loved being a grandmother. And Emma . . . Emma would have shed some of her defenses to help her care for the child, just as she had done when she agreed to join Marie on their failed escape. Marie knew in her bones that it would have been wonderful to raise that baby together, all three of them. They could have had the family she'd been denied.

If it was a girl, she would have named her Alice, just to make her family whole again. Perhaps that would have defrosted some of Alice's hostility, and she would have made overtures toward them again.

Alice. Poor Alice. Least loved by herself. Least appreciated by herself. Overlooked by everyone. Forgotten by everyone. Maybe even by John Hart.

Marie sat up.

Forgotten by everyone.

Maybe even by John Hart.

Alice had been sent to find them. The Dowager Duchess never mentioned her.

Was Alice safe? Had she also been tied up as a loose end?

Would learning that her sister and mother were truly dead make a difference to her now? Could it change her thought?

Could Marie reach out to her? Get her a message? Would Alice even accept it? And if she did, would she do anything to help Marie? Their last meeting hadn't exactly ended well.

Marie searched around the room. Bed. Washbasin. Toilet. No window. A locked door. A small air vent, too small for her to even consider squeezing through, especially since she was destined only to become larger with each day.

And anonymous servants who came in to serve her. The only time the door was ever opened or closed, if only for a few seconds.

Did Marie have it in her?

Could she do it?

She knew that she had to. Knew deep in her marrow that she was carrying a daughter. As the baby became more of a reality than an idea,

Marie's awareness grew. She couldn't feel her child move yet, but she knew, somehow, that it was a daughter.

Marie owed it to her.

She paced the small corner of the room.

Could she do it?

What would she do it with?

And how would she get out once she did?

She shook her head.

She couldn't even think the words to herself. But she forced herself to.

Because the realization hit her like a slap to the face.

No one was coming to save her. There was only one way out of this room, only one way to save her child and, if she was lucky, save herself. She didn't want to do it. But it was the only way.

She was actually contemplating killing someone. Someone innocent.

But she was doing it to protect her child. All she had left. And she had no choice but to spend her last days protecting her. Which meant having to make a very difficult choice.

She looked at her hands, soft and pink, which had never done a day's hard labor in her entire life.

She opened and closed her fists. Clenched them tight as she could until the knuckles turned white and her fingernails cut into her palms.

She stared at them, these hands. These hands that could be weapons, if she tried.

She had run before. Now running wasn't going to be an option. For a member of a species with only two options when in danger, fight or flight, she had only one choice left.

It was a difficult choice.

But given what was at stake, there was no choice at all.

Then she felt it.

The small flutter behind her belly button. She knew what it was, her child urging her to action. She was the mother now, the protector.

She would do for her daughter what her mother had done for her: protect her.

She heard the turn of the lock. In walked a servant, head bowed and covered, as usual, delivering her a meal. Was it the same girl who did it every day? Marie had no idea.

The door was open. Only a crack, but it was open. She could see a sliver of light behind it.

Marie's breath quickened. The girl was small, unarmed, focused on her task. It would only take a second. She looked at her hands again. Could she do it? Do it now? Marie wasn't strong herself, but she was bigger. Strong enough, especially with adrenaline in her system. It would only take a second. A second that was the difference between life and death, freedom and imprisonment, between acceptance and perseverance.

Marie closed her eyes, clenched her fists, and took a deep breath. She imagined what it would be like to overpower or kill this poor girl. She imagined what it would be like to *not* attack her. In the length of a heartbeat, she saw both her outcomes, and made her choice.

She opened her eyes, ready to strike.

The girl was closing the door behind her.

Marie chased after her, but she hit the door just as the lock clicked into place.

Marie choked out a sob, covered her eyes with her hand, turned, and slid down the doorway until she crumpled into a heap on the floor. She pulled her knees to her chest, something she knew she would be unable to do soon. If she was lucky. She felt another kick within her, the baby reprimanding her for her cowardice. *I know, little one,* she thought. *I thought I had it in me too.*

She wallowed there for a few minutes. She'd been ready, but hadn't been fast enough. She couldn't live like this. Who knew how many days she had left?

She looked at the small table next to her, where the servant had left her meal. Watery soup in a white porcelain bowl. Same as every day.

Marie reached out her hand and swept it to the floor. The spoon clattered and the bowl shattered.

And Marie screamed, confident that no one could hear.

Chapter Forty

Time moved even more slowly after that. Recriminations always make the hours grow longer.

Marie heard the door unlock, but she was so numb by that point she did not get up. She couldn't try again and fail again. She lay still as she waited for the expected shuffle of a servant girl's footsteps. She didn't bother to open her eyes. Not worth the effort.

Instead, she heard the unmistakable sound of hard-soled shoes. It wasn't a servant girl, who was meant to be neither seen nor heard. This was the sound of a man who commanded, probably demanded, attention. The sound all women were conditioned to respond to, one they had all learned to fear. It trumped depression, resignation, and despair. She snapped her eyes open and sat up.

A man with a thick mustache, white coat, and black bag entered the room. "Lift up your shirt," the man said without introducing himself.

Marie wrapped her blanket more tightly around herself. Was he crazy? She wasn't undressing for him. "Who are you?"

A servant girl ran in with a chair for the man and set it by the door, and he took a seat. "I don't have time for foolishness," he said.

"But I don't know who you are or why you're here or why you want me to remove my clothes," Marie pointed out.

"Nor is it any of your concern," he told her. "I've been permitted entry to the house and to this room, and you are to do as I say."

"What are you going to do to me?"

He held up a small machine with a coiled cord that connected it to a small wand. "I'm here to check the progress of your pregnancy." It was a portable ultrasound machine.

"You mean, learn the sex of the child?" If it revealed that it was the daughter she knew she was carrying . . .

"There's no need for profanity," he said, referring to the word "sex" spoken by a woman. "I have a schedule to keep, and it's not your place to question me. Now, lift your shirt."

Marie's shaking hands went to her midsection. "But I'm not wearing a shirt, sir. I have a dress on." It was an old, white linen nightdress that had probably sat in a wardrobe for a generation or more.

The man looked at his watch and gave an impatient sigh. "Very well." He opened the door and called to the servant girl. Within a few minutes, she had returned with a shirt and skirt. The man tossed them at Marie, who failed to catch them and they fell on the floor. "Put these on. I'll be back in one minute." He went to the door and barked some more orders at the girl, who quickly shuffled away, then slammed the door behind him.

Marie bent down to pick up the clothes. The shirt was at her feet, but the skirt had slid under the bed. She got on her knees to look for it, and stifled a gasp. There it was, the salvation she had been looking for. She reached under the bed with trembling hands. This had to be a sign. This was it. No time for self-doubt. No more recriminations. She would not get a second chance.

She pulled back onto her heels, but did not get up. She shut her eyes.

Exactly sixty seconds later, the door opened and she heard the insistent footsteps again. She hadn't moved from her spot. The door slammed shut, but did not lock.

"What are you doing?" the man spat at her. "I told you to get dressed. I have a schedule to keep, and you're wasting my time."

She did not respond, and his reaction was everything she hoped.

"Get up from there," he commanded. Marie remained in place. She braced herself.

"I said get up!"

He grabbed at her elbow.

She thought of Emma.

Now.

Marie took the six-inch piece of broken bowl and, without thinking about it, jammed the sharp end into the man's side. With a shout, he let her go and collapsed to the ground. He grabbed at her, but Marie dodged his grip. She ran for the unlocked door, pushed it open, and then shoved it shut. The key was in the lock. She locked it, removed the key, and turned around.

She stood in a corridor that she did not recognize. Definitely in one of the service areas of Grayside. No one was there, but she knew that wouldn't last long. She looked down at her hands. Just a bit of blood, just enough to remind her of what she'd actually done. She wiped them on her white nightdress.

It didn't feel real. She didn't feel sorry. And this was no time to dwell on it. She heard his cries behind the door, and scurried down the hallway. There were few doors and no windows until she rounded a corner. Once she did, she saw a small window to the right, just a little bit larger than her own head. She had to stand on her tiptoes to see out, but she could make out some of the large knotted yew trees that she recognized as being part of the back gardens at Grayside. The ones that had been planted the same year the house had been built and looked as dead and diseased as the family who lived there. Maybe the groundwater had poisoned all of them. The branches were touching the ground, as if the tree were trying to crawl back into the earth and away from this place. Marie had always hated those trees. But they served a purpose. She must be on the fourth floor and, judging by where the trees were, she was just above the rooms where she herself had lived when she had been the Duchess.

Her mind raced. What had been the way from her room to the servants' entrances?

Did she dare chance going out through the house?

Behind her, around the corner, she heard shouting as people realized that something had happened. She heard them frantically trying to open the door.

She looked to her left, the direction from which she had come. To her right, the rest of the corridor, and who knew where that led? Then she looked straight ahead. There was a door that possibly led to a staircase.

She heard footsteps behind her.

She chanced it.

John Hart was about to take a long drink from his glass of beer—the good kind they brewed here at Grayside—when his phone rang. It was the emergency ringtone. He picked it up. Listened for a moment. Spat out his drink. Then threw down both the phone and the beer and raced out of the room.

The door led not to a staircase but to a closet full of cleaning equipment: brooms, dusters, chemicals, rags, vacuum cleaners, rug beaters, rubbish bags, aprons, and a metal squeeze wringer with a mop propped up against it. There was just enough room for Marie to slip inside, and so she did, shutting the door. She heard the trample of footsteps and frantic shouting as people ran past the door. She pushed her hands against it and felt the handle for a lock; there was none.

Marie pressed her ear to the door, straining to hear. She heard low sounds of people expressing dismay and concern. Clearly, they'd learned what she'd done. They would be looking for her.

She felt the blood surge through her veins as her pulse increased. She knew she'd need all the adrenaline her body could produce to get her through this. She'd read once in a book that adrenaline could give a person superhuman strength, and she knew she'd need that sort of miracle. She had no beads with her but began praying the rosary from memory, silently mouthing the words as she waited for an opportunity to carry on with her escape. She couldn't hide in a closet forever.

She slowed down her breathing so that she could hear as much as possible. She heard the commotion down the corridor, but could not detect anyone coming in her direction. If she was going to go, the time was probably now. She wasn't ready, but she had to take this opportunity. She blew out a breath, sent up a prayer, and opened the door.

John Hart was standing in front of her.

Without looking or even thinking, she grabbed the nearest item, which felt like a broomstick handle. She swung it at John Hart's head with all her might.

Except it wasn't a broomstick handle. It was the handle from the squeeze wringer, which was made of metal and had serrated sides. It cracked against John Hart's head, and he fell to the ground. Blood pooled from the wound it left.

Marie stood stunned for a second, and glanced at the wringer, which suddenly looked and felt very heavy in her hands. With a few gasping breaths, not recognizing herself, she dropped the wringer on the ground and stepped over John Hart's body, expecting that he might wake up and grab at her and pull her down next to him, where he could finally take care of her the way he'd clearly wanted to. He did not. She gave him one last look then darted to the left. It didn't take long to hit the corner and realize that this was the direction she had come from, and turn around and run in the other direction. John Hart was still down. She stepped around him and went down the corridor to the unknown.

The corridor had five windows, larger and lower to the ground than the one she had seen a few minutes ago, and they gave her another view of the back garden of Grayside. She stopped, looked at them. Was there a way to get out one of those windows and to the garden, and from there to freedom?

Marie decided to try a window and figure out how she'd get down later. She hoped it wouldn't involve a jump.

She looked for a latch and eventually found one. But it was old, rusted, and wouldn't open. She tried the next window, and the latch broke off once she pulled at it. She hit her hand against the pane, but the glass was old and thick. It had stood there for generations; Marie and her desperate strikes were no match against it.

She tried the latches on the next two windows, but they also held fast. She was losing valuable time, so she raced down the corridor. She was barefoot, and her footfalls made no noise. Another door at the end of the corridor. This was her only chance, and she opened it.

Finally, a staircase.

There was no one on it.

She heard footsteps behind her.

She slammed the door and ran down the stairs and into another corridor. But this one she recognized. Plush carpet with undulating blue-and-white Persian designs that covered the floor from wall to wall—the recently installed carpets that the last of Marie's dowry had paid for. Dark mahogany paneling on the walls. Door after door after door. Oil paintings of Dukes and Duchesses of Suffolk long past. Sconces on the walls that still held actual candles, since electricity could still be spotty, even for a wealthy family like theirs.

This had been where her rooms were, when she was Duchess.

She looked around wildly, panting, praying that she would not see anyone. She could hear them behind her, the cries of discovery at what had happened to John Hart. They would be here soon. But this was good. She knew the way out from here, as long as she was fast enough. She caught up the bottom of her nightgown and began running, her hair falling down her back in long, sweaty ringlets. Her face was pale from weeks spent indoors, away from natural light, and her skin practically glowed white. Sweat ran down her face in tendrils against her flesh, but still she ran.

As she passed her former bedroom, she was so, so tempted to stop to see if the woman who had already replaced her was inside. She was dying to know. But she felt the tightness in her belly and tamped down her curiosity. As she ran past, a figure emerged from the room. She heard her name and stumbled to a stop, whipping around.

It wasn't her replacement.

It wasn't a woman.

It was James. Her husband stood in a doorway, phone in hand.

He gaped at her as if she were a ghost. Which, Marie supposed, she was.

She shook her head at him, but though she willed herself to keep running, she couldn't.

James walked up to her, hand out, not believing what he could see. He put his hand to her face. Marie could not help but press into his touch and close her eyes. It had been so long, and he'd done this so rarely. She sighed, and heard an answering sigh from him. She felt his hand on her stomach, and she covered it with hers. He pressed, the baby kicked, and she felt him shudder ever so slightly.

They lasted like that for only four seconds, but it felt like a lifetime. She wanted to stay, wanted to believe that this moment was reflective of what her life really could have been here, instead of what she'd only dreamed it could be. She opened her eyes and saw that James's face was a rictus of pain and regret.

There wasn't anything left to say to each other. A thousand might-have-beens flashed before her eyes, and she knew that James was feeling the same. Had the relationship been salvageable? Could they have had the rare happy marriage? Marie thought of the humiliations, the isolation, the loneliness she'd felt, and couldn't decide if it would be better or worse if it had all been inevitable.

James looked at her, and then the direction from which she had just come. His Adam's apple bobbed. His cheeks flushed then went pale. He opened his mouth, and she braced herself, knowing that if he shouted for help, this was all over. She would never leave Grayside alive.

James spoke not in a shout, but in a whisper. One word, and it was everything.

"Run."

Chapter Forty-One

She ran.

Her white nightdress billowed out and her hair streaked behind her as she rounded corners and flew down staircases, down one flight of stairs, then another. She ran past gobsmacked servants and puzzled staff. For everyone knew the Duchess had plummeted to her death weeks before. Platters clattered to the ground. Gasps and cries of surprise sounded around her. She heard words like "ghost" and "spirit" and disbelief that she was real. Was it because she had been denied a Christian burial or mass to celebrate her soul, for suicide was a venal sin, that she would wander Grayside like this? And why had it taken so long for her to return?

No matter. Marie was close. She could taste the mossy air from outside. She could feel the salt from the sea sprinkle across her chapped lips, and she relished the sting. On the ground floor, she decided to run opposite the grand double doors in the front and down corridors she had never approached before. It was the kitchen, bustling with activity, but Marie pushed her way through. Scared cooks and assistants jumped out of her way, while those who were not so lucky were shoved aside. She heard dishes break and the hiss of hot liquid splashing on the floor. She ignored it all.

Just as she got to the door, she felt someone grab at her arm, and she yanked it out without looking behind her. With cries of, "She's real!" Marie flew out of the kitchen, out into the gardens, past the big yew trees she'd seen from upstairs. She was outside in the gray light of day. Her side ached. Her bare feet hurt. It didn't matter. She kept going, running away as far and as fast as she could, desperate to disappear for real this time.

Generations of staff would talk about the sudden reappearance of the late Duchess, the Ghost of Grayside, and how those who swore they saw her were disbelieved by those who did not; and the scullery maid in the kitchen was laughed at for claiming she had touched a spirit. But they all knew what they'd seen. The myth would grow over time, with more and more improbable powers attributed to the Ghost. She would be blamed for everything from crop failures to miscarriages to fallen trees until the very last stone of Grayside sank into the sea, which would also ultimately be blamed on her.

She ran through the gardens, past the yew trees, dodging and bobbing and weaving through every plant, building, shed, and stone that would conceal her until she staggered to a stop at the edge of the cliffs— the very same ones from which she had purportedly thrown herself, when this child inside of her had first made her presence known and Marie's role in this life had become irrevocably changed.

She hadn't meant to go to the cliffs. Somewhere in the gardens, she'd gotten turned around. She couldn't run anymore, and had to stop. She fell to her knees, facing the sea, panting and sobbing all at once, in both fear and relief. She might finally be free. She wrapped her arms around her middle, cradling the child, gasping for air.

The roar of the endless ocean crashing against the cliffs was overwhelming. She felt the immensity of the Earth, standing here on the edge of this small island in the cold North Sea. Small and insignificant, hopefully too small and too insignificant to be noticed.

And then, just barely over the sound of the sea, she heard the footsteps crunching on the gravel behind her.

She whipped around at the sound.

It was impossible.

John Hart, eyes filled with venom and teeth bared, was approaching stridently and with purpose. A predator who had finally cornered his prey and was coming in for the kill.

Behind Marie were cliffs five hundred feet down.

And nowhere to run.

Chapter Forty-Two

John Hart was a man possessed. He walked toward Marie with a look of pure determination, hatred, and *purpose*. The hair on the left side of his head, where Marie had hit him, was covered in matted blood. Some of it was still trickling down his neck. It hadn't taken him long to catch up to Marie, who'd been running as fast as her feet could carry her. She was out of breath, and he was hardly winded. Was he even human? It didn't seem possible. She had given it her all. He was going to kill her, and Marie couldn't even stand up to face him.

"I grow weary of this," John Hart said as he got close to her. He grabbed her by her hair and began dragging her toward the cliff. Marie cried out at the pain she felt in each and every follicle that clung to her scalp, feeling many of them being torn away. She clawed at the ground and dug in her heels, desperately seeking purchase on anything to slow him down, but it was no use. They slid across the ground, and the scrape of her feet across the jagged little pebbles sent a jolt of pain and fear up from her heels to her heart. She felt nauseous with the sickening realization that she was about to die, and no force in Heaven or Earth was coming to save her. All she had done, all she had fought for, all she had lost, and in the end it hadn't mattered. Everything she'd ever done in her life, good or bad, would culminate in this moment of powerlessness. She would go over the cliffs after all, the problem finally resolved. The good soldier would go back to his mother, and she would go to her grave. She prayed. She bargained. She screamed. She gasped for air. She clawed at nothing and everything, as if the molecules of air all around them could solidify and give her something to hold on to, but it was no use. She was all out of miracles.

Was this what it had all been for? Had it been worth it? Did it matter? Did anything matter?

John Hart might not be dead, but he was weakened, and this slowed down their process. "You could have just done this the first time and saved us all a lot of bother. Not forcing us to chase you halfway across the continent, taking all sorts of foolish side trips away from where you belong."

"Where do I belong?" Marie asked as she still tried to scramble away, despite having accepted that it was impossible.

"Hell."

Marie tried again to pull away, but John Hart persisted. He gave up on dragging her by the hair and stopped to pick her up bodily. In that split second, she kicked him in the knee and made to run away, but he had tackled her in an instant.

"Just let me go," Marie pleaded.

"Stop asking for ridiculous things," he admonished.

He picked her up in a bridal carry and turned toward the sea and the cliffs. He took heaving steps, panting with the effort of the pursuit and his injuries.

Just as Marie felt he might reach the edge and chuck her over the side, they heard a shout and were suddenly knocked to the ground. Marie and John Hart both cried out in surprise and pain as a heavy weight pinned them down. Marie opened her eyes and was surprised to find that she had not been tossed off the cliff but rather was on the ground mere feet away from the edge. She saw a familiar lock of brown hair and recognized the signet ring with its magpie emblem.

"James?" she croaked out.

Her husband did not respond, but instead pulled John Hart off her and gripped him hard by the arms. Marie backed away but did not run. She crouched at the edge of the cliff, out of their reach. She would have run, but she was still exhausted from running, from fighting, and from growing the child inside her.

"I thought that I clearly dismissed you," James said.

"You might have, but my mistress did not."

"Your *mistress* is no longer the Duchess of Suffolk, much as she has always refused to accept it. And even if she were, I am the Duke of Suffolk. My word is law. And if I dismiss you, you are dismissed. Is that clear?"

John Hart gave a sneer. "You think I'm just some member of staff?"

"I know what you are," James said. "I know why my mother has kept you close all these years. I have heard all the *disgusting* rumors."

John Hart sputtered. "Disgusting?"

"That we share a mother," said James. "The idea that you and I could share blood is inconceivable."

"And yet it's true," said John Hart. "Brother."

"You and I are not brothers. You are the bottom-feeder. The hanger-on. The one who does unpleasant tasks. The one we all prefer not to think about and don't mention in polite company."

"Relegate me wherever you wish," said John Hart. "It changes nothing."

"James?"

The Dowager Duchess's voice carried on the wind. All three heads turned in her direction.

"Wherever I wish," James repeated. He chuckled. "With pleasure."

Tightening his grip on John Hart, who seemed too shocked to stop him, James took several long strides and pushed the other man off the edge of the cliff. With a shout, he tumbled over. But just before he crested the edge, he snatched out a hand and grabbed Marie by the ankle. She tried to grasp at anything she could, but his grip was unyielding. She slid over the edge with him with a scream.

James watched his hated half brother disappear with his wife. He swallowed a lump in his throat.

"James!" the Dowager Duchess repeated. Her perfect hair was still and firm as a helmet despite the wind of the cliffs. "What on earth are you doing out here?"

James cleared his throat and dusted his hands. "Nothing," he said. "Just taking care of loose ends, as you requested."

His mother nodded. "I saw Mr. Hart out here earlier. Where did he go?"

"Go?"

"Yes." His mother looked at him with those eyes, piercing like a shard of ice. "Where did he go?"

James had always refused to believe the rumors. And his mother had never confirmed them, never spoken about them, and always denied them. But here, in this moment, her pleading eyes, he saw a flicker of fear and worry. And in that moment, he knew.

He chose his words carefully. "He has also been taken care of."

Anyone but James would have missed it, the slightest twitch of emotion on her face. He couldn't tell if it was grief or relief. Perhaps it was a little bit of both. She brushed a single stray hair that had fallen out of place back where it belonged. "I see. And your wife?"

James nodded. "Yes."

His mother cleared her throat. "Perhaps you could check, to confirm? We were remiss in not checking for a body last time."

"Of course, Mother."

James hurried over as quickly as dignity would allow. He crouched to the edge of the cliff and peered down.

◆ ◆ ◆

Marie peered back up.

John Hart's iron grip had loosened as soon as his head had hit one of the rocks on the side a few feet down. Marie had managed to grab on to a rock jutting out with all her might and pulled herself up close to it, wrapping both her arms and legs around it. Her hardening belly pressed against the equally hard rock. It was unstable. More and more of this cliffside was disappearing into the sea each year, and if she was not careful, she would disappear into it as well. She was weak, and unpracticed at this. But for now, she was here, and she was alive.

James looked both surprised and relieved. He knelt down and looked down at the ground, but met her eyes again, his expression a question: *Is John Hart gone?* Marie nodded. James nodded back. He leaned forward just a bit more and whispered, "Hold on. Help is coming."

He then stood up and disappeared from her sight. Without even looking at him, Marie knew that he was straightening his jacket and smoothing down his hair. She knew where the priorities lay at Grayside, and appearances were it. "All clear," he said in a crisp voice that cut through the wind like a shard of glass.

"Thank Merciful God Almighty," said the Dowager Duchess. She began speaking about whatever event they had on that evening, and the sound of their voices and footsteps disappeared into the wind as James and his mother walked out of Marie's life forever.

Time moved very slowly after that. Or very quickly. She was in the world of geological time now. It might have been five minutes. It might have been two hours. Stuck with just her thoughts and regrets to keep her company.

She looked up and considered the distance between herself and the edge of the cliff. James had promised her help, but could she trust what he'd said? The conversation with his mother made it sound like she was going to go over the edge, whether John Hart or James had been the one to do it. Were they just waiting for her to finish the job herself?

Marie shook her head at the thought. She'd come this far. She wasn't letting go now.

She wouldn't wait for him. Or count on him. She was going to get out, just as she'd gotten out of the house. Just as she'd escaped the first time. On her own. She considered the cliff before her and how to get from her position on the rock to the ledge above. It didn't look that far. She could climb up there. It just required determination and a steady hand. Anyone could do that with high enough stakes. Determination and a steady hand. She looked down. Gulped and saw stars.

The crash of the waves below mixed with the rushing in her ears. The collective roar so consumed her that she wondered if she'd ever know silence again.

Determination. A steady hand. And not looking down.

She reached out and nearly slipped off the rock. She clung to it again, desperate not to fall. She was recalibrating her approach when the most wonderful sound she'd ever heard carried over the edge above.

"Idiot."

Chapter Forty-Three

Alice's voice was gruff and annoyed. It was the voice of an angel.

"What are you—how did you—what—" Marie sputtered.

"Shut up," Alice cut her off. "Worry about getting off that rock first. You almost fell just now. Idiot." She lay prone on the ground and reached out her hand. "Grab on, I'll help guide you up."

Marie hesitated and clung more tightly to the rock.

"If I wanted you to die, I would have just let you fall."

"I didn't say anything," Marie said. "It's just . . . it's a long way down."

"Which is why I'm trying to help you." She reached out closer. Marie could see the diamond glittering on her ring finger. Her fingernails were perfectly manicured. Like their mother's. "Come on. I've got you." She directed Marie toward her, where to place her hands and feet to pull herself up, and when Marie was close enough, Alice took her hand. With her strong grip, Alice hauled Marie up to the cliff and over the edge to safety. Marie collapsed and panted with exhaustion. She rolled onto her back and began shaking from the comedown as the adrenaline left her system.

After a few moments, Marie put her hands on her forehead and started laughing. Not because anything was funny—not today, certainly, and not at any point in recent memory. To be sure, she was thrilled to be alive. A flutter within her told her that the baby was still okay, and she laughed harder. She looked up at Alice, the least likely savior, and cackled. She was so overwhelmed with the emotions of the day that they had to come out, and they took the form of a laugh.

Alice stood over her, arms crossed, tapping her foot. "I don't know what's so funny, but we need to get out of here, fast. Before someone sees you."

Marie nodded but kept laughing. Tears streamed down her face. She somehow ended up balled in a fetal position.

Alice made a sound of exasperation, dragged Marie up, and pushed her into the back seat of the car that she had driven up to the edge. Marie hadn't heard it approach in the long wait after James and his mother had walked away. Alice tossed a blanket over Marie, not out of affection but to hide her. Marie felt the car move and knew that they had to be driving along the coastline and through the gates of Grayside. And through her uncontrollable laughter, Marie hoped, they were headed to freedom, real freedom, this time.

Once she'd calmed down and wiped the tears from her face, Marie took several long breaths and collected herself. Only at that point was she able to ask the questions that her laughter had suppressed.

"How did you know I was here? And why did you come save me? I thought you wanted me to come back to James."

Alice kept her focus on the road and waited a while to respond.

"James is the one who called me."

Marie sat up at that. "He called you? When?"

"Get back down!"

Marie lay back down and covered herself with the blanket. "You didn't answer my questions."

"Who else would have called me?"

Marie had to concede the point. "I guess I never would have believed it, you and him working together to save me."

"You were wrong about so many things. You should have expected to be wrong about this as well."

"Tell me more about how wrong I was. Tell me everything I was wrong about. I want to know what you talked about."

"He called me, told me where you were, and that I should come get you before his mother had a chance."

She remembered the phone in his hand when she'd seen him briefly at Grayside. Had Alice been the one on the other end of the line?

"I . . . I didn't know you lived so close," Marie said. "I thought you lived down in Exeter."

"I do."

"So, what were you doing here, then? There's no way you could have gotten here that quickly."

"Maybe it's best not to talk more right now," said Alice. She accelerated. Marie figured that they must be on the main motorway now. They sat in silence for a long time.

"I have a lot to tell you," Marie said.

"Later," said Alice.

"But you really do need to know," said Marie. "What we've lost. *Who* we've lost."

"I know," said Alice. Her voice was flat.

"Our mother . . ."

"I don't want to hear it."

"I found her, Alice."

"Stop."

"And . . . and I lost her."

"Stop!" Alice slapped a hand on the steering wheel, stunning Marie into temporary silence. She couldn't even tell her about Emma.

"I'm so sorry," Marie said meekly. She wasn't sure what she was apologizing for, specifically. Perhaps for talking. Perhaps for what had happened to their mother and Emma. Perhaps for everything.

The silence dragged out awhile longer.

"I made peace with the loss of our mother a long time ago," said Alice. "I was the eldest. I was the closest to her, had the most time with her. Trust me when I say that her loss was harder on me than it was on either of you."

Marie chanced sitting up. "I never knew," she said. Alice didn't admonish her, so Marie looked at her sister. She was staring resolutely out the windshield, hands braced on the steering wheel, deliberately not looking at Marie in the rearview mirror.

"Why would you? I never told you."

"I wish you had."

"I'm sure there are a lot of things we wish we had told each other. Things we should have done differently," said Alice.

"After she left . . . I needed a mother so badly. I looked to you and to Emma. And . . ."

Marie trailed off, and Alice did not respond for several long minutes.

"That wasn't my role," said Alice. "It was to make a good marriage to pave the way for the both of you."

Marie looked out the window. It was raining now. Drops raced across the windows like tears converging into rivers on the glass. "I'm glad your marriage is happy," said Marie. "I never knew that was possible."

Alice shrugged. "I was lucky."

"Were you?"

"I knew I wasn't going to attract a Duke or Earl or anything like that. I wasn't going to have a status-based marriage. So I decided to aim for a happy one."

Marie smiled. "I'm sorry we judged you," she said. "We thought you'd suffered."

"When you look the way I look as an aristocratic woman, you learn not to let what you hear bother you. We're like a bunch of crabs in a bucket. All of us trapped, and we keep pulling each other down. If we were just to support each other, we'd be able to get out."

"I never knew you wanted out."

Alice hummed. "Don't we all? You did it. Twice. Was it worth it?"

It was the same question that Marie had asked herself when she was certain that John Hart was going to throw her over the edge. In the moment, she had questioned the idea, wondered why she had bothered with anything. In the end, did anything matter?

Marie thought of her baby. She thought of their mother. She thought of their sister. Who could weigh all of those things against each other and say whether it had been worth it? So she didn't even try, and Alice didn't push it. The only sound that remained was the sound of the wiper blades sweeping back and forth as Alice drove on.

Chapter Forty-Four

After a long time, Alice pulled off the motorway and down a winding road with long stretches of endless green grasslands, farmland, and forests. A few indifferent cows side-eyed them as they drove past, and a rabbit scampered across the road. Eventually, Alice pulled into the long gravel driveway. The farmhouse that greeted them at the end was old, centuries old by the look of it, and long abandoned. Weathered paint that may have been white at one point peeled away to show graying wood underneath. The thatched roof had holes, the weathered wooden shutters were falling off their hinges, and the door lacked a lock or even a knob. The house seemed to be slouching, caving in under the weight of its years.

"We're here," Alice said.

They got out of the car. It was windy, and it blew Marie's hair all around. She shielded her eyes against the glare of the sky; though it was an unbroken blanket of gray clouds from one end of the horizon to the other, the sun filtered through so that she had to squint against it. She wished she had a hat; the worst sunburn she'd ever gotten was on an overcast day like this one. Distantly, she heard a crow caw one, two, three times.

It felt a million miles away from anywhere.

"What is this place?" she asked Alice after taking it all in.

"I'm exhausted answering your questions."

"Given the circumstances, it seems appropriate to ask where I am."

"Get inside," Alice ordered. Marie hesitated. "Don't worry, it's safe," Alice said, with slightly less annoyance in her voice.

Marie took a few steps toward the house, when the enormity of everything hit her all at once. She'd nearly killed a man—twice. She'd nearly died—twice. She'd lost those she loved—twice. It was raining. She was shivering. She bent over and vomited.

She didn't expect the awkward pat on her back. She turned to find Alice with a wrinkled nose. "If you're planning to stay out here a long time, tell me now, because I have no intention of catching cold watching you get sick all over the ground."

Marie wiped her mouth. "Sorry," she said.

"You don't owe that apology to me."

"You're the only one left," Marie said. "You have to hear them all."

Alice said nothing and stalked over to the door. Marie followed her on shaky legs. Alice gave the door an oddly complicated knock before it opened, first at a crack and then fully. Marie's knees gave out when she saw who was on the other side.

◆ ◆ ◆

"Emma!"

Emma was at Marie's side in an instant, catching her before she fell. Whether due to the rain or their tears, their faces were both wet by the time they embraced. Marie had been wrong. There were miracles left in the world. Some were even left for her.

Marie thought of Alice's earlier question. Yes, it had been worth it. Every second of it.

Marie was trying to form sentences, but she was shaking too hard and was in too much shock to be able to get more than a word or two out at a time. Emma soothed her little sister and assured her that she would answer the questions Marie was struggling to ask. But first they had to get inside, out of the rain, before they were seen. The house was far back from the main road and hadn't been touched in years, but one couldn't be too careful when one had multiple people who were supposed to be dead walking about.

Despite its dilapidated appearance outside, and the fact that it had been built long before the electrical grid had been created, the house was heated and had electricity. It was filled with secondhand furniture atop secondhand carpets and had a radio playing soft orchestral music, the sort that Marie had heard back in the days when she'd been a Duchess who went to the symphony, or a girl whose father could afford to hire a private orchestra to play at garden parties. The walls were dingy but not damp, and the fire in the woodstove kept the place comfortably warm.

Emma practically dragged Marie to one of the sofas and sat her down, putting her arms around her. Alice perched next to her sisters, very pointedly not touching or even looking at them.

"John Hart didn't kill me. Obviously," Emma said once she'd gotten Marie settled. Whether from the rain or the shock or something else, Marie was still shaking uncontrollably. Emma grabbed an old blanket from the back of the sofa and wrapped it around her sister's shoulders, but it did little to settle her.

Emma rubbed Marie's shoulders as she spoke. "He shot me. I bled a lot. I passed out. I thought I was gone. But I wasn't. The next thing I remember was waking up in a hospital. Dirk had brought me there. He saved me. You wouldn't believe how apologetic he was. He saw it as a choice between saving us and saving his mother, and of course he was going to choose her. No one was supposed to get hurt. John Hart was just going to retrieve you. He truly believed that."

Marie nodded, still shaking.

"I think what he said about us is true, though, that he lost his mother to us. At least, to him it was true. I never thought about how it affected Jane. Regardless, I didn't want his help after that. I couldn't trust him. I sent him away. He understood. Jane has reached out, but I'm not speaking with her either. Dirk was adamant that she had nothing to do with it, and she'd told him not to do it. I believe them, but if John Hart was able to get to their home and attack them, who is to say that he wasn't still monitoring them through their phones or otherwise. You know?"

"He's dead," Marie choked out through her shudders.

"John Hart?"

Marie nodded, triggering another wave of shakes.

"Good," said Emma. "How?"

Marie shook her head, so Emma continued speaking.

"When I was in the hospital, I tried to think of who I could call. And there was only one person who I thought to contact." She looked at Alice, and Alice looked away. "Which wasn't easy to do, considering we'd stolen her phone! But I got ahold of her. Just as I was listed in the phone book, so was she. And to my surprise, she took my call. I told her about our mother."

Alice closed her eyes and set her jaw. "Just get on with the story."

"We talked for a long time. I think this was the first real conversation we've probably ever had with each other. Something about loss . . . it brings you closer together."

"We got on speaking terms and remain on speaking terms," Alice snapped. "Carry on with what happened next, or I'm telling."

"She had been in contact with your husband previously, and he was just as powerless as you to do anything to free you. His mother rules that place with an iron fist. Well, you know that. So we were hoping there would be an opportunity to get you out of that room. And when you were out, he called Alice to have her come get you."

Marie nodded, still shaking, though not as violently as before.

"I buried our mother alone," Emma said. "In Strasbourg. It was the Christian burial she had been denied when we were children. I wish you'd been there. Both of you."

Marie nodded again. Alice gave a large swallow.

"And now we make things right," said Emma. "I have the proof that our mother was alive." She took out her phone and showed some pictures she'd taken of their mother during their too-short time together. "That's why they wanted to kill me too—I was the proof that our mother has been alive these last years. Which means our father and stepmother were never legally married. Which means that our brother is illegitimate."

At that moment, another complicated knock sounded at the door. All three of them started. Alice jumped up and, after verifying that the person was indeed friendly, opened the door and greeted the person warmly. It was a man, soaked from the rain, but with the same nose and eyes that had inspired terror in the three sisters their whole lives. But the expression was softer than they'd ever known. Emma's face lit up when she saw him.

"If our father had no legitimate heir, our uncle is the real Earl," said Emma. "And we have the proof."

Marie realized this was their father's younger brother, Edmund.

He came over and gave the three a deep bow.

Marie and her sisters barely knew Edmund; Marie wondered if she had ever actually met him. She couldn't recall a time that she had. But she had heard *of* him throughout her childhood. He'd been the strange uncle, the one who was a "confirmed bachelor" and, rumor had it, lived with another man in a townhome in London. Since he'd been cut off from his family, it was entirely possible that they were simply sharing a flat. But it was unlikely. Such things were spoken of only in whispers, if they were spoken of at all. All they had really known was that he was considered thoroughly unsuitable to inherit the Earldom, which was one of the reasons their father had gone to great lengths to have an heir of his own. He hadn't wanted it falling into his brother's hands. Marie remembered their father saying that it would tarnish the legacy of Ellthrop. "I would rather burn it to the ground!" he'd once exclaimed.

"Marie," Edmund said. It was the same voice their father had had, but it was far gentler than they'd ever heard their father use it. Edmund walked over to where Marie sat on the sofa and knelt before her, so they were eye to eye. His eyes had a glimmer in them that had been missing in their father's, and his features were far more relaxed and less severe.

Perhaps it had been the strain of running the estate and the need to produce an heir that had made their father the way he was. Perhaps not.

"Uncle Edmund," Marie replied in a hoarse whisper. He took one of her hands in his, and she found that her shaking subsided just a bit.

While he did not smile, the corners of his eyes crinkled upward.

"We have a lot of catching up to do."

The more they talked, the more she liked him. Marie resented her father back through the years for depriving her of a relationship with her uncle. She could tell they would have enjoyed spending time together. They might have talked after she went to Grayside. She might have been able to run to him and return home rather than following her mother's path. Maybe her sisters would have stayed in her life. Maybe her mother would have too.

Maybe her father had been right. Maybe Edmund would burn it to the ground.

And all the better if he did.

Chapter Forty-Five

The years passed like the pages of a book, one turning into the next.

While none of them held any further trust in Dirk, the picture he had taken of the three of them in that sordid room in Strasbourg, time- and date-stamped, had proven to make all the difference.

The testimony of a woman was never weighed as heavily as a man's, both by custom and by force of law. But a photograph? No one could argue with it.

First the press shared the shocking tale of how the Duchess of Suffolk had faked her own death, only to die for real on those very same cliffs. Then the society pages shared the sordid details of how the Eighth Earl Kenfield had committed bigamy for twenty years, dying from the shock of seeing his lawful wife still alive in Zeebrugge, and how it meant that his long-desired son and heir was illegitimate—just like the other illegitimate sons who had been born during his first marriage. London itself nearly collapsed under the weight of the gossip and scandal.

It would later be said that this single dispute between young Arthur, Ninth Earl Kenfield; his mother, Louise; and his uncle over the true ownership of the estate of Ellthrop and the succession of the Earldom required so many lawyers that it single-handedly sustained the legal profession in Northampton. One could hear people physically cry out in pain when they learned that all testimony was sealed by order of the court, and that the sordid details would never be revealed. Friendships were both formed and broken, depending upon whether one's compatriots were a member of "Team Arthur" or "Team Edmund."

It was also said that when Team Edmund finally prevailed, Edmund, Emma, and Alice personally oversaw the clearing-out of Louise and Arthur from Ellthrop. Edmund prohibited them from taking any property from Ellthrop unless they could prove they had purchased it themselves from their own funds rather than charging it to the estate. They of course could never prove such a thing. All of their staff were fired without notice. Alice personally stood guard while Louise packed all of her clothing into expensive leather luggage, but when Alice saw the embossed "K" on the luggage, she declared that it belonged to the estate, not to her would-be stepmother; demanded that Louise leave the expensive suitcases behind; and thrust some rubbish bags at her to fill after the maid, at Emma's instruction, had hastily unpacked the luggage. Once Louise's clothing had been repacked into the bags, Emma kicked them down the staircase.

"What will you do next?" Emma asked Edmund once the squatters had been evicted and they stood in the midst of the opulence of the entryway to Ellthrop. "There's no heir to the Earldom now."

Edmund smiled at his niece. Over the course of the whole affair, they had bonded with each other, like understanding like, and he had had remarkably sage advice for her. She needn't run away as she had. There were ways to be herself while not removing to the fringes of society, if that was not where she wanted to live. "You can be home again," Edmund told her.

"It never was home," Emma replied.

"Maybe now it can be," he responded.

Once Louise and Arthur lost their case, whatever bargain had been struck with the Dowager Duchess fell apart, and suddenly it was known that the Dowager Duchess of Suffolk had had a son out of wedlock, hastily given away and raised elsewhere. This led to the news that Louise had positioned herself within Ellthrop well before her marriage, and how she had gotten pregnant with the intent of snagging the Earl

Kenfield for herself. The rich and powerful were cannibalizing each other, and the entire nation was enthralled.

Standing on the estate, Edmund considered Emma's question about what he would do about the matter of succession and said, "I think enough lives have been ruined due to a fixation on the succession."

"But you'll have to deal with it someday," she pointed out.

He just laughed, a sound that had been missing in the last decades at Ellthrop. As it echoed through the cavernous home, nothing had ever sounded more appropriate.

"Emma, my dear, I have the best lawyers in England, and I have more money than the Church. If they can't get me out of this entail so that I can name my own successor, what has it all been for?"

He gave her a meaningful look when he emphasized the words *own successor*, and Emma smiled.

"It would be a shame to put half of the bar out of work," she agreed.

"Yes, I imagine this will take some work. But no progress was ever made without an army of lawyers fighting for the cause."

Emma laughed. "That was good," she said. She couldn't wait to share that line with her sisters the next time she talked with them.

Chapter Forty-Six

Gregorian Calendar: Sunday, 10 August 2025 (Feast Day of Saint Lawrence)
Anishinaabe Moon: Manoomin Giizis (Ricing Moon)
Islamic Calendar: 15 Safar 1447
Chinese Calendar: Cycle 78, year 42, second month 6, day 17 (Year of the Snake)
Hebrew Calendar: 16 Av 5785
Mayan Calendar: 13.0.12.14.15
Ethiopian Calendar: 4 Nahas 2017

There was great freedom in death, Marie knew. There was even greater freedom in having died twice. For faking your death once was trouble enough. Doing so a second time? Inconceivable. No one would ever believe it. And thankfully, no one ever had.

She clasped her daughter's hand tightly as she wound her way through the cluttered streets. Years of living in Athens had inoculated them against the stress of crowds, but nothing compared to the chaos of Strasbourg. Since her last visit, the refugee problem in Strasbourg was still much as it ever had been, and she felt both despair and relief at the idea that after more than five years, nothing had changed. Women were still fleeing England via the URN. Marie was grateful that it still existed but regretted that its existence remained so necessary. Perhaps one day it would not be. It felt impossible; but then again, so many other things had seemed that way once.

They finally reached their destination, just where Emma had described it. It was a simple grave, with a simple stone. It was in the middle of the graveyard, between two graves of women who had each died before they were thirty years of age. Marie didn't know what they had died of, but she had her guesses.

She knelt before the grave and made the sign of the cross. Her daughter followed suit. Despite years of living far from the reach of the Church Law, the move was still perfectly practiced. After they prayed together, Marie took her daughter's hand and laid down the flowers at the marker.

The world was different. Edmund and Emma had a platform to reach others, and they used it. Technology had made a small crack in the wall, and information flooded in. There were people like them all over the world, many in societies far freer than their own, and their stories began to circulate within the cloistered world of Europe. The Church silenced many such stories and did what they could to keep them from spreading. But they could not silence them all. It was just a small glimmer of hope, and it made Marie feel safe enough to return. While she had been in hiding, Emma had been changing the world. It was time to stop hiding. But first, Marie had to introduce her daughter to someone very important.

"This is your grandmother, Charlotte," Marie said to her daughter in Greek, the language her daughter learned and spoke outside the home. "She risked it all, and inspired three girls to do more than they ever thought they could. She died twice. Did you know that was possible?"

Her daughter, who shared the same hair as Emma and Charlotte, shook her head.

"Oh yes," Marie said. She squeezed her daughter's hand, feeling the perfect smooth skin between her own calloused fingers. Such perfection, this little girl. "It's not only possible, but sometimes very, very necessary.

Impossible things must happen sometimes. And we are all better for them." She closed her eyes and swallowed the sob that threatened. She wished more than anything that her mother could have met her daughter. They would have loved each other so much. She was grateful that her sisters and her daughter had a strong relationship, despite their distance from each other. It almost made up for it.

"Your grandmother did the most important thing that any mother can do for her children—she lived, and in doing so, she ensured that I would live too. She led by example, and I followed that example. Without it, I would never have had you. She wasn't perfect, of course. She made mistakes. But her mistakes were all made so that my life might be easier than hers. That's what we strive for when we have children. We want them to have opportunities we did not.

"And I want you to know exactly what few freedoms you do have— and you have more than I ever did—have cost people like her." Her daughter's eyes were as wide as the sky, and held as many possibilities as the cosmos.

"Would you like to hear how she did it?"

Her daughter nodded enthusiastically.

"Very well," Marie said. "It all started with a mother who loved her daughters more than life itself . . ."

ACKNOWLEDGMENTS

A brief note on Marie's name: It may seem incongruous that a woman in an England perpetually at war with France would have a French name. I chose it because Marie is my mother's middle name.

Thank you, as always, to the editorial team at 47North for your guidance and effort. I particularly thank Melissa Valentine and Charlotte Herscher for pushing me at every step to make this book better, and to the team of copyeditors, proofreaders, and cold readers who caught so many errors on my end. Thank you to my agent, Sara Megibow, for your unwavering support, and for having more faith than I did that I would finish this book.

Much of this book's itinerary is drawn from my time as an exchange student at Royal Holloway, University of London. Thank you to my friends Mayu Sakota, Yooyi Seo, and Ted Oswald for doing the London-Brussels-Strasbourg-Frankfurt trip with me and the RHUL European Society back in November 2004. Thanks to Yooyi, Akiko Hayakawa, and Yumiko Izuka for also doing London-Brugge with me later that same month with the RHUL History Society. Neither trip was as eventful as Marie and Emma's, but the time we spent together that year was just as life-changing. Thanks to the memories we forged, and to our many photos, I was able to re-create and reinvent these cities in the middle of a pandemic, when I couldn't visit in person. Extra special thanks to my RHUL flatmate and friend Toby Penrhys-Evans, who not only graciously permitted me use of his surname but also generously gave me an evening of his time to take me on the Zoom tour of Suffolk. Any errors are mine, not his.

This book was further brought to you by six years of Catholic school (which included an assignment my senior year in which I was able to find ample support for same-sex marriage in both the Bible and the catechism), various San Diego coffee shops, Panera, Layla's Bakery Café in Sedona, Arizona, and the Sedona vortexes. I had spent months planning to trap Marie in a locked room in Grayside, and was completely stuck on how I would get her out. In February 2022, my husband and I took a weeklong writing vacation to Sedona. Every night, I woke up at about 1:00 a.m. knowing exactly what to write the next day at Layla's. By the end of the week, Marie was out.

Thank you, as always, to my husband, Toufic, and my daughters, Poppy and Lily, for being the light of my life and my reason for everything. I also promised Toufic that I would credit him publicly as the improvised weapons consultant for suggesting the implement that Marie could use to take down John Hart in the closet. Marie and I both thank you for your knowledge of cleaning tools and how, in a pinch, they could be used to try to kill a man. Thanks to you, he went down instantly. If I ever need to incapacitate someone in real life, I'm definitely calling you first.

Finally, thank you to my wonderful cat of over fifteen years, Kitty, who passed away just as we were wrapping up copyedits on this book. Kitty was my constant companion, and she was up with me every night when I wrote the first drafts of *The Peacekeeper* and *The Mother* after my family had gone to bed. Writing can be a very solitary exercise at times, especially when your primary writing time is at night. I was lucky to have a friend with me.

ABOUT THE AUTHOR

Photo © 2011 Toufic Tabshouri

B. L. Blanchard is the author of *The Peacekeeper*. She is a graduate of the UC Davis creative writing honors program and was a writing fellow at Boston University School of Law. She is a lawyer and enrolled member of the Sault Ste. Marie Tribe of Chippewa Indians. She is originally from the Upper Peninsula of Michigan but has lived in California for so long that she can no longer handle cold weather. For more information, visit www.blblanchard.com.